I0763365

Bernado's Circus

James A Calderwood

2018

For Jacqueline

TABLE OF CONTENTS

PROLOGUE

Gunter Khullman scratched hard at the left side of his face with his little finger where his eye and ear had been blown off. This had happened when a Polish soldier had thrown a hand grenade which exploded while on the way to the village of Kostryzn near the Polish and German border. Two of his men had been killed by the grenade.

A piece of red-hot shrapnel from the grenade had torn through his face and had sheared off the three middle fingers of his left hand, leaving him with only the little finger and thumb.

That had happened three years ago at the beginning of World War Two. The itch of the missing eye and ear almost drove him insane even after all these years of fighting.

Now he was hiding in the forest with a small band of SS troops and young Hitler Youth boys, waiting for the Gypsy caravans to arrive. This was a cat and mouse play. A deadly game of hide-and-seek.

Gunter Khullman studied his aerial maps of the forest. The gypsy's horses had been spotted from the air by a small recognizance aircraft two days before.

He tapped his finger on the map, showing a location, then put his hand down on the table and addressed his troops.

“Here is where the Gypsies should be arriving in the morning.” He winced, he then scratched at the mutilated ear once more. He looked across the table.

“What do you think Wolfgang?”

The rugged-looking officer grunted, he then nodded in agreeance. “They would be looking for some green grass to feed the horses in the glade by the river, the distance is right for them to arrive in the morning at the speed they are traveling at,” Wolfgang said with confidence.

Wolfgang took a flask and two cups from his back-pack.

“Would you like some coffee sir”.

“Yes, thank you, Wolfgang”.

The burly man poured coffee into the two cups. Gunter took a sip from his hot coffee. “Thank you, this tastes good.” He said as he drank the coffee.

The forest was pinched into less than a kilometer wide in this place near the village of Slaski, being bordered by a small river on one side and farmland on the other.

Scouts in the forest had reported the caravans traveling toward the small glade. He and his troops were waiting at this place in the forest.

There would not be any sense attacking the Gypsies in the Forrest, as many of them would have escaped in the trees and undergrowth then steal away.

Poland was the first country to be beaten into submission by the German Hitler’s Third Reich. The invasion had taken place on the first of September, nineteen thirty-nine.

When the German troops had stormed through the country many Polish officers in the armed services and officials from cities and towns were captured, and then lined up against walls and shot.

In the summer of nineteen forty-two, a vicious scourge was taking place by the Nazis to rid the Polish countryside of Jews and Gypsies.

The Jews and Gypsies were being systematically executed by Nazi SS soldiers of the Einsatzgruppen acting under orders from Reinhard Heydrich, 'The hangman of Prague',

Heydrich was the head of the German Reich Security.

He was noted for his brutal methods of subduing the population.

CHAPTER 1

People and horses were desperately in need of water for washing and drinking. The water barrels on the wagons were almost empty. The horses also had to share the water. It had been some days since they had been near a river or stream. The line of Gypsy Caravans was moving slowly from the trees onto the edge of a secluded glade in the forest.

Men and boys jumped down from the seats of caravans to guide them under-cover as they stopped moving. The caravans were then carefully backed up to be among the trees on the edge of the green grassy area.

The pre-morning calling of the forest birds was not the usual joy to hear by the people, who were fleeing for their lives. The loud calling was a worry as it masked any other background noises from the forest.

A canopy of tree branches partially hid them from above. There was a small river within one hundred meters. The

The caravans had been painted a drab color over the bright patterns which had adorned them before the war. Dark browns, greens, and greys formed a camouflage to help hide them in the forest.

Fear showed on the faces of the caravan drivers. They checked from left to right in the dim pre-dawn light, straining their eyes, watching the shapes in the forest for any sign of movement. One of the Gypsy men had used a dimmed lamp with a spluttering home-made candle in it. He was the navigator. He walked in the front of the caravans looking for logs, stones, and overhanging tree branches on and above the track they were taking. After walking for some time, a new person would take his place.

A broken wagon wheel or axle would be a huge inconvenience in their flight from Poland.

There was no music or laughter, as was usual when setting up a new campsite. The worried grim look on the people's shadowy faces as the early sunlight peeped through the trees, as the sun slowly rose over the horizon.

The angled sunbeams shining through the trees threw off large shadows which, when the breeze blew the tree branches made them look like a troop of shadowy living beings moving in the new dawn light.

The people were extremely afraid. They had heard tales of the atrocities being carried out against their clansmen by the Nazi SS troops.

The genocide was being carried out from the orders to exterminate the Jews and Gypsies which had been given by Adolph Hitler to Reinhard Heydrich; they were the cause of the alarming situation that the people were living in.

Marko Rominski half stood then carefully looked around before he climbed down from the wooden seat of the caravan; he grasped rail on the edge of the hard-wooden seat and then used the spokes of one of the front wheels as a ladder to reach the ground. Marko was a heavy-set strong man with the dark hair, dark skin, and the Romany features of a Gypsy. His eldest son Ivan and daughter Sasha followed him down to the grassy ground.

They then began to help him unhook the two horses from the caravan.

He called into the caravan in a loud whisper for his youngest son Bernado to help with the horses. The lad was not inside the caravan. He was missing. This was not unusual for Bernado was well known as a good forager for food.

"Where is Bernado?"

Marko quietly asked Krysta his wife as she collected the bowls and spoons for their meal.

"He had noticed a light dimly shining in the distance some way back. He was going to see if this were a farmhouse. He said the farmhouse may be a good place to search for some food he said. You know what he is like; I tried to stop him from going."

Unhitching the horses from the caravans was difficult because all of the chains and hooks had string and strips of material woven through the holes to muffle the ringing noise of the chain as the horses pulled the wagon.

The people then tethered the horses to some small trees, where the tired sweaty horses started to graze on the green grass and tree leaves while waiting for the bucket of water from the nearby stream to drink.

Other horses from caravans were also being tethered nearby. Men and children working with the horses were careful not to make any noise.

Men and children then pulled small boughs from the trees and climbed to cover the roof of each caravan to camouflage them from any aircraft flying above. They talked in muffled tones as they worked. The other women were working taking the cooking utensils out of the caravans. A small fire was lit in a makeshift stove constructed from a small round drum with the top removed. This drum had holes pierced around the bottom to let the air to the fire. This was to minimize the usual amount of smoke from the normal cooking fire.

The fire drum was used to cook with a deep pot which was hung into the top. The pot contained some meager fare of weeds, nettles, and one of the rabbits which had been snared after leaving the previous week's campsite deep in the forest. There was no bread or cheese. These luxuries had not been eaten for many months.

When they were camping at the previous site some days before. A young lad had wandered into the camp from the thick forest.

The two camp dogs noisily announced his arrival.

Georgiou who was from a different Gypsy family, then walked to Marko begging for food.

This poor lad was very thin from living in the forest alone and having to eat bugs and grass. He had to hide in the trees at night in case the wolves or wild boar was to catch him. His legs and arms were covered in scratches and sores, caused by him moving through the prickly shrubs and climbing trees.

His clan had been friends with Marko and the thirty members of his Rominski clan.

Georgiou explained his problem.

"I had been out looking for food when I had heard the sounds of guns firing."

He shuddered at the thought of what he was about to recall. “When I ran back to the camp. I stopped some distance away. I watched my family being murdered by a horrible SS commander and his evil men. I did not see the face of the man telling the men to kill as he had his back to me. He had a mutilated hand with only two fingers. I saw this as he waved his hand to show the men were to attack”

Georgiou started to sob.

“When my parents and sisters and other people were all killed, I watched as some Polish prisoners tossed the bodies of my parents and relatives onto the tray of a large truck. The nasty man had walked away and was standing talking and laughing with his men. I still could not see his face. I was afraid of being caught and killed, I ran away.”

He greedily ate a mouth full of food and drank some water.

“I was sleeping in a tree one night when a pack of wolves started to growl and then try to jump up and climb to where I was trying to sleep wedged in between were three branches came out from the tree trunk. One wolf could almost reach me. I was very afraid as I could not climb any higher into the tree as there were no branches to grab onto. They had finally left me. I was scared about getting down the next morning in case they were waiting for me.”

Marko talked to other members of the clan. A decision was made. Georgiou was taken into the clan by Marko and his family.

Marko and his extended family of three brothers and his two younger sisters, and with their husbands, wives and children made up the clan. There were six caravans, two wagons, a goat in milk, and fifteen horses.

The family had heard rumors of the Nazi atrocities against the Gypsies and Jews some time ago. They were extremely worried that they may also be caught.

Marko was plotting a course toward Hungary. He had heard from the few other Gypsy clans that they had met that this country had not yet been invaded by the Nazis. This involved traveling during the moonlit nights and keeping in the forests and sparsely populated areas so they were not seen.

As they ate their meal, one of Marko's sisters Aasha stopped eating. She had a long-hooked nose with a thin face and a shock of unruly grey hair. She could pass for a witch with the right clothing. She then spoke to the clan in a soft voice "I had a bad vision last night. I could see people with guns and young boys running from one person to another with knives and cutting them while laughing. I saw this man with three fingers missing from one hand and only having one eye and ear. This was an evil man."

Aasha was one of Marko's sisters who in better times had been a fortune-teller at fairgrounds and other events they had frequented. This vision worried the people of the clan; they discussed this in whispers amongst themselves as they ate from their bowls.

Bernado was just twelve years old. He was walking through the forest toward where the dim light had been. He was navigating by the stars. His eyes had become accustomed to the gloom after the moon had set. The brilliant starlight from the sky helped him to see. He left the forest then climbed through a wooden rail fence then walked across a freshly plowed field toward the farm. He had run into a gorse bush and had some spines in his ankles; these would have to wait until morning when he returned to the camp.

The farm-house was carefully avoided as it would surely have a large dog sleeping outside. He could just make out the outline against the bright starry sky, of what looked like a chicken coop some forty meters from the house. He crept carefully toward it trying to not make any sound. He made sure he kept downwind from the house and probable large dog.

The horses and other animals in the barn nearby made contented noises as they slept.

When he arrived at the coop, he could hear the rustling of feathers and the soft sleepy cluck of some of the chickens inside. Bernado lifted the latch on the gate and then entered the wired coop. He went into the henhouse then carefully opened the door; he quietly stepped inside, felt amongst the sleeping chickens as to not wake them. He slowly put his hand around the head of a chicken holding its beak closed.

He then pulled it into the folds of his thick coat to stop it from making an alarm call or flapping its wings. A few of the chickens were disturbed somewhat, but they still clucked quietly.

As he left the chicken house and was crossing the plowed field back toward the forest he looked at the twinkling stars netted in by the tangle of tree branches. A shooting star drew a line of light across the sky just above the tree line before it vanished and died.

He twisted the neck of the chicken. The chicken made a loud noise which started a large dog barking back at the farmhouse. Bernado climbed the wooden rail fence and re-entered the forest. He was heading toward where the caravan tracks should be; he navigated by the star-light once more.

The first rays of sunshine were now peeping over the horizon. This made finding his way through the forest far easier. After a short time, Bernado found the tracks of the horses and wagons. He felt proud that he had caught some decent fare for the pot and food for the clan.

He had been walking for almost an hour along the trail left by the horse's hooves and wagon wheels. Suddenly in the near distance, the sound of gunfire broke out.

Bernado dropped the dead chicken and then headed toward the sounds of screaming and gunfire, he was running as hard as he could through the undergrowth in the forest.

Marko's two large dogs were barking and the horses were screaming in pain.

In the small clearing where the clan had stopped to make camp was a horrible scene. Nazi soldiers were shooting at his family. Flame spat from the muzzles of their guns as the bullets sped to his family.

The soldiers had the family in a cross-fire with soldiers firing from two sides of the camp. There was no avenue of escape.

Young lads not much older than he, dressed in the khaki uniform of the Hitler Youth were running and laughing as they slashed at the people with knives as they lay dying on the ground. The lads were covered in blood from the people they had stabbed.

Mixed in with the noise of the screaming people and barking dogs was the shrill noise of wounded horses, as some had been shot in the crossfire by the Nazi soldiers.

A single shot in resistance was fired from one of the caravans. This was from the ancient muzzle loading rifle which was used in some of their poaching forays. The rifle had been aimed at the Nazi commander. This man had swung around to shoot at another of Bernado's relatives; the bullet had hit the man behind him in the shoulder. Machine gun fire was directed at the Gypsy caravan from where the shot had been fired. Marko's brother pushed the rear door open, he then fell backward from the rear of the caravan, missing the steps; he still held the old gun in his hands. His body was torn to pieces by the concentrated machine gun-fire.

Ruffo one of Marko's dogs leaped onto one of the boys and bit hard onto his neck. One of the other lads ran to help the bleeding boy; he stabbed the dog through the chest. The dog opened his mouth and then fell to the ground, writhing in his death throes. The lad was bleeding profusely from his wound. The other lad who had stabbed the dog wound his neck scarf around the wounded lad to stop the bleeding. Marko's other dog had now been shot.

Directing the operations Bernado spied an evil-looking man dressed in an SS uniform. His grey peaked cap was pushed back on his head. He had the look of arrogance about him. This man was directing the operations. The man had three fingers missing from his left hand which he was waving to direct the soldiers to a hiding person, he held a Luger pistol in the other hand and was firing at the Gypsies, he yelled in a loud nasal voice as he did so. The man then turned, he showed the left side of his face which had an ear missing and a patch over his eye. Bernado felt the evilness of this tall thin man. A cold shiver ran down his spine.

As he lay deep in the thick bush he watched as one of the young blond-haired boys in the Hitler Youth uniform cut his mother's throat, blood gushed out of Krysta's throat onto the green grass, she began shaking from the lack of blood as her lifeblood spilled out, then Ivan and Sasha were stabbed and killed as they ran to their mother's aid. Bernado almost fainted from the grief he held back in his heart. He had an urge to run to his mother's aid also but knew better than to sacrifice himself.

The lad was laughing and mocking the Gypsies. The smell of fear and the smoke from the guns was taken from Bernado's nose to his brain. He almost screamed in grief. Silent tears streamed down his face wetting the collar of his vest.

When the human carnage was ended, the soldiers then shot the horses and goat.

There was a noise of some heavy vehicle crashing through the undergrowth toward where he was hiding. A large truck with wooden sides on the tray was driven past where Bernado was, nearly running down the thick bush he was hiding in, as it crashed past him through the short shrubbery. The truck stopped in the clearing near the bodies on the ground.

Ten Polish prisoners of war in striped uniforms jumped down from the truck and started to drag the bodies to the truck. They then picked up the corpses and tossed them onto the truck tray. Two of the prisoners climbed back onto the tray and dragged and stacked the bodies. The men were covered in blood from the dead Gypsies.

When the job was finished a soldier walked to each of the caravans, he had a backpack with a hose leading to a gun-like device, as he walked to the first caravan he fired a stream of flames into the van from the flame thrower. This was done to all of the vans, each one was well alight.

Two people who were hiding in the vans ran out with their clothes well on fire. One of them was Georgiou.

The Hitler Youth boys ran to these two people as they lay on the ground writhing in pain from the burns of the fire which had been squirted into the van, the boys stabbed each one many times.

A few minutes after the carnage was finished and the Nazi's were congratulating each other, some prisoners went to the dead horses. Two went to the dead goat. The dead goat's belly was slit, it was then gutted. The goat's carcass was towed across the ground to the dead horses. It was then tossed with the large pieces of meat which were cut from the horses. This was then tossed onto the truck with the dead Gypsies. This was going to be used to feed the prisoners who had been working throwing the bodies onto the trucks.

The truck drove off through the forest. Crashing through shrubs and small trees until it finally stopped in another glade in the forest. Bernado extricated himself from the bush he had been hiding. He then followed the crashing truck as it mowed down the small trees and shrubs. He was careful to keep far enough from the scene not to be seen.

The truck came to a halt some three hundred meters away. Vehicles were parked here, two small amphibious rear-engine vehicles and another large truck with a covered tray.

Bernado again hid in some brush as the men stopped fleetingly near the other vehicle. When they started to move again, he extricated himself from the bush he had been hiding. He once again followed the crashing truck as it mowed down some more small trees and shrubs until it came to a larger clearing in the forest.

The Nazi Commander screamed some orders; the Polish prisoners jumped down from the truck and undid a box running along with the chassis of the truck. Spades picks and shovels were tossed out on the ground. The emaciated Polish prisoners selected tools. The Nazi commander paced out an area to dig and had one of the prisoners follow him to mark the corners of the soon to be grave with a pick. He dug a shallow hole on each corner of the rectangle which had been stepped out.

The men started to dig in the moist soil, digging the hole some five meters long by three meters wide. The soil and clay were tossed out on three sides of the hole. The men sweated profusely as they worked, A young soldier watched them would menacingly point his gun and then occasionally yelled at one of the men to work harder. The bodies and meat on the truck were covered in green flies. The people's bodies started to swell. Bernado could not bear to watch. He was transfixed by the horrible scene but was afraid to move. In his mind, he was formulating horrible curses on all of the SS soldiers.

After an hour and a half, the commander returned with some of the men to check the depth of the hole, it was nearly two meters deep. He yelled in his nasal voice for all of the men to get out of the hole, it was deep enough.

The men were helped over the rim of the hole by others pushing them up the slippery bank. The men out of the hole handed the handle of a long-handled shovel to the men to hold as they left the grave.

One man was left in the hole without another to help him up. "Hey Yarko, what say we leave you there. You can stay with the dead Gypsies and keep them company in the hole." The man in the grave yelled back some abuse. The men laughed as two of them reached down and grabbed an arm each and towed Yarko over the side of the grave. The prisoners were extremely thin and grubby.

The Polish prisoners then tossed the bodies from the truck into the hole. Bernado watched as the members of his family were thrown so the bodies were in line, with their heads up to the other side of the hole. The truck was started and moved farther along the edge of the hole. Bernado had tears streaming down his face. He could hear the moan of one person who had not yet died.

The truck was driven away when all of the bodies were thrown from the truck. The prisoners then set about refilling the large hole.

His dead parents and relatives then had the dirt thrown over them as the prisoners toiled with large shovels. Bernado shuddered as his mother's face was covered with a shovel filled with dirt. He felt numb with the horror of watching his whole world collapse in front of him as all of his family was destroyed by the evil man.

The SS officer was laughing with the troops and boasting. "Hey, Wolfgang. These were the easiest we have had to kill. I wish some of the others had been this simple. Only one person fired a shot."

Wolfgang smiled and nodded,

"how easy has it been to kill this mob, hey."

He said to Wolfgang his second in command.

The soldiers and Polish prisoners climbed into the trucks and finally drove off.

After they had left the scene Bernado walked to the mound atop of the mass grave and collapsed to the ground and sobbed. Being a Gypsy sobbing was not normally a thing done. In his clan, it was a sign of weakness. Bernado found it difficult to move from the mound of dirt which had engulfed his family.

Feeling an extreme sense of guilt and sorrow, he then walked back to the burnt-out caravans, smoke was still rising from the ashes of the vans.

He found nothing worth salvaging as all clothes and timber had been burnt. The springs and axles with the rings which had been the tires on the wooden wheels and the clasps and chains from the bridles and other saddlery were all that was left of the wagons.

A few pots and pans and crockery lay in the ashes. He found the blood-smeared patches on the grass where each member of his family had been systematically murdered. He sat near where his mother was killed and the tears streamed down his face and mixed with her blood on the grass.

The stench of death filled his nostrils. It was like having sniffed chili powder, it burned to his brain.

Bernado suddenly realized how hungry he was. He had barely eaten for the last three days they had been traveling. He ran back to where the dead chicken from the morning lay and bought it back to the clearing. He pulled the dry feathers hard and found it tough to remove them from the now cold dead bird.

He then searched through the ashes and found the blades of some burnt knives. He then remembered that his father always kept a sharp knife in a scabbard on the halter on one of the horses. This was to be able to cut the rope in case they had to flee in a hurry. He walked to the dead horses still tethered to the trees and found the knife.

The horses were starting to swell up; green blow-flies had found the cut off sections and were accumulating in large numbers. The smell of terror still emanated from the horse corpses. These horses had been part of the family as well as the dogs.

There were some coals among the ashes where one of the caravans had been burnt; he found warped steel handled pan. He then cut the chicken into pieces ready for cooking

He placed this on the coals and then started to cook the pieces of the stolen chicken,

As he watched the chicken pieces sizzle in the frying pan. He turned them over with the large knife he had found. His thoughts went back to his murdered family and friends, as he studied the scene of carnage, he hoped in his mind that this had been a terrible dream and he would waken to find his family cooking and tending the animals.

He had never been left alone before in his life. He did not like the feeling. The thought then hit him. He was the last member of the Rominski clan.

As he ate the hot chicken pieces, he thought hard, his thoughts went to the present situation. The memory of how weak and ill Georgiou had been from hiding in the forest for three weeks, and the tales of wild animals foraging around looking for prey, was on his mind.

After pondering further, as to where he should go, he deducted that if he were to follow the small stream as it meandered down through the countryside there surely should be a village or some farmhouses along its course.

Before setting off, he meticulously checked the burnt wagons again to see if he could find some coins or any other valuables, he could sell to buy food. He knew where the strongbox was situated in his father's van where any money would have been kept.

He dug around and found the hinges and lock of the box, there were a few coins, these were misshaped by the heat of the fire, any paper money was burnt to ash. The jewelry had melted and any precious stones had disintegrated in the heat. The wooden caravans had burned with very high heat.

A feeling of dread overcame him as he thought of his family working to set up camp just three hours ago. He had to move away from this dismal bad place.

CHAPTER 2

Bernado walked for four long hours; keeping the stream on his left side. He walked in an almost straight line, sometimes a reasonable distance from the stream. He had not discovered any habitation in the forest near the stream. The night was quickly approaching. The tales of the wild boar and wolves in this area from Georgiou weighed heavily on his mind. He had listened to the Wolves bay at the moon on some occasions when sleeping in the caravan with his family.

The gorse spines in Bernado's leg had started to fester. They were very painful. He sat down on a rotted tree stump and studied the festered lumps. He took his father's knife from his clothes. The black spots of thorns showed in the festered pimples. They were carefully removed with the knife-point, and then the pimples were squeezed with his thumb and the back of the knife blade.

He then walked and checked the low shrubs in the forest. After carefully looking for some time he found the one he needed. He walked to the bush and cut off a small sprig of leaves.

The bark was pared off the stem, and then the juice oozing from the stem was dripped onto the area with the pimples. This stung his leg as it seeped into the open pimples.

With difficulty, Bernado then climbed into the fork of a large oak tree, as night was falling. He was hoping this would deter unwanted visitors during the night. He broke off some small branches and used them to cover himself during the cool night. He had his father's large knife lying loose at his side ready for any problems which may arise.

He was woken once during the night by the grunting of some wild boars which were foraging in the dark eating some of the fallen acorns at the bottom of the tree. He did not hear any sign of a wolf pack. He went back to a tortured sleep.

The heavy overcoat had kept him warm during the night.

He had resolved to try to find some sort of shelter he could camp in during this day, for the coming night, as he climbed down from the tree.

At dawn, he started walking along the edge of the running stream, still hoping for a house or village, somewhere to try to beg for assistance. He felt very lonely.

About noon there was the smell of cooking wafting through the air blowing from the direction he was walking. After a short while, he could see an old farmhouse that was surrounded by trees. He had eaten some more of the chicken to fill his hollow stomach. The smell of the farm's food had a far more alluring odor.

The forest gave way to farming land. As approached the house, the large dog laying on the doorstep guarding the doorway to the farmhouse had its hackles up. It rose and was growling as he walked closer. Bernado did not show any fear as he neared the house.

He was frightened inside his head by this dog, but knew if he were to run the dog would most surely attack him.

As he walked to the growling dog, he pulled a chicken leg out of his coat pocket and called to the grumpy dog.

“Here dog, come for food.”

The dog stopped growling and sniffed at the air; he then walked timidly, with his tail between his legs to Bernado, he peed on the ground and then took the food, and then nervously jumped back.

The door of the house was opened by a large man with a huge brown mustache peppered with grey. He had a pair of red braces over a checked shirt holding up his heavy trousers. “What do you want?”

He said in a loud gruff voice as he glared at Bernado. “I have been lost in the forest all night. “Bernado said. “Where did you come from? “The man asked in a loud voice.

“A long way up along the river,”

Bernado pointed back from where he came. The man’s attitude softened somewhat. He studied Bernado with critical eyes,

“Are you a Gypsy?”

Bernado did not know what to say but nodded yes. “I have no time for thieving Gypsies said the man, as he turned to re-enter the house. “Please, wait! I want to tell you what has happened.”

As he said this the man’s wife appeared at the door. She was a kindly looking plump woman with blond hair, which was plaited and wound around the top of her head. She was dressed in a blue house dress with an apron covering the front. The apron had flour dust covering it in places from her preparing to bake bread.

Bernado related the story of how his clan had been murdered the day before by the Nazi soldiers. He described the young lads stabbing his family and how he had watched his mother die. The large blonde woman had a look of compassion come over her as the story was told; even the large man looked sorrily at Bernado. “You must come inside and have some food lad,” The woman said.

The man stepped back to let him pass.

The kitchen was warmed by the large cast-iron stove at the wall. A pot sat on the side of the stove to keep the food warm.

The woman took a clean plate from a cupboard and then ladled a large spoon of delicious spicy smelling food onto it. She then cut a thick slice of crunchy crust bread from a freshly baked loaf on the table and added some slices of cheese.

Bernado sat at the table and started to eat the meal with a spoon. This was some of the tastiest food he could remember having ever eaten. She gave then him an apple when he was finished. Bernado was overwhelmed and thanked her.

The man looked at Bernado.

“I am taking some pigs to the village market in Slaski tomorrow. If you would like to sleep in the barn and help load the pigs I will give you a ride. I want nothing to be stolen. You hear me?" Bernado nodded and agreed to this.

The man and lady sat and talked to Bernado after they had eaten. The lady explained how her three sons had gone to join the Polish army to fight the German Nazis as they had advanced through Poland. At least they had been told they were still alive some weeks ago, even though they were now slaves for the Nazi's. They had news of this when another lad had managed to escape some weeks before. He was lucky and had found his way home, he lived nearby. The family talked long into the night with Bernado after the evening meal. It was interesting for them to try to understand the Gypsy's nomadic lifestyle.

The man then rose from the table.

"Come with me boy, I will show you to the barn where you can sleep".

Bernado followed the large man outside, the man took a kerosene lamp from a hook outside of the door. He lifted the glass then fumbled for a box of matches in his trouser pocket. He struck the match on the box then lit the lamp, He then trimmed the wick to stop it from smoking.

They left the house and walked briskly to the barn.

The man stopped, then with effort opened the door of the barn.

They then walked inside.

There were animals in wooden stalls making the noises most animals make when sleeping. The man hung the lamp carefully on a long nail in a post, he pointed to where he Bernado could sleep; there were piles of warm straw to cuddle up in. The man gave him a horse blanket to sleep on and fold over himself to keep warm. When he was settled in the man left for the house, taking the lamp, then closing the barn door behind him.

The horses made comforting noises during the night which reminded him of when he was living in the caravan with his family.

The noisy rooster woke Bernado.

Soon after the man came and opened the barn. He then went to a rail supported by two splayed legs on each end in the barn, this rail had saddles and bridles for horses laid over it. A saddle and bridle were selected, it was then taken into the horse stall. He put the saddle blanket, then the saddle onto the horse. The bridle with the long reins for the cart had the bit fitted into the horse's mouth. He then took the horse from the stall to hook it onto the wagon. Bernado had experienced a bad night dreaming of being chased by the one-eared and eyed man. He would never forget his evil image as long as he lived.

Bernado was standing behind the man as he worked.

"Here boy, help get the horse into the cart."

Bernado had done a lot of work with the horses; the horse and wagon were soon hooked up. The cart was backed up into a ramp adjoining the pig-sties.

The pigs were sorted from the smaller ones. They were not keen to climb up the ramp into the wagon, it took a lot of pushing and yelling to get the ten medium-sized pigs on board. Some of the pigs would squeal and snap at him as he tried to push harder. Finally, the grumpy pigs were loaded. The rear gate on the cart was closed then tied with a length of stout cord. Bernado climbed onto the wooden seat next to the man.

As they left for the town the lady came out of the house, she walked to Bernado and gave him a thick cheese sandwich and another apple. The bread was still hot from being baked in the oven.

During the two-hour trip to Slaski, Stanislaw talked about when his boys would come home. News of the war had been passed from word of mouth through the country. He and his wife were desperately looking forward to seeing their sons if they were still alive. The horse plodded slowly toward the town in the distance. This area had no strategic need for the Germans, so they had been mainly left alone.

On some occasion's food was annexed for the troops.

The steel tires of the wagon chattered over the cobblestones of the road as they entered the main Slaski village road. When they finally arrived at the market Bernado was contemplating his future, moving to a bigger town may have more opportunities to find food to keep him alive.

The pigs did not like the chattering vibrating tires as the wheels ran over the rounded cobblestone road in the town. They started squealing and fidgeting in the wagon.

The wagon was driven through the food and produce stalls. When they stopped, people milled around the wagon prodding their fingers through the slats on the sides of the wagon at the pigs. The pigs were squealing and snapping their teeth at their fingers as they did so.

Stan reached for the steel rail on the seat He hauled himself up then stood on the wagon tray amongst the pigs. He scanned the crowd with his eyes and then in a booming voice offered his pigs for sale. He auctioned them to the customers, one at a time. The people would pick which pig they wanted. Certain marks were made on the sold pigs with blue raddle on their back, The Stan would ask for bids on the remaining pigs again.

When each of the deals was done, Stan would crouch down; both the buyer and Stan would spit on their hands and clap each other's right hand together. Some pigs were tethered and towed away by people in the town. Some were transferred to another wagon.

Bernado helped transfer the pigs.

When all of the pigs were sold, Stan bid Bernado farewell. He gave Bernado some small coins to help with food just before he left.

Stan then drove off in the wagon to the store to get some provisions with some of the money he had earned.

As he walked around the small town Bernado was looking for some deserted building to stay in before moving on to a larger town. He had no idea where the roads led off to. He would camp somewhere. Then the next day tries to find some information about where to go.

Bernado noticed an old woman was standing on the footpath in front of a shop. She was studying him intently. She smiled at him, then walked over near to him in the street. She looked over at him, thinking deeply. She had the look of a Gypsy by the clothes she wore and the two large gold rings in her ears. She then walked to Bernado.

“Hey young boy, I have seen you with Marko and his family.” Bernado looked up at her but did not recognize her.

“My name is Zelda. You must remember me! I am the best teller of fortunes that there is. I have visited your people and have eaten with them. I last visited them just two years ago after a fair. How is that sexy Marko?”

Bernado had a huge lump in his throat.

“My father and all of our people were murdered by the German Nazi SS three days ago.”

He described the carnage at the hands of the Gestapo when his family was murdered,

Zelda had a look of horror on her face as he recounted the grizzly story of the murder of his people.

When he finished telling the story, she put her large arms around him and pulled him to her ample breasts.

“Oh, poor lad. We live in such terrible times.”

As he finally stepped away, she reached and gently took his right hand, she carefully turned it palm up,

” I will see what the future holds for you.”

She then bent over closer as she studied his palm.

“I can see you will have revenge in a bad way on the man with his eye and ear missing. You take comfort from this lad. It will not happen straight away. You will be there when it does”.

She dropped his hand, then asked.

“Would you like to come and live with me in my small house by the river?”

Bernado was overtaken by the offer of hospitality.

“Yes, please Zelda.”

“You will not be getting free board and lodgings I tell you. You will have to work hard”,

“I am not lazy and I am strong. I will help you.”

She turned toward the road leading out of the village.

“Well, come along lad, I will show you my house.”

The walk and constant chatter from Zelda affected to lift Bernado’s spirits somewhat. She pointed out the different birds and butterflies that they saw along the way.

A small path led from the road some three kilometers from the edge of town. This led to a small run-down cottage with a thatched roof.

As they neared the house there was a lot of barking from dogs and noises from other animals.

As they walked closer to the house, a large Irish Woolf Hound ran down the lane to meet them, when he saw Bernado, his hackles rose upon his back, he growled a menacing growl.

” Hey Pepi this is my new worker.”

Zelda took Bernado’s hand and held it out toward the large toothy mouth. Bernado did not show his fear. He was really afraid, being confronted by this huge dog. Pepi came and sniffed his hand and reluctantly gave it a lick with his long tongue. “See, now he knows you, he will not bite you now,”

When he pulled his hand away Bernado was still not too sure of this. The dog was licking his lips in anticipation, he thought.

The house was small, but the inside was cozy, it had a smell of herbs and perfume from flowers. There were rows of sachets and small jars lined up on a long table by one wall.

The embers of the fire in the hearth still had enough coals to rekindle the fire. Zelda put some kindling wood, then a log onto the coals. She bent down and blew onto the kindling to help it catch fire. “I do not let this fire go out Bernado. This will be one of your jobs. I have had the same fire going for fifty years.” She turned away from the hearth.

“Come outside and look at my animals.”

They walked through the house. The back door creaked as she opened it. There was a dry-stone walled yard that ran down to the small stream.

In the yard, there was a menagerie of different animals Cats, Dogs, a goat, and some tame birds sitting in the trees, even a large owl. The owl glared at Bernado with huge eyes. ‘Who! Who! said the owl.

“The people here think I am a witch, so they keep their distance from my home, except when some person is sick or they feel as if there has been a spell set upon them. This keeps me in provisions and some money to live.”

They returned to the house. After they had entered Zelda took a large round loaf of bread from a box then cut off four slices. She put the bread back, she then found some cheese in a pretty blue bowl with a lid on an old kitchen dresser. They sat at the heavy wooden table, as they ate Zelda made Bernado an offer.

"I will teach you some of the black arts, and ways to heal. I will also teach you to read palms and minds. I am an old woman and I would like to have someone to be my pupil. I do not have children, I never could. I am barren. When I have gone, all my learning will be lost." Bernado was pleased and grateful to have a place to sleep and to be able to continue his Gypsy heritage.

The days were enjoyable. He rose at daybreak every morning as the multi-colored rooster extolled the beauty of the new dawn with his loud crowing. His first job of the day was to rekindle the fire from the coals which lay deep within the ashes.

Bernado became very fond of Zelda. He had many chores to do.

Trapping rabbits with snares and keeping the firewood box filled. He would scour the forest near the cottage then cut the dry fallen tree branches with the large axe, they would tie the branches together with twine, and carry them home on his shoulders.

He was always on the lookout for mushrooms and herbs to add to the pot to flavor the rabbit stews.

Many days were spent walking in the forest where Zelda showed him where there were different herbs used for healing and other spells.

"You must always look under logs and pieces of bark. Some of the fungus which grows there is good for medicine."

She turned over a rotting log to show the red fungus.

They would always come home with a large basket filled with a different fare.

Usually, the herbs bought a wonderful aroma to the cottage; some potions surely did not when Zelda was boiling them in a special pot. Bernado spent many hours crushing the herbs in a large mortar with the pestle to reduce them to paste or dust to mix into the salves or medicines.

Pepi always accompanied them as they roamed through the forest. He still glared at Bernado when Zelda was doing something and could not see.

"Hey Pepi, come now, you be friends."

Pepi would come to Bernado and lick his hand. Bernado always felt as if he tasted him ready for when he took a piece out of his hand. He was under the impression he was just tolerated by the large dog. The smaller dogs and other birds and animals had long since accepted Bernado as their friend.

The small dogs of which there were five ranged from the size of a large cat to an Alsatian. Pepi was different; he towered over all of the other dogs; he was boss. Bernado still treated Pepi with great respect; Pepi treated Bernado with condescending contempt, barely tolerable.

Over the following months, Zelda taught Bernado many things, the art of fortune-telling.

"You must always look into the person's eyes. You can see when you have touched on a subject close to their heart. Telling a good fortune helps people cope with the problems we have with the world and our lives. Now we have the German soldiers to add to our every day worries."

A pretty young blonde woman knocked on the door one morning. She explained that she was in love with one of the local boys; he did not even seem to notice her. Bernado asked her to come into the house and then to sit at the table, as she sat down, he sat opposite her. He gently took her hand, then turned it palm up, and then studied her palm and the lines for some time; he then told his first customer what she wanted to hear about this boy.

"I am sure this boy would be proud to talk to a beautiful young woman like you. I would think that he may be afraid to talk to you because you might make fun of him. Just look at this man in the eyes with your beautiful blue eyes. He will be smitten. I have a potion here that will make you look more beautiful to the eyes of this young man."

Bernado selected a small vial from the many on the long shelf and sold this to the young woman.

Zelda had been listening from another room. She complimented him and gave him some of the money.

"This girl is just too shy to approach the boy. What you have told her will make her less timid, she will take the medicine, then usually she will talk to the boy and then the birds and bees take over."

After dealing with his first customer, he was now making and dispensing medicines to people of the town and also advising about the black arts of curses and other similar arts. There were many visitors to the cottage to purchase cures and ask about setting spells and curses. He was now skilled enough to advise some of these people of the remedies and cures which were available. There were small bottles and sachets of powder and other substances to cure most ailments.

Zelda told him a story one day.

"The human body is a strange thing. If a person is given something and is convinced that this will cure them, the body takes over and the cure works. In some places in the world a person can sing another to death, even pointing a bone at a person will cause them to die in some societies if they know they have had the curse put on them."

Bernado had taken to trying to train the dogs. They had all been strays which would have usually have been taken and shot. Zelda had asked the Dog catching man to keep any healthy dogs for her to keep.

He started to teach them to do cunning tricks. Pepi was not included in these lessons, as he had refused to be taught, if Bernado had tried to include him in any lessons he would growl menacingly and show his large teeth, he would then sit and watch. Any more effort from Bernado caused Pepi to become nasty and snarl menacingly, showing his large yellow teeth again with a more menacing look.

There was an old gramophone in the house and three records with stirring marches on them. Bernado asked Zelda if he could use it to try to train the dogs. He would use the music to teach the dogs to pair up and dance together.

"I never use it Bernado so it is yours."

Bernado thanked her.

Training progressed. The dogs would look forward to the gramophone being taken outside for their lessons.

Zelda was quite fascinated by the dancing dogs and commented to Bernado that he should take the troupe of dogs to town and start to earn money by showing their acting to the people.

The war was still raging and German troops had started to move through the country headed for Hungary. This was a very worrying time for the Polish people in the area, who until this time had almost been ignored by the Nazi regime. The roads to Hungary were nearby.

One morning Bernado was away from the house and walking through the forest alone, checking on the snares he had set near some rabbit burrows.

He had caught two nice fat rabbits and was heading home to the house. He heard the deep barking of Pepi in the distance. The barking had a more urgent sound than normal. Bernado had a feeling of dread come over him as he ran through the trees toward the house. There was the sound of some gunshots. This bought back memories of his family and the terrible massacre which had occurred.

As he neared the house, he saw that Zelda was lying just outside the door of the now burning house. When he ran closer, he noticed that she had been shot through the head. The gold earrings had been ripped from her ears. Pepi was lying next to her and had also been shot. The thatched roof over the cottage was well alight. The eaves were hanging over her dead body and were beginning to drop burning pieces of thatch down on her. The searing heat kept Bernado from Zelda's corpse. There was nothing he could do to help, he ran around the house, keeping his distance from the searing flames.

The small dogs had been shot, any animals which could have been used for food like the goat and chickens were missing. The large owl was looking down from his tall tree, he looked down at Bernado and said who, who, Bernado certainly knew who. Nazi soldiers had raided the house looking for food and had murdered Zelda and her animal friends.

He sat in front of the burning house in a state of shock. His body was shaking. There would be nothing salvageable from the burning house. Bernado felt a deep sense of loss once more. The last nine months with Zelda had been a very rewarding time; she had been a very good teacher. He waited until the roof finally collapsed inwards on the house. Zelda's and Pepi's bodies were smoldering from the heat. The roof had not fully covered then when it collapsed.

As he set off for town Bernado contemplated what his future might hold for him, he had the feeling that the two disasters had followed him and that he was somehow in some perverse way the cause of all of these terrible events which had happened.

He had a really bad feeling of dread as he slowly walked toward the village. He once again felt the horrible pain of loss. He screamed out loud and asked himself what would be happening to him next.

CHAPTER 3

Nazi troops were in the village in large numbers. They outnumbered the people in the street, as many local people were keeping off the street and were in self-imposed hiding. Children were kept inside the yards and houses, especially teenage girls.

In previous trips to the village with Zelda, Bernado had spied a tumble-down cottage, which had a yard filled with tall weeds.

He sneaked through the main thoroughfares, avoiding areas with the troops, and found the small house.

The small cottage had no glass in the front windows and the door was askew, but the thatched roof looked like it would keep off the rain. Bernado entered the cottage, pushing the door, which was missing one large hinge open. There were pieces of broken furniture and some old rusty cooking utensils next to the fireplace. The windows which had the broken glass had wooden shutters that looked as if they would still work to keep the cool wind out. The rear of the cottage had two windows which were not broken, and a door that would still work.

He was still carrying the two dead rabbits which had their legs tied together with a piece of string; this was around Bernado's neck and the rabbits hidden under his coat. He walked out to the rear of the cottage through the old door, its hinges groaned at being used for the first time in many years. He took his father's knife from the folds of his clothes, then skinned the skin off the rabbits, and then gutted them, tossing the smelly gut a long way from the door. It was cold in this old cottage. He walked to the front of the house and with much effort finally shut the rotting shutters to keep the wind out, the door with the broken hinge was pushed shut and latched with the rusty latch. He then walked to the rear door of the cottage and walked inside. Shutting the shutters on the broken widows and closing the door kept most of the cold wind outside.

Bernado had seen some members of his clan make fire by rubbing two sticks together when it was needed as one of the fires had gone out, Bernado scraped some of the old dry wood off some broken timber which had been furniture with his father's knife, and had a small pile of scrapings, he then split a piece of wood off a larger piece ready to kindle the fire.

After a lot of effort rubbing this piece of wood in the middle of the larger piece, he finally had some smoke. He blew onto the smoking tinder, a small flame appeared which was fed with more dry wood shavings; he soon had a small fire in the old fireplace.

The rabbits were cut into pieces and then cooked in one of the old rusty pans. He turned the pieces over with the stick he had started the fire with. The warmth from the fire finally started to warm the small room.

After this meal, Bernado thought about the learnings and good times with Zelda. How could such a bad thing happen twice to him in such a short time?

The cold morning air woke him, Zelda's house had always been warmed by the fire in the fireplace, and the little fire he had used to cook had long since lost all heat.

Having ventured outside from the rear door to see what the day would bring, and also relieve his full bladder in the roofless old toilet, he went back inside and took a large pot and placed it outside under the thatch of the roof where there was water running down from the light cold rain. He would need some water to wash himself, and for drinking.

Making sure he was not near the streets where the soldiers were, he scouted around the town looking for something to keep himself warm during the frosty nights.

As he walked along a rear laneway he kept looking every way to see if he could find something which would keep him warm at night. He noticed that there was a damp rug hanging on a clothes-line wire in the frosty sun to try to dry it after having been washed, Bernado reached over the fence along the laneway and slowly pulled the blanket into the lane. He then rolled it up and carried it back to his new dwelling place. Few people were out in the street in the bleak cold wind.

Later that day he checked the rubbish bins at the rear of the restaurant where the soldiers had been eating. There were vegetable peelings and some bones. He took them and wrapped them in a small hessian bag from the trash can, which had held the vegetables when they were delivered.

On the way, back to his new home, he noticed a dead tree branch hanging down on a tree. He grabbed the end of this and pulled it back until it snapped off the tree. The small branch was added to his needs for the cold night.

He took the fire-making timber and made a new fire, a stew was made with the remains of the rabbit, vegetable peelings, and water from the bowl outside. It was quite bland without any seasoning but it was food. The room was warmer with the fire going.

Bernado was worried; he thought his prospects of surviving were fairly bleak in the cold damp cottage by himself.

The next morning, he was foraging for food again. He had the sack inside his heavy coat. He walked into a small shop. The small dark-skinned shopkeeper glared at him, he did not take to the look of him.

His eyes followed him around the store like a hawk looking for prey. "What are you looking for?" He yelled to Bernado.

He did not answer.

A fat lady came into the shop and was talking loudly to the man. He took his eyes off Bernado, this was his chance, and he slid a large box of matches, some salt, and curry powder into the bag and was searching for more food.

Unbeknown to him the lady had left the counter and was looking at something in another area of the shop. The man yelled at him as he noticed him slide a can of fish into the bag. He yelled again and ran toward him,

Bernado was used to being chased, he ducked past the shopkeeper and fled onto the street, he ran back to the old house. Two days later he was scouting another part of the village He had stolen another blanket from a clothes-line and had been spotted by the house owner.

The plump woman ran onto the street yelling

"Thief, stop the thief. "

She was repeating herself very loudly as she ran after him. Bernado turned to look over his shoulder behind him to see if this lady was gaining on him. She was running faster than he thought she could have. She was catching up to him. He sped up, looking frantically over his shoulder.

He turned a corner of the road. Thud! He fell to the ground dazed; a large hand reached down and picked him up.

It was a Polish policeman. He wriggled and kicked at the man, there was no way that Bernado was going to break the hold of this large man.

The puffing lady arrived at the scene; she had a very red face as she took the blanket back from Bernado. She swore at him in a screeching voice and then shook her fist in his face as she left. The old tall policeman's grip tightened as he dragged him to the police station which was three streets away.

When he had finally dragged Bernado inside, he took him into the open cell; he then quickly stepped out and shut the door.

"We have a little robber in town and it seems to be you. What am I going to do about you?"

Bernado looked at him with a surly look on his face; he then turned away to the bleak wall of the cell.

The policeman went to his desk and started to study a sheaf of papers.

He then left the station.

After a while, he returned with a pot filled with some potato's meat and thick gravy. He placed the pot just outside of Bernado's reach. "I think you might have a good story to tell me." He kicked the food slightly closer to the cell door.

Bernado knew there was no way out of this situation, he resolved himself that he had been caught, possibly lucky he had been caught by the local police instead of the German soldiers.

"Please sir I will tell you my story!"

He first told the story of how he had watched as his parents and relatives were murdered.

"The man who was directing the soldiers was deformed with scars on his face, and had three fingers missing and had lost an eye and ear."

The police-man was horrified to hear this story.

"That murderer was Gunter Khullman. If I were ever lucky to set eyes on him I would shoot him like a rabid dog." The Police-man said, with emotion in his voice.

Bernado then told of how he had been living with Zelda. The policeman pushed the pot of food under the cell door. He took the pot and started eating ravenously.

He finally stopped eating.

"I was alone and met up with a nice lady with the name of Zelda. She was teaching me to become a healer. I was training her dogs to do tricks and helping find food and herbs in the forest. I came home with some rabbits I had caught and found her shot through the head, she was dead and her house was burning."

The Policeman turned his head, he then spat toward the door. "I curse Hitler and his murderers. Zelda has helped many people in this town. She was a good woman. We found her yesterday after one of the town ladies went to visit for some medicine. There was nothing left of the house and her burnt bones and the big dog bones were found in the ashes near the door. We have sent a man to dig graves for both her and her dog." He spat at the doorway again.

"I hope I will live to see the day when these thugs have to pay for what they have done. I would especially like to see all of the Nazi murderers like Reinhard. Heydrich, the Commander of the murderers, and also the person who killed your parents Gunter. Kullman faces the hangman."

The look on the policeman's face softened.

"There have been so many orphaned children since the cursed Nazis have taken over our country."

He thought for a short while,

"There is a good place run by the church for children like you, in the large town of Rybnik twenty kilometers away."

Bernado did not know what to think of this idea. He was surely going to have problems looking after himself.

"What is this place like?" "It is run by some nuns and two priests. The children are well fed and have good clean clothes, so I have been told. The children have to help with the washing, cleaning, and cooking."

Bernado thought for a while, he then agreed to go to this place. If it were run by the church he should be protected from the German soldiers.

The policeman said he had business in the town in three days he had to stay in the cell until he was ready.

During his wait, the Policeman bought good food and some bread and cheese. They had spent many hours talking of Bernado's life as a Gypsy, and his life as a policeman.

CHAPTER 4

The Policeman walked to the cell, opened the door with the large key, and let Bernado out.

"I want your oath that you will not try to run away. I do not think you could survive alone in this or any town. I am afraid that most people would not take a Gypsy child to be with their family. If the Nazi soldiers caught you, they may kill you, or do other despicable acts to you."

They both walked out of the police station. There was a black car outside.

Bernado had never ridden in a car. He had seen some scooting along the roads, rudely tooting their horns to get the horses and caravans to move off the road.

The car was an old shiny Model T Ford with a black box with bars on its windows, mounted on the rear of the vehicle.

"Do you want to be put into the back in the box or sit in the front with me? I do not want you to try to escape. I want your solemn oath that you will not run away."

The policeman stressed again.

Bernado thought deeply before he answered.

"I agree to this, I do not want to hide from the Nazis, they would probably kill me like a dog if they caught me."

The policeman opened the door and followed Bernado into the car. The car tipped over somewhat when the large man swung himself into the seat. The man switched on the ignition switch then pressed the starter button on the floor with his large boot. The engine spluttered to life. The man selected a gear from a pedal on the floor.

The car started to move from the police station.

He felt a bit nervous at first sitting in the noisy contraption. As the trip went further, he became more at ease and was enjoying the scenery as it whizzed by.

As they turned a corner in the road there were some German army vehicles parked next to the road. A beam of round timber was across the rough gravel road and was blocking their path. Two German soldiers stood in front of a small shed next to the checkpoint. They had a fire burning in an old oil drum to keep themselves warm. One of the soldiers sauntered over to the vehicle. The other stood by the fire casually holding his machine gun.

The policeman stopped to show his papers at this checkpoint on the outskirts of Rybnik. The trooper asked about Bernado as to where his papers were.

The policeman explained as to there being a bad house fire as to the reason for not having papers. After some talking, finally, the other man slung his gun on its strap over his shoulder, then went and unhooked one end of the beam and carried it off the road.

The car drove between the posts then pulled back onto the road and headed through the houses toward the middle of the town.

There were German troops everywhere one looked.

The old car threaded its way through the trucks and tanks and artillery guns on the street.

After driving for some time up and down streets with many wrecked or damaged houses there was a large drab-looking building. Joining it further up the street was a large church with two tall steeples on its steeply sloping roof. The policeman drove off the edge of the road and parked his car in front of the church.

They both alighted from the car and walked to the large doors of the church.

Bernado looked up at the front of the church which had a group of two carved angels above the doorway. The clouds streamed past the tall steeple making it look like the front of the church was falling, he felt giddy.

The policeman opened the large church door.

"Come Bernado, I want to introduce you to the priest." Bernado turned back and followed the policeman through the heavy door to an office. A nun was sitting at a desk writing notes on a piece of paper, she looked up at the policeman and Bernado, she had a frown on her red face.

"Can I help you?" she asked in a terse manner.

"Yes, I have a homeless orphan with me whose parents have been killed by the Nazis."

The fat, sour-looking, red-faced nun studied Bernado through her glasses with contempt. "I will go and get Father Paul."

She rose from her seat with effort and waddled down a hallway to a door and knocked. A thin unsmiling man opened the door and then walked into the room. He looked piercingly at Bernado. "Good morning officer I see you have another orphan for the church."

The policeman told a brief history of Bernado. He did not mention the gypsy connection; just the two bad situations which had happened to Bernado in the last few months.

“Thank you, officer, the boy can come with me now.”

Bernado thanked the policeman as they left to walk inside of the church.

As they walked into the church Bernado was overawed by the size and beauty of the huge room with its painted altar and golden figurines. Rows of candles burned on a table in front of the altar.

“Have you never been in a large church before?”

“No never.”

Said Bernado as he was transfixed by the altar and the carved Jesus nailed to the wooden cross. He was going to ask who the man on the cross was but thought better of it.

When they walked from the church Bernado noticed a pathway bordered by rose bushes leading to the large building that they had passed on arrival at the church. Father Paul took a large key from his pocket and unlocked the door leading into this building.

They walked past two offices with three nuns working at desks. The nuns stood and crossed themselves when the priest passed. A door led into another large room which had long tables and forms to sit on, this room smelled like rotting food.

A door on the side of this room led to a paved quadrangle with buildings on all four sides. A large crowd of boys played in this area. As the priest walked through the children, they crossed themselves. They entered a door on the other side of the quadrangle; three middle-aged nuns were busy mending clothes,

" I have another boy for you." announced the priest.

The nuns looked up from their work, turned up their noses, and scowled at Bernado. The Priest then turned and left him with the three nuns.

One nun stood up, she glared at him through her glasses.

"Follow me. I will show you where to clean yourself up, you smell like a Billy goat." She ordered.

She took him to a room with a series of showers along a wall. "Right boy, take those dirty clothes off, I will take them and wash them."

Bernado was loath to take off his clothes in front of this strange woman, plus he still had his father's knife secreted away in the folds of his coat.

"I do not have all day to wait for you, don't worry boy I have seen it all before, you are no different."

Her menacing tone made Bernado obey. He slowly peeled the layers of clothes off and handed them to her. He took the knife, as he handed it to her, he pleaded.

"This was my father's knife please do not lose it. It is all I have left to remember him from." "We will look after it for you." said the nun with a lack of conviction.

The water was freezing. The soap hurt his eyes when he washed his hair as he had been told to. Bernado had his first reservations about his new home.

As he dried himself with the dirty thin towel, the nun returned with some clean clothes, she studied his body like a vulture.

"How old are you, boy."

"I am thirteen years old miss."

She looked down between his legs; she kept staring and then muttered.

"You look like a very big boy for thirteen", she could not take her eyes from his large penis.

When he had dressed, she said in a bossy voice.

"Follow me."

He followed her out into the large quadrangle surrounded by high stone walls. She walked with him to a door.

She pointed to a door further along the wall.

"When the bell rings go into that door and you will get fed."

Some of the children were watching Bernado as the nun left. One came over and held his hand out.

"I am Nicola." Nicola was a slightly built lad with red hair and freckles

Bernado grasped his hand.

"I am Bernado."

The other two boys came over:

" These boys are Walther and Yanko." Both the boys were taller than Nicola and had dark hair like Bernado.

Bernado shook both of these boys' hands.

” Why were you bought here,” asked Nicola.

“My family were all killed by the Germans”.

“So were ours, we were left alone with no one to care for us,” said Nicola.

A bell started to toll. All of the boys hurried through the door to the mess room, Bernado stayed with the other three boys. They sat at the forms along with the tables.

The old Priest came out and sat at the head table with another younger priest. Two red-faced nuns in a more elaborate dress sat with them. Starting from the first table the boys filed past a small wagon with a large cast-iron pot sitting on it. In front of the pot on a shelf were piles of wooden bowls, next to them were wooden spoons. Each boy took a bowl and a spoon. The bowl was filled with a ladle from the pot by two of the older boys.

It was finally Bernado’s turn to have his bowl filled. The food was finely cut peel from potatoes and some grains of swollen wheat floating in it. It did not smell very nice at all.

As he walked back with the three new acquaintances, he noticed that the priests and nuns had roast meat, potatoes, and green vegetables with thick gravy; they also had crusty bread and cheese.

Bernado was going to start eating;

“Wait for the Priest”, hissed Nicola

He stopped the spoon in mid-air and waited.

The head priest stood and recited grace in a droning voice. As soon as he finished the boys all started to eat.

The food was not very nice at all, it was bitter and smelled as if it had been boiled many times. Bernado forced himself to eat his as he was hungry. He recoiled from the smell of the food as he ate it. When they had all filed outside of the mess room, he felt squeamish from the food.

"Is the food always this bad"?

"Sometimes it is worse"

Yanco answered

"Do we ever get outside in the town?"

"Very rarely, only on special occasions."

Suddenly he felt an urge boiling up in his gut.

"Where is the bog, I feel sick?"

Nicola pointed to a doorway in the wall halfway along the other side of the building.

Bernado took off in a quick trot. He ran into the room. Rows of dirty toilets without any walls or doors for privacy lined the walls, there was a long trough with taps above it every meter was along another wall. A long single urinal was past the trough. Some of the other boys were also using the toilets.

The room had a nasty smell of its own, dirty unwashed toilets, and the smell of rancid urine in the urinal. Bernado sat on the filthy seat-less toilets and in one heave emptied his body. Some small cut pieces of newspaper tied with a string sewn through the corner where the toilet paper.

During the day Bernado had three more visits to the toilet, his anus felt like it had been moving gravel through it. Yanco said this always happened to new boys. He would be fixed in a few days.

The evening meal was a sort of porridge with some of the oat husks still in it, small pieces of some sort of meat floated in it, this meal smelled stale also. He forced himself to eat it.

After the evening meal, a bell carried by one of the nuns was rung loudly as she walked through the quadrangle. The boys were all ushered inside to the dormitories.

Rows of rusty iron beds with a folded thin blanket on each one under the uncovered striped pillow lined each wall. There was barely room to fit between each bed. Bernado was in the same room as his new-found friends.

The room was cold and smelled like urine and feces as the toilet block did. He later found the lumpy hard mattress also had a population of moving small biting bed bugs to keep him company. He slept very restlessly.

As the sun rose the nun with the bell walked through all of the dormitories loudly ringing her bell. Bernado woke with great reservations about his new home. His body was covered by red lumps from the bug attacks during the cold night.

Breakfast was a thin gruel of oats and water. All of the other food he had eaten the day before the food had a similar bitter taste as the cooking pot.

After the meal, he had the urge to run to the toilet again. This urge happened three more times during the day. His anus felt as if he was passing sharp shards of broken glass out of it now.

Nicola had an old worn tennis ball with which they played catch. They would run around the quadrangle tossing the ball to each other and bouncing it off the walls. Some days they had competitions with other boys playing catch and chase plus other ball games.

The bedding in the dormitory was still filthy after the first two weeks and still smelled like urine and sweaty bodies. It was not taken to be washed. The bugs were still trying to eat him as he slept. The one thin blanket certainly did not keep him warm. Occasionally one of the nuns would open the door and walk through the room with a dim torch, counting heads as she did so. There was a rush for the freezing communal showers in the morning. The lye soap burned his eyes when he was washing his hair. It stung the welts where he had been bitten by the bugs during the night.

Bernado noticed that most of the boys had red lumps where the bedbugs had been biting them.

Sunday morning after breakfast the boys were all dressed in better clothes and had to go across to the church for mass. As the boys filed into the church they all dipped their fingers in the holy water and crossed themselves in front of a statue of the Virgin Mary. Bernado just walked past this, he did not know what to do.

A short distance past the doorway was the young priest. As Bernado walked past, he reached out and grabbed his arm, he then forcibly dragged him into a small room.

" You did not cross yourself in the presence of the Virgin Mary."

"I did not know what to do."

"I will teach you what to do so you remember."

He offered. He grabbed Bernado by the neck in a vice-like-grip and forced him over the desk in front of him. He then reached over to a long cane which was nearby in the corner of the room. He swung the cane back and hit Bernado very hard on the behind three times. This hurt and bought tears to his eyes.

"Now you might remember to show some respect for the Virgin Mary and the church."

He let Bernado go. He wiped the tears from his eyes on his sleeve before he walked out of the door.

The church service had started. The orphanage boys sat together in the front rows of the church. Members of the public sat behind them, leaving two empty rows between them. This was evidently to keep away from the poor smelly orphans.

The older priest was ranting in Latin. Bernado found a seat at the back of the church and listened to the service. It made no sense to him. He had trouble sitting on the cut marks from the cane on the hard-wooden church pew. He had to change sides as he sat on the red marks from the caning.

When they filed out of the church his three new friends caught up with him.

"Wow, you were brave not to cross yourself before going into the church."

"I did not know what to do."

"I bet you do next time, that Father Mark loves getting the chance to hit us."

It took three days before he could sit without feeling the excruciating pain. When he walked past Father Mark, he crossed himself as he had been taught by Nicola, the priest had a smug look on his face.

"I think you may finally learn if you meet up with my persuader a few more times." He said with a smirk on his thin face.

One day after lunch, two weeks after he had arrived at the orphanage, one of the sour-looking nuns took Bernado's hand. "You will come with me boy I will cut those long locks of greasy hair off. "

He knew it was no good arguing. He was sat on a chair while she took a rusty old pair of hand clippers. She cut all of his hair off to the scalp, as she did so she pulled at the clippers pulling hair out before it had been cut. She then had a small round tin can with holes in the top, it was marked DDT; she then shook some white powder on the bald head to kill lice. Bernado looked at his mane of black hair on the floor. Itchy hair was down his neck and back.

As he walked out of the door the waiting boys came to him and studied the white bald scalp.

"Hi baldy, looks like you have had the treatment, you have blood running out of cuts on your head;" said Nicola.

"We all have had this before; your hair will soon grow. We think they wash the hair and sell it for people to make wigs." Bernado's head felt as if it were freezing.

Bernado was assigned for kitchen duty washing the spoons and bowls after the meals. Ten other boys were also doing this with him.

The muck in the large cast iron pot was tipped out into a bucket and kept to be mixed with the next meal.

The bottom of the cooking pot stank like rotten food when it had been emptied; no amount of washing took the smell away.

Some of the boys in the orphanage had taken other boys into a group and had formed gangs. These boys were usually larger than the others and enjoyed trapping some smaller children and then beating them. The smaller child was herded to a secluded part of the quadrangle and thrown into the ring with the bully. The bully usually had his way and beat the smaller hapless child. The nuns could see this happening on many occasions and took no action. They just did not care.

One afternoon Bernado was walking to the school-room to meet up with his friends. A ring of children suddenly surrounded him and forced him to a corner of the quadrangle. A tall nasty dark olive-skinned large boy called Billy came to Bernado. He taunted him, "Dirty thieving Gypsy."

Bernado was in the circle of boys who had joined arms to act as a fence. Bernado tried to no avail to push his way through the boys.

They kept pushing him back into the middle of the ring. Billy came to Bernado and pushed him to the ground. He kicked him in the side two times.

Bernado had never had this treatment before, he jumped to his feet. Billy came toward him once more, he was taunting him again. The lad was considerably taller than he was. He had a smirk on his face.

Bernado threw a punch with all of his strength; he hit Billy right on the nose. He felt a crunch as Billy's nose broke. Billy recoiled back and fell to the ground on his behind. Blood gushed out of his nose; tears poured out of his eyes and ran down his cheeks.

Bernado turned to the mob and with his fists up ran at the smallest boy. The lad pulled back from him and broke the boy's fence grip and ran away. Bernado ran through the gap. He ran to the school-room. "Where have you been?" asked Walther.

"I was nabbed by the gang who get around with that nasty Billy."

"What happened?"

"Billy pushed me over and started to kick me in the guts. I jumped up and punched him on the nose. I think I felt a bone break when I hit him, I must have broken his nose."

"How did you escape?"

"I ran at the little Jani, He was frightened by me running at him, he broke the chain of boys around me. I ran away".

A short while later, the door of the school-room opened. A red-faced Father Mark entered. He came to Bernado.

"Come with me, your a young trouble maker. You have been fighting".

Bernado looked at Father Mark defiantly.

"I did not start the fight, it was Billy."

"I do not care who started the fight, you have broken the nose of the other boy".

Bernado was dragged along the corridor by one arm, then into a room. He was pushed hard across a desk and given six hard cuts with one of the many canes he had stashed throughout the orphanage's rooms.

When he returned from the room to the school, he had tears in his eyes.

"What happened to you. Did the priest hit you again? "Nicola asked. "That mongrel gave me six cuts with the cane for defending myself." He winced in pain.

"I will get to him one day."

The bully Billy had also been to see father Mark and had the cane treatment. He was seen walking around the quadrangle for the next two weeks with a large bandage stuck to his nose. His gang had deserted him.

The seasons were changing. The days were getting colder. The first powdering of snow was on the ground outside. The windows of the dormitory were covered in ice on the inside; the thin blanket on the bed did nothing to keep the cold away. The nights in the freezing dormitory were now punctuated by the coughing of sick boys.

When a child was very ill, they were taken to a sick-bay and fed on slightly better food and given a bitter green medicine which tasted like tar.

Some of the boys did not recover. They died. Their bodies were placed in a deal box and taken from the orphanage by a hand cart towed by a gaunt-looking old man.

Just fewer mouths to feed thought Bernado as he watched the cart being towed out of the door one day with a chanting Father Mark following behind it. The bodies were buried just outside of the walls of the orphanage in unmarked graves.

One morning three Nuns came into the dormitory. One had some tins filled with white powder in a bucket.

Every boy had to stay in the dormitory and had to strip their beds. The three nuns had shakers filled with the DDT lice powder and shook this over the beds. Each boy then had to turn the mattress and pillow over as well as lay-out the thin blanket for the treatment. Little black bugs started to climb out from the bedding and drop on the floor. Some of the boys had brooms and were assigned to sweep them up.

When they were out in the quadrangle Nicola said.

" I wonder if they put the bed bugs in our next lot of food, they sure don't waste anything here".

"It's a pity we could not serve them up to the priests and Sisters on the head table"

Bernado said.

" I would like to see that Father Mark get one stuck in his neck".

The routine of the orphanage carried on, working at cleaning, washing the bowls and spoons, bending over large tubs with scrubbing boards in the laundry. They were always overseen by one of the priests or nuns. The blankets were washed every three weeks. The smell of the dirty blankets when they were wet almost made Bernado gag the first time he had to do the job.

Bernado's thick black hair had grown again. The days were finally getting warmer. Bernado had three more episodes with Father Mark's persuader, as had many of the other boys. This man seemed to enjoy this kind of work. He had persuaders secreted in many rooms of the orphanage. There were arguments and even some fights between some of the boys in the quadrangle. One was a brawl between two different gangs of boys. The result was a meeting with father Mark's persuader for each of the boys. This was done outside over a table, which two of the boys had been told to fetch. All of the boys were commanded to watch. The only winner was father Mark who enjoyed the job. He was puffing from the effort of caning the twelve boys.

There was one area of the orphanage that the four boys started to have some sort of enjoyment. This was the afternoon lessons conducted by two grumpy nuns and Father Mark.

Bernado could not read or write.

Nicola had gone to school before being placed into the orphanage. He was very proficient at reading and writing.

He took it upon himself to help Bernado and the other two lads to learn.

After a very short time, the lessons began taking effect. Bernado and the other boys were reading simple school books with ease. This kept the boys out of the quadrangle, and also away from the gangs of trouble makers. It also stopped some of the mischief-making they were becoming involved in. There was a library of old worn children's books which could be read in the dusty room.

Bernado was leaving lessons one day and was following Father Mark, going down the four steps to the quadrangle to go to lunch, his foot slipped on the top step.

He grasped the stone wall in vain to stop himself slipping. He careered into the Back of Father Mark; he tumbled to the ground with Bernado on his back.

Most of the children in the quadrangle stopped playing, they watched Father Mark struggle to heave Bernado from his back then regain his feet. As they watched the scene unfolding, they then all started laughing,

Father Mark turned extremely red. He grabbed Bernado and dragged him up the steps; his face was still a crimson red color.

Bernado was saying he was sorry all of the time.

"You little Gypsy bastard, I will make you pay this time, I will not be made a subject for laughter" he yelled, as he shook Bernado violently.

He dragged him back inside the door, then into a small room with a desk. He had been here before and had met one of the priest's persuaders.

The priest kicked the door shut, then bent him over the desk, and instead of reaching for the persuader, he pulled Bernado's trousers down, tearing off the top button as he did so.

Bernado was terrified. The priest held his head down on the desk with one hand while he fumbled with his clothes. "I have something that will teach you a lesson here boy." The next thing Bernado felt was something being rammed up his behind.

He screamed with pain as the skin tore.

"You can scream, Gypsy no one cares what happens to you here." The priest kept pushing and grunting, Bernado was still screaming with the pain.

"If you tell about this, I will find out and your life here will not be worth living. You hear me?"

Bernado, still sobbing, nodded his head. The priest pulled out his now flaccid member and tied up his trousers.

"You remember boy this is between us. If you behave you may not have this happen again."

As he opened the door the priest reminded him.

"Just remember what I said, no one cares about you, I am a man of God, you are just a Gypsy boy, they will believe me over you."

Bernado staggered out of the door holding his trousers up. He felt the hot blood dampening the trousers as he carefully walked to the toilets.

The boys came across to him as he slowly walked to the toilet. "What happened, you're bleeding from the bum?" "I would like to kill that Priest;" he said through gritted teeth.

The boys followed him into the dirty toilet block. Bernado sat on one of the toilets and when the bleeding stopped, he washed his behind carefully. His trousers had a dark red stain of blood on them.

"What happened to you?"

"The rotten priest stuck his tool up my behind. He tore a lot of skin. Hell, it hurts."

"I have heard he has done this to other boys. Two boys went to Father Paul. They each told on him, and then they got six cuts each from Father Paul for trying to cause trouble by telling lies."

That evening after the meal Bernado went to one of the nun's, Sister Mary who seemed to be a nicer person than most other nuns. "I had a button ripped off my trousers today. Could I have a needle and cotton to sew it back on please?"

"I will do that for you."

She found a needle and thread and a small chocolate tin filled with various sized buttons. She selected one which fitted the buttonhole and started to sew the button back onto the top of Bernado's trousers while he still wore them. When she had finished, she looked hard at the bottom of his clothes. "What is on the bottom of your trousers it looks like blood?" "I fell over and cut my behind on a sharp rock. "Bernado lied.

After the meeting with Father Mark, Bernado tried to avoid him. He always tried to keep a lot of distance between himself and the priest. This did not work; He was walking past the small office one day. Father Mark opened the door and grabbed him from behind before he could run away. He dragged him inside then kicked the door shut, He raped Bernado again. This did not hurt as much but it disgusted Bernado just by the filthy crude act.

"You remember what I said before. You know what will happen if you tell."

Bernado ran past him outside to the quadrangle.

"That rotten mongrel nabbed me from behind and did me over again."

The other three tried to console him.

"He had better not try again. I will get him."

One day about two weeks after he was raped, a cart had come into the quadrangle through the gate, which was usually locked; one of the nuns had opened it. The cart had a load of wood for the kitchen fire. A skinny tired-looking horse pulling the cart, and a tired grubby looking old man driving it. One of the nuns called Bernado over to help unload it, and carry the wood inside to keep it dry. One of the pieces, which had come from a bombed building, had a six-inch nail in it. This was an old flat steel nail, not a new round modern one, the head of the nail was a piece stepped out on one side.

He hit the wood on the stone of the doorway, and the piece split letting the nail fall out. He had not been seen; he put the nail into the pocket of his trousers.

When he was with the boys, and when alone during the next week he would rub the nail on a sandstone block on the building foundation. The nail was honed to have a sharp point and shiny sides.

"What do you want this for?" asked Nicola.

"If that rotten priest tries to rape me again, I will try to get him," said Bernado, with vengeance in his tone.

He then bound some old material from rags used in the kitchen over the nail head, then with some string he had found in the kitchen, he wound this round and round to secure it together. The nail looked like a small stiletto. Bernado thought about what he would do with his newly acquired dagger. Possibly use it to jab in the priest's eye may get a better result. The length of the nail was not long enough to use elsewhere. The dagger was hidden in his clothes from that day. The priest must have found some other young boy Bernado thought, as there had been no other attacks with him. He had started to become complacent; it was three months since the last encounter with Father Mark.

There was some good news about the war at-last, one of the boys had been told by one of the nuns that the German army was in bad trouble, and the soldiers were now retreating to Germany. Thousands of Germans had died in Russia during the freezing winter.

Bernado asked Sister Mary one day if this were true. She had a cutting from a newspaper in her handbag. She took it out and showed this to Bernado. On the page was also a report of how one of Germany's heroes had been killed by cowardly patriots who had ambushed him while he was driving to work. As Bernado scanned through the writing the name of the person jumped from the page. The war hero was Reinhard Heydrich. The man was The Hangman of Prague. He had been blown up by having a bomb tossed into his car. He had died in hospital three days after the attack. Bernado felt a wave of elation at hearing the man who had ordered his parents and friends killed had been killed himself.

"That man is the one who ordered my parents to be killed;" He said to Sister Mary.

"Maybe God had something to do with his demise"

She smiled, then took the cutting from the newspaper from him, then placed it back into her handbag.

"The news is not that good. The Russians are coming after the Nazis. They are just as bad."

She had heard that the Russians had also killed millions of Jews, Poles and, gypsies, as well as many of their Russian people as well.

The mood lifted somewhat in the orphanage as the boys thought they may be let out and taken to a more humane place with better food and conditions.

Bernado was walking to meet the boys after he had finished working in the kitchen. He passed the small, office without a thought that Father Mark may be there. He usually passed this place at least twice a day. The priest must have seen him coming and was lying in wait.

As he passed by, the slightly ajar door opened fully; before he could run away Father Mark grabbed him and dragged him inside the room. He struggled violently as Father Mark pulled his trousers down. When he tried to loosen his clothes, the hand on Bernado's neck slipped, Bernado bit down on the priest's middle finger, he would not let go.

The priest screamed and went to hit Bernado with his other hand, Bernado moved, opened his teeth to let the finger slip out, and reached into the top of his shirt and got the nail.

He lunged at the priest aiming for his eye. The priest twisted slightly and the nail missed. It slid into the skin and embedded itself from the eye to the ear under the skin. The nail must have cut an artery as blood pulsed out of the wound, squirting over Bernado's clothes.

The priest held the bloody eye with the nail still embedded under the skin; he screamed oaths that no decent priest should have ever known. Bernado quickly slid out from under the priest, then pulled his trousers up, he ran out of the room and headed for the office with the door which led outside on to the street.

He was still holding his trousers up as he was too frightened to stop in case Father Mark was close on his heels.

He passed the two nuns sitting at the desk. He had blood from the priest's finger and face all over the front of his shirt.

This must have been his lucky day because when he arrived at the doorway, he heard a key rattle in the lock; Father Paul opened the door to enter the orphanage. Before the two nuns, who had been sitting at their desks could rise and catch him; Bernado pushed past him knocking him down on the floor and, then ran out onto the street. He kept running until he was puffing madly.

When he finally stopped running. He was puffing profusely. He gasped, trying to get his breath. It was only now that he looked behind himself to surveyed the lay of the land around him.

This part of town was a residential area with two-story buildings lining the street. Some of the houses had been bombed when the Germans had invaded Poland. The bricks from the ruined houses had been carried off the road and were tossed back into the wrecked buildings. This was not where he wanted to be, he wanted to be where there were markets and shops. The time was now mid-day; the clock in the Town Hall had just chimed twelve times. The boys used to hear this clock in the orphanage. Bernado headed for the sound of the clock.

He went down many streets and alleyways. He could hear the sound of traffic in the distance. Finally, after a half-hour walking, he started to see people hurrying along the street, and a few cars and busses moving.

He did not see any German uniforms among the people. Bernado was now fifteen years old. This time he would try not to get caught by the police, he considered that he was old enough to work and look after himself.

As he walked his thoughts went to the kindly old policeman who had taken him to the orphanage. This man had honestly thought the church would look after and care for the children who were alone in the world.

CHAPTER 5

The business part of town had fared worse from the artillery and bombing than the residential areas he had walked through. Some of the taller buildings had pieces missing from them; others had been demolished and were piled up to keep the road open.

Bernado thought that there should be some places on these buildings which he could live in. A lot of people had been killed or taken away and murdered by the Nazi's, there would be no problems with owners wanting to evict him.

A dark-haired strong-looking man with bright clothes had a stall selling food in a temporary type of market area where some of the bombed buildings had been cleared. He had a large cart with a roof, similar to a Gypsy caravan, but with canvas sides. These were rolled up to display the vegetables and fruit. A horse with a nosebag filled with chaff stood nearby. The horse had a pile of manure behind him. Bernado walked to the man and asked if he needed some help with his business. The man laughed and said.

"Boy, I have six kids who help me, they are all mine and my wife's. I certainly do not need another helper."

He laughed with a deep voice. He then looked at Bernado. "You look very skinny, are you hungry? Do you want a few of the bruised apples to take with you?" He pointed to the pile of horse manure.

“Would you please shovel that horse poo into a bag so I can take it home for my garden;”.

“Yes, I would like some of the apples please; I am looking for somewhere to live.”

“If I were you I would look at some of the empty buildings which would probably have water and maybe even power turned on still. You may even find one with some furniture inside. Many people have gone missing since those cursed Nazis came.”

Bernado took the shovel and bag and was soon finished manure shoveling chore. The man gave him the bag of apples.

He then left the fruit seller.

As he walked through the small market, he asked others if they could help with work for him. He also discussed the fact that he was looking for somewhere to live.

One old man offered Bernado some bread and cheese from his stall. He cut two slices of bread and some cheese and handed it to Bernado. Bernado thanked him, he then walked on.

Another thin old man selling second-hand clothes from a four-wheel cart called to Bernado as he walked past. He knew of a place he could live in.

“The people who had lived there have been taken by the Nazis; I think they have been taken to a nearby gas-chamber;” he said.

Bernado had never heard of this before and asked the man what the gas chamber was.

“The cursed Germans build places where they take people who they loaded into cattle cars on the railway. They are taken to these places, where they are taken to rooms, where they are told they were going to have a shower to get rid of lice.

There is no water in the showers there is only poison gas. The people are poisoned with gas.” “How any could people do this?”

“Ask the damned Adolph Hitler, if he is still alive. I curse his soul.”

He looked at Bernado, sizing him up.

“Are you strong enough to pull the cart for me when I go looking for clothes to buy?”

“I am looking for any way to keep myself alive. If you want me to help, I will try hard.”

He stayed with the man as he sold some of the clothes to the needy looking people.

“I will show you this small house if you pull this cart home to my house tonight. I have arthritis and my back hurts when I drag the cart.”

They talked while waiting for customers. Bernado offered Stefan one of the bruised apples. Stephan took the apple, bit into it, he then thanked Bernado.

As he pulled the cart, Stephan walked next to him and started talking.

“My wife had been killed in the street when a German bomb had hit a building near where she was walking.” Stephan Said. He had a sad look on his face.

“My wife and I could not have children. So, I am all alone in the cold world.”

Bernado marveled at how the old man had coped with pulling the heavy cart to work. His house was a long way from the market. They talked on the way. Bernado told him of the terrible thing that happened to his family. He also said about the orphanage and the priest.

“I have lost faith in god. My wife and I went to church every Sunday, and I paid tithes to the church from my wages as a clerk in a drapery shop every Sunday. Look at the world today. Look what the priest did to you in the name of god.”

Finally, they came to his small house. They left the cart parked inside his gate and then walked three doors down the road. These houses were joined together in blocks of four. They were one room wide with a top story.

“Here is the house where my friends lived.”

The door was ajar. They walked inside. A narrow hallway passed a small room this led off to the stairs.

The house had been ransacked but there were some pieces of furniture. They walked upstairs to find a bed and some dirty bedding covered in dust. A few clothes lay around the room from where they had been sorted through by the looters. There were two upstairs rooms.

The old man tried a light switch. The bulb came to life with a dim light shining through the dusty globe.

“People have not been checking electricity and water meters. They have been trying too hard to stay alive.”

They walked down the stairs. The kitchen had a built-in stairwell along one wall it had cupboards in it. There were some pots and pans which were rusty and some cracked cups and plates in these cupboards. A small rusty, single hot plate electric stove with a small oven was in a cupboard. Through the door was a small walled area with a brick toilet at the back corner.

Standing up hooked to the wall under the eaves was a galvanized iron sit bathtub.

"I feel great sadness about coming into this house. Many nights my wife and I shared a bottle of schnapps or vodka and shared a meal and laughter with my friends, now they have been murdered. I have not laughed since they were taken away."

Stefan walked outside to the road. He coughed up some phlegm and spat it on the road as he turned then walked back to his home.

" I will see you in the morning."

He said and then turned back toward his house.

There was a lot of tidying up to do before he could sleep that night. He picked up some of the dusty men's clothes and held them to himself; they looked as if they may fit.

The woman's clothes were piled in the corner of the bedroom for Stefan to check out. He ate two of the apples and then lay on the bed and drifted into a contented sleep. Many things had happened that day.

The next morning Bernado dressed in the other man's clothes. His were covered in the priest's blood. While waiting for Stefan to show, he found a broom in a cupboard in the stairwell in a corner of the kitchen.

Starting with the bedrooms upstairs and working down the stairs then the two rooms of the ground floor he carefully swept the dirt. The table was swept off of the three years of grime. This was picked up with a small broom and pan and taken outside and tossed into the yard.

"Are you ready for work "Stefan yelled.

He walked along the road carrying the women's clothes which he added to the clothes in the cart.

"I would feel guilty selling Eva's clothes, poor woman, but she will not be wearing them now."

As they walked together in the street Bernado pulled the cart while Stefan yelled.

"Buying and selling good clothes."

The occasional man or woman would come out of their house and catch the slow-moving cart either to buy or sell. Bernado could see there was very little money to be made in this trade, but there was just enough to keep Stefan alive.

When they arrived at the market Bernado bid Stefan goodbye. "I will see you tonight; I want to check to see if I can find some way to earn some money."

As he walked along the streets he noticed a large hand cart parked next to a ruined building, an old man was trying to pull pieces of timber from the piles of bricks. "Do you need some help?" Bernado asked.

"My wife and I have a wood stove for cooking, wood is very expensive and hard to find. This wood will probably be heaped up and burnt if people ever start to rebuild the town."

Bernado worked hard for the old man to finally fill the cart, when the job was done the old man pulled some bank-notes from his pocket, he counted them out carefully and then gave him ten groszy.

This was at least a start. Further along the road, there was a gang of men and a few women loading bricks on a wagon to clear off a site on which had a burnt-out house on it. He asked the man who seemed to be in charge if he could help.

"I pay ten groszy an hour if you are prepared to work," said the burley-dark- haired man. He had a voice that sounded like gravel rolling in a concrete mixer.

The man looked at his watch then asked Bernado his name. The starting time and Bernado's name was entered into a small book. After working for two hours, while he pulled the bricks and charred timber from the house he noticed something gold shining in the ashes, he picked up a brick and slid it over the gold and picked it up so he could not be seen.

When he tossed the bricks onto the wagon he held the gold with his middle finger. He reached into his pocket and took a piece of rag to wipe the dust out of his eye; the gold went back into his pocket.

He kept working with his eyes peeled for more booty,

Late in the day when a large amount of the site was cleared, the remains of a body were found, a bag was found in a box under one of the wagons, and the bones were carefully packed into the bag. This was a common occurrence from what the workers were saying.

Bernado was paid for his work.

” Excuse me but is there more work tomorrow?”

“Just down the road there” the man rasped. He then pointed to another burned house site. “You look like you are keen to work for a kid, I’ll see you tomorrow.”

When he left the site, he took the rag from his pocket, inside was a gold ring with a large diamond set in it. He would surely be back the next day.

Stefan was waiting when he finally arrived at the market.

“Sorry Stefan, I found some work today.”

“This is good Bernado. If one wants to get dirty there is usually some work-around.”

He did not realize how much black the charcoal from the wood had covered him. “You look like a man from Africa.” Laughed Stefan.

Bernado had never heard of Africa.

“Where is that?”

He asked as he dragged the heavy cart homewards.

“It is a country a long way from here where the people have black skin.”

Bernado was no wiser, though before the war he had seen some people like that when they were performing and playing drums and music and dancing at a fair.

When he cleaned off a mirror in the bedroom, after arriving at his house, a strange black face peered out at him.

He went down and took the tin bath off the wall and bought it into the kitchen.

He had not tried the water tap before. He turned the tap on, luckily it worked. The rusty water dribbled out of the tap. After a minute, the water began to become clear. He filled a large saucepan with water. He then took the old stove from the cupboard and placed it near the sink. He plugged it into the power, turned it on, then felt the top of the stove. It was beginning to warm up. He then took the saucepan and put it on the top of the stove. In a short while, the water was hot. While waiting he had searched the cupboards under the stairs and found some bars of dried up soap.

When he stripped off his clothes, he tossed them in the bath then tipped the hot water onto the filthy clothes; he then joined the clothes in the tub. He washed the clothes as well as himself. He wanted to try to get the bad smell of the orphanage out of his clothes and skin. A piece of cord he had found was strung from a hook on one wall to a doorknob; the clothes were hung on this cord to dry.

He ventured upstairs and tried on some more of the clothes of the man who had lived in the house before. They were not a perfect fit but would do the job. He realized how hungry he was by now.

The small shop which was on the corner of two streets beckoned him. There was cheese, crusty bread, and some canned meat and fish. He bought a loaf of bread and a large piece of cheese and two cans of fish.

When returning home, an unkempt looking stray dog timidly came up to him. Bernado looked at the poor dirty dog. He broke a piece of cheese off and held it out for the dog to take from his hand. The dog took the cheese then ate it ravenously, it then came and licked his hand in appreciation, as he walked home the dog followed him, he would stop and break some more cheese to feed it to the dog.

As he opened the door to the house the dog was hesitant to enter, it dropped its tail between its legs and stopped. Bernado fed it some more small pieces of the cheese; the dog then followed him inside the house.

While he fed himself from the thick sandwiches made from the fish and cheese, he shared his meal with the small dog. He spoke to the dog as he did this, the dog would cock its head to one side and listen to him as if it could understand him.

When he met up with Stefan in the morning, he told him about his new friend.

"You have a dog! Why do you want a dog? They are like filthy pigeons. They are everywhere."

As he walked towing the cart he kept talking about the small dog. He had never had a pet of his own before, just borrowed ones.

The work was similar to the day before. Picking up bricks and placing them into buckets to be lifted onto the horse-drawn wagons.

The wagons were very high. Especially to him as he was not fully grown yet. As he worked, he noticed one of the other workers make a find, they were careful not to show any other person. When he put the water into the bath that night, Yanko his new friend was let inside the house from the yard. He had not been sure about leaving him inside in case he made a mess.

Yanko was pleased to see him and wagged his tail madly. Bernado took a piece of cheese from the large covered pot and broke a small piece off, in no time Yanko was walking around on two feet following the held piece of cheese.

Training had started.

When Bernado had finished washing his clothes and himself, he dressed, he then took Yanko to the tub. Yanko had been tied to a length of cord; he did not like the soap and water.

The water reminded Bernado of the orphanage by the foul smell. The dog was lightly dried with some rags, when he was let go he ran around shaking himself and rolling on the stone floor.

The dog looked like a completely different animal; his fawn fur gleamed in the weak light. Some small black animals from his coat, which did not like the strong soap, were lying doing backstroke on top of the bath-water.

The water was tipped into a bucket, then taken outside and tossed on the ground among the weeds.

Bernado shared his meal with Yanko. The dog had very good manners when eating. After the meal when Bernado was cleaning the dishes and pots Yanco went to the back door and barked two times, he then scratched the door and barked again. Bernado walked to the door and opened it; Yanko went outside to the back corner of the yard and relieved himself. He trotted back inside the room and licked Bernado's hand then sat down.

This was not a wild stray dog Yanko had been someone's pet.

Stefan was told of the dog's antics; he showed a muted interest as to the dog's tricks.

" You will find hundreds of dogs who probably came from good homes. The Nazi's used to shoot them. The Polish police are doing it now. Half of them probably have rabies or some other nasty disease."

Bernado did not care. He left Stefan at the market then walked off to work.

His fingers were getting sore from lifting the rough bricks, the skin was wearing down. He did not slow down though, as he lifted some bricks into the bucket he noticed a leather pouch, he made as if he had tripped and fallen on it, as he pushed himself up he had the pouch in his hand. He reached to his pocket and took the rag and made to wipe his eye, he dropped the pouch into his pocket. He felt the pouch was very heavy.

"Are you OK, "Rasped the boss,

"Yes, I just slipped on some slippery pebbles on the floor, no damage done."

When he left work and was walking home he took the pouch from his pocket to study the contents. There were ten large gold coins in the pouch. These could be worth a lot of money. He had never seen gold coins before, only silver ones.

After he met up with Stefan to drag his wagon home he showed him one of the coins.

" You have had a lucky find; this coin is very old and will be worth a lot of money, they are very rare. A friend of mine before the war had a shop selling books and coins."

He put the coin back and said no more about the other nine. When he went to the shop that night he stocked up on some more essential goods, like some soft scented soap and seasonings for food. He also bought some pasta and vegetables plus some big meaty bones to make a stew.

Before cooking all of the bones with the stew, Bernado trimmed some meat off one bone and then gave the trimmed bone to Yanko to chew on outside while he prepared the meal.

The bone was left on the outside of the house; Yanko did some more lessons with some cheese while they were waiting for the stew to cook. He was improving and had started to dance in circles as the cheese was moved in front of him. As he rotated Bernado said "dance boy."

The job was quite lucrative; occasionally one of the workers would be busted by the boss.

"Hey! Stevo show that thing you just picked up to me."
"Ok boss."

The worker would give the piece of jewelry to the boss. Jobs were hard to find, it was better to comply than argue with him and be looking for work.

Bernado had found two more dogs, both of these had the bath treatment with the old strong soap, these two were larger than Yanco. One was a female. She was called Esmerelda and the male Punka. They instantly went into training.

Three weeks later, when coming from the shop with food, a large dog came out of an alley-way. He was growling menacingly. He evidently could smell the food.

Bernado looked closely at this dog. A cold shiver ran down his spine, this dog was a perfect match for Pepi; this big Irish Wolf Hound dog was very emaciated, its fur was all matted together.

Bernado carefully put some cheese on the ground then stepped back. He wanted this dog. The dog stopped growling and with his tail between his legs, ran in and took the cheese, then quickly stepped back.

He did this at numerous times while walking home, the dog was following and getting braver, so was he, the dog took a piece of cheese from his hand then quickly stepped back, he still followed but more closely.

This poor dog had been beaten by some person and was very wary of humans.

As he entered the door of the house he turned, he then held some more cheese out in front of him, he walked back through the doorway. The large dog entered the house. The other three dogs growled and cowered in a corner as far from him as they could get. Bernado closed the door. The big dog looked around as if he had been trapped. In the bag of food were some large meaty bones. Bernado took one out of the bag and walked to the back door and opened it wide. The big dog walked nervously to the door and smelled at the bone, Bernado walked outside and gave him the large bone.

He then had a flash in his mind and thought of a name, Shandor, this meant proud, and with the right treatment, this dog could be just that. He just hoped he did not jump out of the yard and run away. He then went inside and filled a large saucepan of water and took this to the dog. He was contentedly chewing his large bone.

When the other dogs scratched the door to go outside Shandor would growl well back in his throat, the smaller dogs would keep well away from him. When he returned towing Stefan's cart that night, he had reservations as to whether Shandor may have jumped the back gate and run away. When he opened the back-door

Shandor was still there; he even gave a slight wave of his tail. During training times Shandor would watch the other dogs. They had reached an understanding and tolerated each other, Bernado was able to pat Shandor and make a bit of a fuss of him. He was finally starting to trust him and would lick his hand.

While waiting for the boss to find another contract to clean a building site, Bernado scoured some of the junk-yards for props to use to train the dogs. He had bought some hoops and had found a child's three-wheeler bike with a tray on the back. This bike did not have the pedals on the front wheel but had pedals like a normal bike and a chain to the large rear wheels. Bernado would like to teach Shandor to ride this bike.

During training, it was obvious that the bike was too short, the seat would have to be removed and the frame lengthened.

That night he had a pencil, ruler, and a writing pad he had bought. He copied an image of the bike onto the paper. He then measured the frame in front of the pedals. The frame needed to be lengthened by at least thirty centimeters. He made drawings of the pedals with a raised surround to take the large dog's feet.

When walking to work on the demolition sites Bernado had found a workshop that did welding and repairs.

The next morning bike was tossed on the wagon among Stefan's clothes on the way to work. He had asked the boss about arriving late; he did not care as Bernado was working on an hourly pay rate. He left Stephan at the market, and then carried the bike to the machine shop. He had the drawings of the finished bike, and also the surrounds to be put onto the front of pedals so Shandor's feet would not slip off. After talking to the man and explaining the drawings, the man seemed to know what he wanted and would have the job done that night.

As he walked to the machine shop in the evening after work, he thought of the new bike design. He hoped his measurements were right.

Bernado walked into the shop filled with grinders, welders, and, a lathe. He inspected the bike, then paid the man. He picked up the modified bike. He complimented him on the good job he had done. The man had matched up the paint of the bike frame where the new extension and pedals were fixed. With the modified pedals, he could see no reason why the large dog would not be able to hold the handlebars and steer the bike.

Shandor studied the new bike suspiciously; it was now different from the one that Bernado was trying to teach him to ride. With, the seat was missing, and no longer the big dog fitted onto the frame better. He even pushed the peals three times to keep the bike moving. Bernado was excited to see the dog now trying to keep the bike moving. He fed Shandor with a small handful of the dried liver.

By this time, he now had the four other dogs doing tricks.

He had found Carmen who was a similar size to Esmerelda. She had been walking on the streets also.

When searching for new props for the dogs He had also found an old gramophone and some records in a junk shop. They were bought for the dogs to dance to the music; the dogs were starting to do a good job.

Finally, Shandor took his first ride on the bike without Bernado having to help him. Bernado was overjoyed and made a huge fuss of the large dog. He now had a constant supply of dog goodies like small pieces of dried liver that they liked to eat, in his pocket. Stephan had seen the dogs put on a show and said he was very impressed.

Shandor was quite clever; he had mastered the steering of the bike. He no longer just pedaled to the end of the yard. He would turn corners and keep driving the pedals with his large feet.

As Bernado was training the dogs some of the children from the local area would knock on his door and ask if he would let them watch the training sessions. They would make a fuss of the dogs when the sessions were ended. Even Shandor would sidle up to them to have a pat. He was nearly as tall as some of the smaller children.

Bernado bought some collars and chains, so he could move through town with the dogs. A small four-wheeled wooden wagon was added to the props. This had wooden spokes and steel tires like the larger wagons did, similar to Stephan's cart.

Bernado took Shandor and the cart to a cobbler and had a fitting made to take the small shafts of the dog trailer so he could tow it along.

The bike, gramophone and records, and other props were loaded onto the trailer. Shandor pulled it with ease.

Shandor pulling the cart was a good advertising ploy, as the load was different from the normal cart-load, people tended to follow the troupe until they set up the show. The wagon was painted red. He had Stefan paint Bernado's performing dogs on the sides of the cart. Stefan was far better at painting the names than Bernado. He had painted advertising signs in the shop where he worked before the war.

The shows were usually near shops and schools where children congregated.

Bernado would set a large pot for donations. Children were enthralled by the bike-riding dog, plus the dancers; there were the hoop-jumping and a conga style dance, where even Shandor joined in as head of the line.

The hard times had eased up a little and people liked to have some entertainment, especially for the children.

Bernado was making as much money on the weekend with the dog show as he was making with his hard work during the week.

The problems of his past, his parents and friends being murdered, and the terrible orphanage experience were not gone but had lessened in his mind.

The dog shows had been running most weekends for over five months. The dog's act was improving as the dogs learned how to do the difficult tasks set for them

One sunny Saturday, a man dressed in showy clothes was intently watching the show when they were performing in the town square. After the dogs finished acting and were being chained together and the cart loaded with the props he approached Bernado.

Bernado eyed the man suspiciously. 'What does he want', he thought? He is possibly some town official trying to cause trouble, looking for money for a performing license or some other charge.

The man introduced himself.

"Hello! Stefano is my name. I have a circus which is traveling to this town soon. I am impressed with your dog act and would like for you to join our circus."

"What sort of circus?"

Bernado asked, with a suspicious tone to his voice.

"It is The Famous Martino Brothers Circus."

Stefano said proudly. He rolled out one of the advertising posters he was carrying for the show.

Bernado had seen the ads through town. This was a reasonable size circus with lions, tigers, clowns, and horse acts, even a large elephant.

He thought intently,

"How much would you pay?"

The man offered a probationary figure. This was a lot of money. "If your act suits the audience, we will offer a third more for a full-time contract."

Bernado thought for a short time and after weighing up the offer in his mind, agreed to join the circus. The man Stefano was the ringmaster of the circus. He explained to Bernado where the circus was going to be situated in two days. They then shook hands on the deal.

Bernado thought deeply about the new job offer as he walked home with the dogs. When he arrived home, he fed the dogs then walked across the road to Stephan's house. He knocked on the door and asked Stefan to come for a meal the following night. He told Stephan about the circus job he was offered.

He walked to the shop the next day and bought some meat and vegetables for the evening meal. During the afternoon, he chopped the meat and vegetables and made a nice pot of goulash. During the meal, he talked to Stefan about the job and what Stefano had offered him as wages to join the circus.

Stefan was amazed at the wages figure.

"Before I leave, I would like for you to have something to help with your money to live on."

Bernado climbed up the stairs. He then returned after a short while and then handed Stefan one of the gold coins.

"I can't take this. This coin would be worth a fortune."
"I have enjoyed our friendship; your help was very much appreciated. Take the rest of the goulash with you when you go home. It is no good for the dogs, the last time I fed them goulash leftovers they farted all night. I had to put them all outside." Stefan laughed and grasped Bernado in an embrace before he took the coin and pot and left for home.

Stefan offered to keep watch on the house for him when he was working away.

He was sad to leave the house. The neighbors on the other side house wished him well and also offered to look out for the house when he wanted to return. The people had two small children, who had always been fascinated by the training sessions with the dogs.

Shandor was yoked up into the cart carrying his bike and other props. The other four dogs were on leashes.

The small cache of jewelry, money, and coins was secreted into his pockets. As he walked out of the house, he looked back at the rundown house with sadness at leaving.

His thoughts went back to the orphanage with the horrors he had experienced there. He wondered what had happened to his three friends Nicola, Walther, and Yanco. He hoped that seeing the war had ended that they may have been let out.

He thought of Father Mark. A shiver ran down his spine as he recalled the treatment he had received from this bad priest. It was very hard to erase this bad person from his mind. His name sat on a special place in his brain with the name of Gunter Khullman sitting above it.

When sitting alone or lying-in bed the recollection of these two people haunted him.

CHAPTER SIX

There was a long walk for him and the dogs to the small field where the circus Big Top tent was being set up. Shandor was puffing from the effort of pulling his wagon for such a long distance. The thin steel wheels' rims had clattered for a long-time sending vibration back through the shafts. They had stopped on two occasions when Shandor had been unhitched, the dogs fed and given a drink of water.

The circus was situated in a small field on the edge of the town. Lines of cars, trucks, and Gypsy looking caravans on the rear of motor trucks were in one corner of the field. Some of the trucks had large cages on their trays with animals in them.

As he came closer, he could see the ringmaster Stefano who was overseeing the erecting of the large colorful tent. He was checking the tightness of the ropes. There was even an elephant helping to pull some of the heavy ropes, Bernado had never seen an elephant before, and was amazed at the huge size of this animal. His dogs certainly did not know what to think of this huge beast.

Stefano looked up from his work and noticed Bernado and the dogs. He came over and shook his hand. Bernado looked more closely at Stefano. He was lean, medium height with slightly greying hair at the temples. He looked like a man who would not be able to sit still. His eyes kept darting back to where the men were working." Welcome to my circus, as you can see, we are very busy." He yelled over the noisy workers.

“Hey, Julio come and take the man and the new act, and show him where to store his things. This is Bernado and his dog act we were talking about.”

A small wiry dark-skinned man left his work, then ran across to them. He shook Bernado’s hand vigorously.

“Julio’s the name. Follow me.”

As they walked, the small man studied the dogs.

“Nice looking dogs you have there.”

They wended their way through boxes of props for acts, past animal cages. Bernado was enthralled by all of the different animals he had never seen before. He did not even know what a monkey was.

The dogs did not like the roaring lions; they cowered as they walked past the cage, Bernado was not very keen on seeing the large teeth when the lion opened its mouth to roar.

The men walked out of the animal enclosure, and then came to a line of the caravans like Gypsy caravans built on the back of motor trucks. They were all painted red with the name of the circus painted in bright yellow and orange on them.

Julio stopped at one of the caravans, then climbed the short rear ladder and opened the door. “Hey Bernado this is your new home” He followed Julio into the caravan.

Memories of the caravans of his childhood flooded back. This was very similar to the caravan he had lived in as a child. “I grew up in caravan very much like one of these. Ours had two horses pulling it.” Bernado Said.

“I lived in one as well. We lived in Romania; my parents were Gypsies.”

Bernado had a feeling that Julio could be a good friend. They could have a lot of heritage in common.

Nicola was fidgeting; his eyes kept looking back to where the tent was being erected.

“Right, I have to go back and help get this tent up. If you need anything just come and find me,” he climbed down the stairs and ran off.

The dogs were tethered under the truck with their food and water bowls. People were moving around everywhere he looked. Some were dressed in costumes.

He asked a man dressed as a clown where to get water. The man pointed to a truck with a round tank on its back.

There was a bucket in the caravan; he climbed back into the caravan and picked up the bucket, then walked to the tanker and filled it with water.

Some people were carrying bales of straw and some bags of chaff to feed the horses which were tethered to a long rope between two trucks. They all seemed to be hurrying to finish their work.

There were also some pretty girls in skimpy costumes practicing an act, as he looked around, there seemed to be pretty girls everywhere.

The dogs were fed and watered; he had bought some of the rusty saucepans as water bowls for the dogs. He could see Shandor was not too sure of what to think of the surroundings. Bernado went to him, then unhooked his chain off the truck and clipped a long leash onto his collar, then led him through the busy menagerie of animals and people.

The people seemed very friendly, although they were wary of Shandor, his size was rather intimidating.

One pretty girl asked if she could pat his dog. Bernado had a good look at the girl in the skimpy costume. She was a very pretty blonde with a lean strong body.

"I am not sure about him. If you put out your hand carefully, he might lick it or growl."

Shandor looked the girl up and down. He had a silly doggy smile on his face; he also agreed with the look of the pretty girl, finally he tentatively licked her hand.

"Hi I am Bernado a new act; this is Shandor my star of the act, he's very clever, he rides a three-wheel bike." They shook hands.

"My name is Lilly I have a rope climbing act. I have got to go. I have to do some work on my act in the ring. Come into the ring soon and have a look."

As he explored his new home and work-pace, he met a lot more of the friendly people as he walked the perimeter of the site. Shandor seemed to be settling down now. He took him back to the caravan.

The dynamic circus atmosphere sent his eighteen-year-old brain working. If he were to dress as a clown with the dogs, he could incorporate more acts into the routine. He thought of Shandor taking a chair as he was to sit on it, picking up a bag or satchel and running so he could not catch him. The other dogs could chase him barking as they went. He could not wait to see what the acts were the other people did. His thoughts went to Lilly the pretty girl. He hurried back into the ring to watch her act.

Ropes were hanging from the structure between the two main tall poles of the huge tent. People were erecting the tiered seating. The inside of the tent was a hive of activity. Some clowns were doing a tumbling act on the grassy floor of the main arena.

Lilly waved to him. She took hold of one of the long ropes, and hand over hand she pulled herself up without using her feet. She then turned upside down and hooked one of her feet into the rope and started to spin around, he was fascinated with the act, and he had never seen anything like it. He thought she must have something sticky on her skin to be able to hang onto the ropes.

Stefano had walked over to where he was watching Lilly.

"Have you ever been to a circus before?"

"No, I have been to plenty of fairs with my parents. I have never seen anything like this before."

"I think you will find that there are a lot of things you have never seen before."

He said, with a chuckle and a smile on his face. Stefano looked over to a group of workers near the tent entrance.

"I had better go and check on something else, I don't like seeing men standing around when there is work to be done." He walked off chuckling to himself.

Lilly slid down from the rope. She walked over to him.

"What did you think of that?"

"You must have sticky glue on your legs?"

She laughed,

"No of course I don't, you feel my leg."

She took his hand and pulled it to her thigh near the edge of her costume. The silky skin had a strange reaction on Bernado, he did not want to take his hand away. He rubbed closer to the inside of her leg. Lilly laughed and wiggled a bit in jest.

" You had better take your hand away now" She laughed again; she looked down at his crotch, and then added.

"Wow, big boy, is that all you?"

Bernado was extremely embarrassed; he had not had this treatment from a pretty girl before.

"Bernado, I think you are going red in the face".

She laughed again and walked off.

She called back to him.

"I will see you later tonight".

He felt as if every eye in the tent was looking at the huge bulge in the front of his trousers.

Stefano found Bernado checking the dogs,

"Is everything Ok with your new home? "" Yes, it reminds me when I was a kid, we lived in a caravan like this".

"Were you a Gypsy?" He raised his eyebrows.

"I was until the Nazi's murdered my family when I was very young. I was caught by a polish policeman and taken to an orphanage. The policeman thought the priests and nuns were all nice people." "I bet that was crap," said Stefano.

"I would not feed my dogs on what we were fed on. The food was rotten and stank. Most of the nuns were nasty, and one of the priests was something else. He was screwing the young boys. I escaped three years ago."

Stefano went to look at the dogs.

"You look after them well, their coats are nice and clean and they look healthy. Would you like to give them their first trial in the big top?"

"When would you like me to come and try them?"

"We have finished setting the tent up. Now would be a good time." Bernado went back to the caravan. The dogs were fidgeting as they were pleased to see him. He put the harness on Shandor and hooked the cart onto the big dog. The bike and props were still in the cart. They all walked toward the tent.

"I have thought of some variations to the act."

Stefano answered,

"Just show the activities you do at present. I would like to see what the dogs do in the ring. It is a lot different than performing outside." He thought for a while.

"We have to get you some better clothes; we should have some to fit you in the props department."

Bernado started the dogs doing their routine. He was pleased and surprised at the way the dogs performed in unfamiliar surroundings. He went through the routine without a hitch. He pedaled his bike around the edge of the other dogs as they danced and did other tricks.

The workers and performers who had stopped to see the new act clapped their hands enthusiastically when the dogs finished. The dogs milled around Bernado looking for some tasty treats from his pockets.

Stefano walked over to him. “Congratulations. The dogs performed better than I thought they would. You never know what to think about animals performing.

sometimes they do not like to work in strange new places.” Stefano started to walk off, he turned back,

” You know about the mess tent for the meals. Ask Nicola here”

Lilly came over, she had changed to normal clothes a blouse showing some cleavage to her bosom and a tight pair of blue slacks. “Your dog act is really good; I will save you a place next to me at dinner tonight if you would like to sit with me.”

Wow, thought Bernado things are looking up.

“That would be very nice Lilly, I have not met many people here”.

Nicola walked over to explain how the mess tent worked.

“You are a fast worker. I have been trying to get onto Lilly; she won’t even look at me.”

“I have never had anything to do with girls. I was in an orphanage for boys for three years.” Bernado answered.

“She must think you are a virgin. Follow me I will show you the tent”.

Bernado hitched up Shandor to the cart, then put the leads on the other dogs and walked out of the ring.

He and Nicola walked to his caravan. He tied the dogs back to the truck. He then followed Nicola to see the tent.

The long tent had forms and long tables like the orphanage, this bought back bad memories. Outside the tent was a wagon with a large stove and smaller tables set up around it. The smell from the cooking was certainly not the same as the orphanage. Quality food was being cooked. Cooks were busy preparing the meals.

Later when he walked into the tent Lilly half stood, and then waved her hand to show where she was, she had saved him a seat. Waiters came around the tabled with the meals; there was a choice, an aromatic Goulash or slices of meat and gravy. Baskets of bread bowls of vegetables were lined on the middle of the tables. There were baskets of apples and oranges and some nice cheeses for after's.

Lilly grabbed the top of Bernado's leg and rubbed it when they had finished eating.

"Would you like to come around to my van for a cup of coffee?" "Thank you I would appreciate that".

The throbbing member problem started again. Most people were leaving the table. Bernado bent slightly in the middle to make the bulge less obvious as he followed Lilly.

When they arrived at the caravan Lilly climbed up the steps Bernado followed and appreciated the view of her perfectly shaped bottom as she wiggled her hips climbing the five steps.

When in the van with the costumes and other clothes hanging along the wall, she lifted the glass flue on a small kerosene lamp then reached for a box of matches on a shelf, and then lit the wick, the glass flue was replaced. A dim flickering light came from the lamp. She then reached back and grasped Bernado's hand, dragging him to her bed at the end of the van.

When she lay back on the bed, she reached out to him, she then pulled him next to her. She undid her top letting her tight round breasts spill out. The pink nipples stood dark pink and hard from the desire in the dim lamplight.

Bernado took a huge gulp when he saw them. She then lifted her rear and wiggled out of her slacks then panties. Bernado saw the brown triangle of fur between her legs.

She took his hand and placed it on the fur and then opened her legs slightly. He slowly rubbed the fur and felt the moistness coming out from under it.

Lilly then reached for the front of Bernado's trousers. She had great difficulty undoing his buttons as there was so much pressure pushing on them. Finally, the huge penis popped out and stood tall.

"Mother of God, I have never seen one like this before,"

She smiled, then reached out and softly grasped the long wide tool. With some difficulty, she managed to get Bernado between her legs. The huge tool seemed to get in the way; finally, it was lined up with the home spot.

"Slowly push it in, take care don't hurry",

Bernado slowly pushed the member into the warm moist spot; it seemed to hit the bottom and would not go further.

He Shuddered violently and thought he was going to faint.

"Just slowly move, take your time, this is not a race".

Lilly was starting to moan at every movement.

"Slow down and make it last." She whispered in his ear. "I have never done this before" He muttered.

"Well, I have, so just take it slowly."

As soon as Bernado started to quicken the stroke, she told him to slow down. The urge was too great, he could not stop and quickened the pace, the tool was forcing deeper. She yelped with pain, and involuntarily backed away slightly, but told him to keep going.

Suddenly there was a gigantic explosion in his head. She started to yell for him to keep moving. Finally, it was all over. Bernado lay on top of Lilly. He did not want to remove his tool from the warm home.

He was worried that this experience may only be a one-off, and she would not allow him to re-enter her.

They lay together joined together for some time after. Before too long his tool started to grow strong again.

During the night, it grew six times. He pulled back from Lilly, he then slid the flaccid tool out, Lilly was moaning contentedly at his side.

At the break of dawn, they made love again.

"That was the best that I have ever had," she said as she snuggled into his side.

Bernado climbed down from Lilly's caravan and unsteadily walked back to feed the dogs and fill their water bowls.

He then staggered to the meal tent. He felt as if he had been run down by a team of wild horses.

As Lilly came into view, she was talking to three other girls, as they walked, they were giggling She made a gesture of something very long with her hands, Bernado had a feeling it may be the part of him that he used for the first time the night before. She left the other girls and came to sit next to him.

"Boy, that was a great night. Thank you. Phew, I feel a bit sore now. I think you stretched me inside when you got excited" she sat down, on the form next to him and moved closer.

" There is going to be a matinee and a night show for the circus today. Are you working?"

"I don't know I haven't been told yet."

Nicola caught up with Bernado and asked him to come to the wardrobe caravan to find some decent clothes. "The boss seems to think you and the dogs may be OK to have a try with your dog act today."

He winked at Bernado,

"I hear you have had a bit of fun last night".

Bernado went red and grunted

"Yes, it was pretty good."

"You're a lucky sod"

Bernado had been given some gold shiny trousers a white shirt and a green vest. One problem with the clothes was the part between the legs showed the large mound,

Nicola stared at the mound between his legs.

“Boy is that all you, or do you keep your socks and undies all hidden in there,” Nicola said.

He checked the front of Bernado’s new trousers. He then laughed.

Bernado was embarrassed and felt his face redden.

“If you have got it, flaunt it,” Julio said.

When he was getting the dogs ready for their act at the caravan some of the girls just happened to pass by, they introduced themselves. He noticed that they looked at the bulge in front of his new uniform. One could not seem to keep her eyes off it. There were some very pretty girls in skimpy costumes in the circus. Bernado was both pleased but worried about this.

He was very proud of the dogs. They performed without a hitch. Shandor was proudly riding his bike like it was a natural thing to do. His front feet on the handlebars guided the bike all over the area of the ring he was working in.

The crowd erupted into spontaneous applause. The dogs all bowed to the audience, even Shandor bowed.

Lilly asked him back for supper after dinner. There was no food on the menu. This was very different; he had a great liking for her supper. The next morning, he did not feel so exhausted. Lilly had tried some new positions. She rode him like a horse for a while.

Lilly made the situation quite plain to him. This was just really good fun, not love or anything stupid like that.

In his spare time, he was working on new parts for the act. One was for one of the smaller dogs to come to him acting lame, He would get up from a chair, Shandor would sneak in from out of his sight, and he would then pull the chair away. He would sit down to find the chair missing, and fall backward. He would then chase Shandor who would run away with the chair. The other dogs would chase him yapping at his heels. This bought out huge laughter from the crowd, especially from the children.

Lilly said she had a date one night she was going to have dinner with one of the town dignitaries. They were going to an expensive hotel.

Later that day red-headed Martha came up to him.

"Lilly told me you were going to be alone tonight."

She looked him up and down zeroing into the bulge in the front of his pants. She smiled with a wicked smile and then asked him if he would like to come back to her caravan for supper after dinner. Bernado had seen her coming from her caravan on some occasions and had noticed her good figure and looks.

Martha worked a high wire act with another woman. She was an extremely attractive woman.

Bernado sat with Martha at dinner time. He could see a bit of talking amongst the other girls, as they looked his way.

Sultry Martha's caravan was different. The clothes were neatly folded. There was more room inside. She stripped off her clothes, just after the door was shut. Bernado looked at her perfect body with lust.

She slowly undid the buttons on his trousers. This took some effort to do, as the pressure behind the buttons was quite immense, as the last button popped, it shot out She jumped back to get a better look. "My god was your father a horse or something," She giggled.

As she stood in front of him, she reached forward and held the tool up, while she guided it inside under her warm mound surrounded with red curly fur; Martha then held Bernado's neck with both hands, as she wound both of her beautiful legs around him. She wriggled her bottom.

"Now carefully lay me back onto the bed."

She yelped a short squeak, as it filled the void, and then more.

"I will teach you the arts of lovemaking."

Martha must have done a university course on the subject, she did not stop teaching him for very long at all that night, it was almost straight back to work. He could not remember the number of times they climaxed, Bernado lost count. He felt very seedy the next morning at breakfast.

During the next two months, Bernado had been invited to supper with most of the girls.

One assignation with a small vivacious brunette was almost a disaster. The bubbly smiling girl had a problem. As much as she and Bernado tried, his tool would not fit inside her. He felt very sorry and certainly did not want to hurt her.

“I have not had a night without a woman in the last two weeks, I am looking forward to just lay with you”.

They caressed and cuddled through the night, Tonia still had two orgasms during the stroking and cuddling as she rode him without him entering her. It was still an enjoyable night having her warm naked body next to him.

The dog act had some new acts in the show. He had a burning hoop. And some more props. There were multi-height chairs which the dogs would jump up, plus a broomstick on top of adjustable poles like a high jump. Bernado would set this up and just as the first dog was going to jump, Shandor would rush in and run away holding the broomstick in the middle with his large teeth.

After three times, he would sit back and let the small dogs jump. This bought the house down with laughter.

There was one girl which had made suggestive remarks to Bernado when Stefano had gone to the next town they were going to perform in.

The beautiful blonde woman Marta was the woman who lived with Stefano in the large caravan. Bernado had to carefully try to get out of the situation without offending her.

“Look I am so sorry but Lilly and I have a thing going now, and I do not want to do anything that would bust this up.”

“I have seen you with the other girls also. “

“They are friends of hers.”

This was getting a bit hard to work out what to say next, he did not want to make an enemy.

“Marta, you are a very beautiful woman, but you are the boss’s girl, as much as I would like to be with you, I am frightened of Stefano. I am only a young boy.”

Marta laughed. “Well young boy, it is there if you want it, but I suppose I will not die of craving for you,” She walked off laughing.

Later in the afternoon Strombolo the Circus strong man walked to Bernado. Strombolo was built like a Battleship. He had muscles bulging out everywhere.

On top of this huge body, there was a very small head sitting on his thick neck, he sounded like Donald Duck when he spoke with his reedy squeaky voice. He did not portray an image of being over-endowed with intelligence. “I would not advise trying anything with the Boss’ girl.” He said with a serious look on his face.

Bernado was intimidated by this huge man.

“Look! Strombolo I got a shock when she made some suggestive remarks. I have enough sex with the other girls without being stupid like that. I told her that she was a beautiful woman, but she was the boss’s girl. I have had enough problems keeping it up with the other girls. She laughed at me.” Strombolo laughed.

“Bloody women are never satisfied. You did well.” He was chuckling with his squeaky voice, as he walked off. He sounded like a quacking duck.

Bernardo had noted that Strombolo had been very serious when discussing Marta. He certainly did not want to be beaten up by this man.

CHAPTER 7

Stefano met Bernado when he was feeding his dogs. He asked him to come to his office in about half an hour. The caravan was near the entrance to the tent. He was worried that the refusal of Marta's favors might be the subject. He knocked on the door, Stephano asked him to come in. Bernado tentatively opened the door then shuffled up to the desk. Stefano pulled a piece of paper from a sheaf of documents on the side of his desk.

" I am very pleased with your act! I want you to sign a contract. This will mean that you will get more wages."

Bernado was relieved that this was what the meeting was for. He slowly read the contract and signed it with a shaky signature. "Your act is very popular with the children. I like some of the new acts you have added." He sat back in his chair.

"By the way, I have heard Marta made a pass at you. Thank you for not taking up her offer. Bloody women, some of them, they can never seem to get enough sex. If I find that you have been with her though I will give you to Strombolo to do some practice on." He then laughed. Bernado knew that he meant this. He had noticed that when some of the animals he had been training acted up he was very vicious with the whip.

The circus had crossed the border into Germany. This part of Germany was under the control of the Russians. They were more prevalent than in Poland. A lot of Russian soldiers and their girlfriends attended the circus every night, as they moved from town to town over the next month.

Bernado had a vivid dream one night after one of the girls had left his caravan. This dream was about a money-making scheme, outside of the circus act.

The dream involved a plan to teach the dogs to steal. He had dreamed of how Shandor and Esmerelda worked so well in the act with the lame whining dog routine.

The dream involved taking the two dogs out after the show during the night to some of the poorly lit areas of some of the towns when people were coming home from working late, the circus, or shopping, he would send Esmerelda out onto the pavement and have her approach people. People like women with handbags or men with bags or cases.

Esmerelda walked with her foot held off the ground whimpering to the person, as she had been taught to do in the circus act. The person would put down his or her bag and look at such a pretty dog to see what was wrong with her paw. Shandor would run in and take the bag. If the person would chase, he would drop the bag and come toward them snarling. Bernado was hidden in an alley to keep watch.

He woke early the next morning trying to remember all of the details of the money-making dream. Finally, the details all came to him.

The dogs went into training. After three weeks Bernado was sure the dogs could work the stealing act on the streets.

He was ready to try his new money-making scheme. After the show one night, he left for the streets with the two dogs. They were all hiding in an alleyway near the main business and shopping area of the town.

After a short while, an old well-dressed woman came into view. She was looking behind her and sideways. She was wary of any people at this time of night.

This was the first test of the new money-making scheme . He held the collar of Shandor. He told Esmerelda to go, she trotted out of the alley, whimpering as she did so. She trotted on three legs to the hurrying woman and followed her closely. The woman stopped walking and looked at the dog; she bent to look closer, putting her handbag on the pavement as she did so.

"Poor little doggy, what has happened to your paw"?

She asked kindly.

Shandor ran out of the alley and snarled at the woman, showing his large teeth. He then picked up the bag then ran off. Esmerelda followed him.

The woman was yelling loudly as they disappeared around a corner.

The dogs met up with Bernado who took the stolen handbag from Shandor. The noise of the yelling woman faded in the distance as they ran off. The three were well gone. When they arrived back at the circus the dogs were tied up. Bernado patted both of the dogs and praised them, then carried the stolen bag to his caravan. Bernado opened the handbag, he had no idea what women carried in their bags. The contents of the bag were carefully removed near the lamp on the small cupboard. The normal lipstick handkerchiefs and compact for powder were sorted to the side. A purse bulging with money was opened. Bernado counted out the money, there was a large sum of money. He then searched the pockets of the bag. Two large diamond rings and one other with a large ruby in an ornate setting were found. He had hit the jackpot. The contents were in his estimation worth more than a month's wages.

He found it very interesting what the women carried in their handbags. There was usually quite a large amount of money and some diamond or other gem jewelry.

After this first dog robbery, Bernado found the spoils, which were the result of the robbery were different. Occasionally it was jewelry, some gold with diamonds or other precious stones in it. Some other times it was large amounts of money. Occasionally there was only the handbag with very little value in it. He learned to watch what the people looked like. Some did not look at all wealthy.

Usually, he and the dogs waited for a prime looking victim. One evening there was a smartly dressed woman hurrying along the street. She carried a briefcase. Esmerelda had hopped alongside her for a while until she must have felt empathy for the limping dog. She put down the briefcase then patted Esmerelda. Shandor then rushed in and stole the briefcase.

This woman had a voice like a siren. She chased Shandor along the street screaming. Lights went on in some of the house windows. Eventually, Shandor lost the screaming woman and met up with Bernado three streets away.

Bernado had whistled loudly a few times to give him bearings as to where he and Esmerelda were.

The woman must have been a salesperson for a jewelry company. This briefcase was half-filled with gold jewelry and the other half money rolled up with rubber bands around it.

Bernado realized why the woman had chased Shandor and had screamed so loudly. There was a small fortune in this case

One other night the dogs tackled a well-dressed man on a

Wednesday night. The man had a shiny black briefcase with him.

He had gotten very angry when Shandor had run off with this case. He chased Shandor for some distance; the dog had stopped and growled, he put the case down, the man had lunged for the case, Shandor had bitten the man's wrist badly. There was a lot of blood.

The yelling man bound the wounded arm with his handkerchief.

Shandor picked up the case once more and was well gone.

This night the case must have contained the wages for the week for a factory or some other larger business. There was a very large amount of money in the case. This cunning robbery was not committed more than once in any town and was usually the night the circus was leaving.

The girls were complaining of being neglected. Bernado said he was training the dogs for a very complicated new act.

As time passed, and the robberies continued, Bernado was accumulating a large stash of cash and jewelry.

He had walked into town from the circus ground one morning and visited a hardware shop. He searched through the tills and strongboxes. He selected a heavy medium-sized steel strongbox; he then bought a heavy padlock to fit the box, some tools, and some long wood screws.

The box was in a cardboard carton. One of the girls noticed him carrying the heavy box and asked what it was.

"I found something in town which I could use in my act" was his reply.

When he climbed into his caravan, he stripped his bedclothes and mattress off, then stood the bed on its end. This box was screwed to the floor of the caravan under his bed. The large padlock was fitted to keep out unwanted people. He took the bag filled with the money and jewelry and transferred it to the strongbox. The box was locked and one key was hung around his neck on a strong piece of twine. He then went outside then crawled under the caravan, near where the dogs were tied up. He tied the other key to a wiring loom leading to the rear of the truck. It was pushed out of sight behind the wiring.

One evening while doing the act in the big top in a medium-sized town, Bernado felt a strange urgency to look up into the crowd. He usually concentrated more on the way the dogs were doing their job. What he saw in the crowd of people tore so hard on his heart. It skipped a couple of beats, he nearly fainted.

Sitting three rows back from the ring was Gunter Khullman the man with the patch on his eye and the missing ear. The man lifted his hand to show the three fingers. He then scratched at his missing ear. Bernado had no doubts as to the identity of the man even after nearly five years. The image of this monster was burned into his brain.

It took all of his effort to finish the act. When he did so he hurried back to his caravan and tied all of the dogs up and fed them all, except for Shandor. He then waited with Shandor half-hidden by his side outside the tent until the last acts finished.

The crowd began to slowly file out. People were walking slowly and talking to each other about the circus's acts.

Bernado felt like screaming at them to hurry out of the tent. He wanted to see the man who had murdered his parents and family. After waiting impatiently for some time, he noticed the thin one-eared man walk out of the tent.

He was alone. Bernado was sure he would have a car or some other transport and he would lose sight of him.

The man walked past the parked cars and in a quick walk headed down a road toward a dimly lit part of town. He still walked with the arrogance and swagger he displayed when he was murdering Bernado's family, his head held high, his nose in the air.

This was Bernado's lucky night. Gunter Khullman did not have a car.

In a state of anticipation, Bernado and Shandor followed a safe distance behind him. Bernado was careful not to lose sight of this monster.

The man lived a long way from the circus ground. Finally, after wending their way through dingy streets, the man walked out into a dark moonlit stretch of street with no houses. There was a small stream on one side of the street.

Bernado reached down and undid Shandor's collar. He then sent Shandor off.

"Attack and kill," he said quietly in his ear.

"Get him." Shandor ran toward the man. Gunter heard the running footsteps of the dog and turned to look behind him; the large dog had leaped and was in mid-air, Shandor's huge mouth then grabbed his throat. Shandor held him with a vice-like grip as the man was taken to the ground.

He landed heavily, knocking his wind out.

The man hit out at the dog. He could not scream as Shandor's grip prevented that. The man tried to gouge his eyes. Shandor shook his head, as he hung on tightly to the man's throat.

Bernado walked to the struggling man and dog.

"You murdered my parents and relatives I hope the devil and his hounds of hell chase you for all of eternity. "He said loudly, with hatred in his voice.

This bought a look of fear into the man's eyes. It showed in the moonlight, Shandor had severed the main artery as blood gushed from the deep wound. Still, he held on and shook the man's head.

There was no fight in the man now.

"Stop now."

Shandor had no intention of stopping. He reached for his neck and pulled back. Shandor would not let go He then slid Shandor's leash around his neck and twisted it between his fingers and hand, Shandor gasped for breath then finally let go.

The man was not moving. Blood was everywhere, Shandor was covered in it. Bernado was careful to not get blood on his clothes.

Bernado re-attached the collar around Shandor's neck. "Come, Shandor, you are a good dog." He then praised Shandor.

"Thank you, Shandor. You have done well; you have avenged my parents and friends."

There was the stream near the edge of the road where they had followed the man. Bernado carefully took Shandor from the road, being careful not to get blood from Shandor on his clothes. He then stood him in the shallow cold water just below the stone-paved area next to the road. He flicked water over the dog with the palm of one hand. The blood had not dried so most of it washed off.

"Good boy, let's go home."

As he walked towards the circus ground, his mind went back to Zelda's prediction when she had read his palm, all of those years before. She had predicted that he would find Gunter Khullman, and then be able to exact his revenge. He was engulfed in a wave of sadness at the thought of the loving woman who had taken him in when he was all alone

Upon arriving at the circus Lilly was waiting by his caravan. "Where have you been?"

She said tersely

"I have been waiting to give you your eighteenth birthday present." The floodlights of the circus were still on as men were working making the tent and other facilities secure

Lilly looked at the large dog,

"Shandor has blood on him."

Bernado, when he had seen her, had been thinking she might have bought the subject up, and was ready with an answer.

" Bloody dog! When I unhooked his chain, he ran off. I found him down the road with a stray bitch. He was joined to her and another dog was attacking him. I was lucky I did not get bitten." "Sounds a bit like his owner with the ladies" Lilly laughed.

Bernado was not very interested in having sex with Lilly, he felt both exhilarated and exhausted from exacting his revenge on the evil monster. He thought briefly again of Zelda and her prediction when he was thirteen years old.

Lilly stamped her foot. She insisted. They entered his caravan; he undressed and lay on his back while she helped herself to his body. He tried to think about other events of the night to stop his member from growing. This did not work Lilly had secret ways to give him an erection. In the morning, he made love to her properly, she left satisfied.

During the day as they packed up the circus to move on. Bernado's thoughts were on Gunter Khullman. He would never forget the fear in his eyes which showed in the moonlight. He did not feel any guilt of ridding the world of this evil monster.

A new troupe of girls who had a tumbling act joined the circus; the leader of this act was a very rare beauty. In Bernado's eyes, she was the most beautiful woman he had ever seen. Bernado talked to her and made some suggestive remarks. He pushed the front out on his gold trousers. She looked at him then told him to take a hike; "I have more things to think about at present than a horny young man." she was not interested.

The refusal was a huge dent in his male ego. It seemed as if the lady was not interested in any of the postulating males who followed her like puppies. Her friends in the tumbling act were of a different ilk.

Heidi a Swiss blonde was his first conquest of the new girls. She had a nice tight figure with just the right-sized breasts; she was smitten by the bulge in Bernado's tight pants, she could not keep her eyes off it. He asked her to have some supper with him after dinner.

She winked and asked where she would find him.

"I will take you there after dinner."

"Shall I bring some food?" she asked naively, with a mischievous smile?

"No, I have some in my caravan for special occasions."

After dinner, they went to Bernado's caravan, when they entered Heidi smiled and asked where the food was. Bernado undid the buttons of his trousers.

"My god this looks like a giant stick of Bierwurst" She laughed.

"I will have to taste this and see if it will be OK."

She bent down showing the cleavage between her breasts and kissed the end of the Bierwurst stick. Heidi then took her clothes off slowly to tease him. As she took each item off, she folded it carefully and placed it on a benchtop. He stroked her bare breasts as she did this. This was a real turn on, not like just jumping in. When they were undressed, he lay back on the bed. She then mounted him and rubbed her warm spot under the blonde fur across the end of his tool. This was driving him crazy.

"I know what I am doing trust me."

This went on for some time. She then let a small length of the tool inside her, she would then pull back.

"Slow down. I guarantee that you will enjoy this. Kiss my nipples." He kissed her large tight pink nipples and was about to climax. She pulled away.

"You will not forget this one for a long time."

After a short while, she resumed. His testicles were starting to ache. She then slowly slid her body right down over the long Bierwurst. She started to move more quickly. She was yelling. She then started to yodel loudly. One of the dogs barked then howled, all of the other dogs joined into the chorus. The other animals joined in, even the lions started to roar. Bernado thought the explosion the first time he had sex with Lilly had been good. This one was a Block Buster bomb.

The next time they made love it was a more normal way.

"Where did you learn to do that?"

"I just taught myself. It is far better to take one's time than just jump in."

"What are you doing tomorrow night?"

"We shall see."

This was not the answer he wanted. When Heidi left at dawn, he felt like he had been working loading the bricks all night. He would have to wait all day to find out.

He walked to Heidi as she entered the dining tent.

"I think I will give supper a miss tonight. I will catch up with you later."

Bernado was disappointed; He noticed that Lilly had just sat at the table. He sat next to her.

"You and the new girl woke everyone up last night. Even your dogs and all of the animals joined in. What were you up to? We heard yodeling during the night. I think they could have heard it back in Switzerland." she laughed.

"I had a very different lesson last night; would you like to come for supper. I will show you."

"That could be interesting, but I don't know how to yodel."

” I am sure you will learn quickly; you will be surprised.”

Bernado took the role of tutor. They both undressed and lay on the bed, Bernado slid in between Lilly’s legs. Lilly raised her knees, he just touched the entrance to her warm spot, and he wriggled his tool up and down lightly.

“Put it in! “

Lilly demanded.

“This is the secret” he rubbed it more then pushed a tiny length inside. He then pulled it out and rubbed more. “I want it inside me she demanded. “Wait it will get there later.”

“I am getting angry,” she yelled.

Bernado pushed some more in and still worked around the entrance. Lilly started to moan softly.

“Please put it in” she blubbered. Bernado slowly slid his tool to the full depth inside her, she screamed over and over as they headed for the climax.

“You rat, how you could do that, it was fantastic.”

“I would not like it that way always. I think you woke the dogs though” he laughed,

“They will probably make me move my caravan near the lions and other animals, so everyone is not woken up. You should have been an opera singer. You sang a couple of arias.” They spent the rest of the night sleeping.

A week later, on Saturday evening Bernado was tying the dogs up. He undid Shandor from the cart; Shandor pulled his head back from the chain and ran away. He called to him as he ran away. Bernado tried to chase after him. Shandor did not look back and disappeared around a corner some distance from where Bernado was running.

He stopped running and cursed the dog soundly in its absence. He was worried about this escapade.

He stood well out from the circus tent and called over and over, finally, Shandor arrived carrying a large handbag in his teeth. He had a small amount of blood around his mouth. Bernado realized that he may have created a monster.

After Shandor had escaped that night, he always hooked his leash on his collar before taking him from the cart. He did not want to find he had been attacking and hurting people, or worse, killing someone.

The box under his bed had a small fortune in cash jewelry and the gold coins growing by the week. He was worried that someone may steal it. He decided to empty the box and take the booty to a bank in a large town when they finally returned to Poland. He was working with the dogs on a patch of mowed grass near the circus when Rina the beautiful tumbler walked over and watched the act. Bernado thought that trying to talk to her would be a waste of time.

"You have very clever dogs. I have been watching your acting and the children in the audience. This act has the best applause of all. You are a very clever boy Bernado."

He was flattered that she would talk to him; she was so aloof with all of the men.

"I have now finished teaching my girls the right ways to do their act. I was not satisfied when I first came to the circus. I was wondering if you could come to my caravan for some supper tonight after dinner."

Bernado was going to play this out, and refuse her. These were his thoughts. He heard his voice say

"This would be marvelous; I will see you tonight."

Rina opened the door, she had changed into a really lovely dress and had made herself up, and she looked ravishing in the flickering lamplight. The small table in the caravan had some small biscuits and two small coffee cups on it; she poured the coffee and served out the biscuits onto dainty plates. Bernado was disappointed; this was not the usual supper in a caravan.

When they had finished the biscuits and coffee, she cleaned the table then excused herself; she pulled a curtain over the end of the caravan at the end of the bed. He could see the curtain move as she was undressing or some other thing behind it; he was puzzled as to what she was doing. The curtain slid across.

She had changed into a see-through gown held together with a row of six buttons down the front of it. The top of the gown was held from her by the erect nipples on her beautiful breasts. She came to him and asked if she could undress him.

Slowly Rina removed the top part of his clothes.

"Stand up now."

She undid the buttons of his trousers. His throbbing tool shot out to attention.

"I thought this one would be worth seeing, you are a very lucky boy to have been given this by your parents."

He did not know what to do next. This entire act was different. It was like playing a role in an erotic movie. He had not read his lines.

"Now come next to me and lay on the bed."

She lay back; she undid the six buttons, the gown opened up around her, and looked as if she were lying on a cloud. She slowly took her arms out of the sleeves. Bernado was on fire.

"Lay next to me now, we will play a little game."

He was ready to pounce on her like a tiger and take her.

" Hold my breasts and then lick my nipples." she reached down and slowly stroked his tool. Her touch was so soft, like stroking a pussycat.

Bernado's head was buzzing with desire.

"Now you can carefully get between my legs".

He awkwardly rolled on top of her and knelt between her legs. He lined his Bierwurst stick with her warm moist spot. "You must be slow and take care."

The long Bierwurst slowly slid into her. She moaned loudly. "It has been a long time since I have made love. Take your time and do not rush."

As soon as he showed signs of speeding up she yelled.

"No."

This was a marathon. Finally, she started to hump her hips and scream. Bernado kept pace with her. The fireworks in his head had been lit and the rockets exploded with sparks and flames. The whole lovemaking had taken two hours.

Rina moved from him then sat on the edge of the small bed. She turned to him.

"Thank you so much. I would need to sleep now, could you please leave."

As he walked unsteadily back to his caravan he met up with Julio. He had been on a similar visit. He had just come down the steps of Heidi's van.

"Bloody hell, she is good. I have a job to walk. She nearly deafened me when she started to yodel. Where have you been?"

"I have been with beautiful Rina."

"What was she like?"

Bernado thought for a second, he smiled broadly.

"Hmmmmmmmmm."

He staggered past the dogs and climbed into his caravan.

From that time, he and Rina would both be an exclusive pair. They would trade caravans on a nightly basis.

Bernado asked Rina to have dinner at a good hotel one evening when the circus was just in the setup mode and there were no performances.

All eyes in the dining room of the Grand old hotel turned to Rina as she entered.

Tonight, she had excelled herself. The clothes she wore made her look extremely elegant and beautiful. Bernado had never been to dinner with a beautiful woman before. He had not even been inside of this type of establishment. Rina looked as if she fitted in with all of the well-dressed people. Bernado felt embarrassed by his old clothes.

Rina noticed his discomfort.

"It is not the clothes that make the man. It is the man in them that matters. Boy, there is a lot of man in yours." She winked at him with a yearning look.

Rina ordered the meal for him. The meal was very new to him; he was used to the circus meals and the performers and workers he knew so well. The etiquette of cutlery choices was a new experience. Rina was very helpful in teaching him what to use for each course of the meal.

CHAPTER 8

The weather was turning colder. The circus was slowly heading back to Poland where they would stay for three months until the snow and cold abated. There was a huge amount of maintenance to be done through this winter.

The Big Top tent was starting to tear when it was windy, this could cause a huge accident if it were to collapse. There were a lot of skills needed for building a new tent.

All of the ropes and most of the props had to be replaced, Posts repaired, plus the high wire cage and other props Repaired and repainted.

Some years the circus traveled down through Spain and worked along the edge of the Mediterranean. From Spain, they headed through France to Italy following the sun.

The last show for the season was a somber event as many of the performers would be leaving to return home to their families.

Bernado and Rina had just made love. Rina had spoken of her home in Romania. She asked Bernado to travel back to see where she had come from to meet her brothers and sisters.

Her parents had been killed during the German Occupation. They had been caught running a black-market cigarette and food run.

Bernado agreed to the offer. He would like to travel and see her part of the world.

That night after making love he sat up in the bed.

" I am sorry I have changed my mind. The dogs are a problem, I cannot leave them."

He was especially worried about Shandor. If he were to leave him with the troupe, he may escape and return with a bag or case. He would be found out; the robbing dog which attacked people would be common knowledge.

Rina was upset at his refusal to accompany her to Romania. Bernado explained again about the dogs. They were his income source and friends. Taking them was also out of the question. "How long would you want to go to see your relatives?" Rina dried her eyes.

"About three weeks would be enough to catch up with friends and family."

"That would be ok I could do some work with the dogs, and help around the circus while you are gone."

"What about the other girls?"

"Most of the girls are going home or some other place. What about some other men when you are away?"

The performers at the circus had mostly left to visit friends and relatives,

Bernado accompanied Rina when she left the circus.

He carried one of the suitcases and a kitbag as they walked quickly from the field to an area where they could hail a taxi.

The old driver strapped the luggage to the rear rack on the old car as it went to the railway station. Bernado held Rina's hand. She felt his Bierwurst stick with her other hand as the Taxi slowly traveled to the Station. "I am going to miss our nightly meetings, Mr. Bierwurst," She said in a husky voice, as she snuggled up to Bernado. The Bierwurst rose for the occasion. Bernado paid for the Taxi on arrival then helped unstrap the suitcases. He was with her as she purchased the ticket. He followed her to the gateway. He kissed her on the lips and held her for about two minutes, rubbing his erect member discreetly against her. As she walked through the gate, he felt an empty wanting feeling. He watched as she entered the train to go to her home in Romania. Bernado felt a deep sense of loss when the train carrying her finally

turned a corner and disappeared from view.

Lilly had also left for home as well, as most of the other girls were also traveling to see loved ones during the winter. There was only one beautiful woman left, Marta. There were some of the female cooks and other female helpers with the props, there were no ravishing beauties among these women.

Bernado felt alone, after the last nine months of having the company of the beautiful girls. Marta sidled up to him two days after the last girl left.

"Looks like you are going to miss out on your supper meetings. That is unless you would still like to have a try with me." She winked lewdly at him.

"You know I can't do that. Stefano said that he would give me to Strombolo to practice on if I did so." "Stefano does not own me." "I know that but I am scared of Strombolo" She laughed.

"Looks like you miss out again."

He went to work with the men painting and repairing broken or worn props, as well as starting to teach Shandor and the other dogs a new routine.

Julio and he would go into the business part of town some nights to a small club with a band and dancing and meet up with some girls. There were always some girls willing, especially if Bernado wore his gold trousers with the huge bulge in the front. Julio was never too proud to have a second choice.

Bernado was counting the days in his mind to when Rina would return to the circus. If she kept to her timetable there were ten more days to wait.

Stefano was in the circus ring attempting to teach a new young horse to fit into the three-horse act, where the three horses ran around the perimeters of the stage and had two of the girls change places from one horse to the other as they stood on their backs. This young horse was a bit skittish. Stefano was holding a tether from the horse's bridle.

He touched its rump with the whip to try to keep it in line with the other horses. The young horse swung around and kicked out; she kicked Stefano above the knee then knocking him to the ground.

Stefano hobbled over to the horse and caught the tether rope and pulled it toward a post. He tied the rope to the post; he then proceeded to lash the horse with the whip. The young horse reared up and screamed with pain.

Shandor had been performing one of the new routines. He looked across and stopped the routine.

He then ran off to Stefano and bit hard just above his knee. Stefano went to the ground with the dog firmly latched on. Strombolo had been painting nearby, he ran across and grabbed Shandor's collar and tried to pull him off. Stefano screamed with pain.

"Get the stick and rope," Strombolo yelled.

One of the helpers came running with a long pole with a noose on the end. Shandor was now gasping for breath. He let go of Stefano's leg, the noose was dropped around his neck and pulled tight.

Stefano was bleeding profusely from his wound.

"Take him and lock him in the spare cage," he yelled.

Bernado protested

"You shut your mouth your dog tried to kill me."

One of the other men who were working nearby took the long stick with the noose still around Shandor's neck. He dragged the choking dog out of the ring toward the animal cages.

Strombolo helped Stefano to the first aid area. Stefano was showing signs of shock. Marta had appeared and was helping hold him up.

Bernado was very worried. He took the other dogs to the caravan and tied them up. What was going to happen now he thought? There had been no way that he could have stopped Shandor, he had moved too quickly.

Marta ran out of the tent. She found one of the circus cars and drove it into the doorway of the circus tent.

Stefano was carefully helped into the car. Marta reversed the car out of the tent and then drove off.

Marta returned to the circus in the car. She had been gone for two hours. Stefano was with her in the car. He had a crutch to help him walk. His leg had a large bandage on it.

"Come here you." He yelled to Bernado.

He gestured to him with his arm. "Do not go near that killer dog of yours, he is mine." Bernado thought of protesting but just nodded his assent.

The freezing wind swept through the high cage. The other dogs howled in sympathy with him.

Bernado was not allowed near the cage; He stood hidden in the darkness some distance from the cage and watched. Strombolo would come to check to see whether he was near, He would wait hidden for a few minutes then walk off.

The next morning Strombolo came to him at the breakfast table. He looked down at Bernado as he sat eating.

"If I catch you near that cage with your dog, the boss told me to thump you"

He said in his reedy voice.

Shandor was not being fed; he was licking the rainwater off the floor of the large cage. This was mixed with the manure and urine. Shandor was becoming emaciated. He was very weak after being locked in the cage for a week.

Bernado took some meat and smuggled it to Shandor one night. He could not bear to listen to the howling of the large dog. He had just watched him eat it when a hand grabbed his shoulder, then an arm was around his neck.

"I tell you, stupid fool, not to come near the dog," a voice squeaked in his ear.

Strombolo swung Bernado with all his might against the cage. Bernado felt his lower arm snap. Strombolo then kicked his feet from under him and began to systematically kick him. Bernado blacked out from the pain.

When he finally opened his eyes, he was in a small hospital ward with a plaster cast on his arm. The doctor was waiting for him to regain conciseness.

The story he had been told was that he had a run-in with one of the circus animals when he had entered its cage. He knew it was not going to do any good telling the real story as the employees from the circus would back up Stefano's version of the tale.

Julio came to see him that evening and told him he had been feeding the four other dogs for him.

"Stefano had climbed into the cage with Shandor as he thought he was too weak to fight back. He was whipping him when Shandor grabbed his ankle. He shot Shandor through the back and had left him to die. I will help you, but my job is with the circus. I don't want to lose my job."

Bernado agreed with this.

The next day he let himself out of the hospital and asked where the circus was, the nurse protested saying it was too soon to leave the hospital. When she saw he had made his mind up to leave, she told him it was not very far away. She drew a map on a piece of paper.

The broken arm was in a sling to hold the heavy plastered arm up. It was very painful as he slowly walked back to the circus. The pain from the kick marks on his back and sides did not help.

Work was going on. The roof of the Big Top was laid out on the ground. People were cutting and sewing the large canvas roof as it was being made. Stefano hobbled over to him as he walked to the dogs.

"You can get your things and your dogs and go; you are not wanted here anymore.

"Great, where does this leave me?"

"I do not care, your dog tried to kill me." He thought for a second. "I will give you two week's extra pay. I want you out of here by tomorrow. Come to the office in an hour." Stefano hobbled off, back to the working men.

He looked at the four dogs; they had been fed and watered. He then went inside the caravan to get the strongbox.

Things had been moved around in the van. The top was off the bed and the holes in the floor where the strongbox had been, showed in the torn wood, marks where a lever had prized the box showed in the wooden floor.

His savings from working and the proceeds from the dog crime had all been stolen.

Julio came over to him. He walked into the caravan.

"What did the boss say?"

“I’ve got the sack. Some rotten bastard has stolen all of the money I had saved.” “I wonder who would have done that?” “It could have been anyone that’s the trouble.” “I have to go,” Julio went off back to work.

As he walked to the office Marta came over to him.

“Looks like I am not going to get to try that weapon of yours after all. That’s a pity.”

“Yes, the pity is that some rotten thief has stolen all of the money I saved up from working the last nine months,” the smirk went off her face.

“Oh, I am sorry about that. Some of the people working here are not very honest; Gypsies and other robbers seem to like this circus lifestyle. It keeps them moving from the law.”

He walked up the three steps into the large aluminum caravan.

Stefano was sitting in the office behind the desk.

“I was robbed of all of my savings when was in the hospital.” “Well, I cannot help that.” He thought for a while.

“I am sorry about that. You did a good job and helped the circus while you were here with your good act. I will pay you another two weeks' salary to help you out”.

“Thanks for that.”

Bernado noticed an edge of a gold coin showing out from under a sheaf of papers on the desk. He was going to accidentally move the papers but thought better of it. Stefano counted out the four-week pay and gave it to him. He did not want another meeting with Strombolo.

As he walked back to the dogs and caravan, he felt extremely angry, he walked over to Marta who was standing near their caravan.

"I would not want to leave you wondering, come to my caravan at ten o'clock tonight. You may have to help yourself because of my broken arm." Marta smiled.

"I'll be there".

The bed had been put back and caravan tidied. There was a knock at the door.

Marta stood outside in the moonlight.

She was dressed in a harem outfit with her midriff showing. She had a loose cape over her shoulders for warmth in the cold night air.

Bernado looked past her to see if she had been followed, then let her inside. They both stripped their clothes off. He winced from the pain as he carefully removed his coat and vest. She lay back on the bed with the soft moonlight on them. Bernado was going to give her the tease treatment so she would never forget him.

This would be a payback for the boss. In the dim moonlight showing through the window, she looked very beautiful; she reached out and held his tool.

"My god this is bigger than I thought it would be, it might not fit inside me."

His arm was very painful, but the job at hand took precedence. He slowly moved the tool around the entrance to the warm home.

"Put it in or I will scream." She hissed.

"If you scream you and I will probably get beaten up, or killed by Strombolo."

It was nearly half an hour before Bernado finally pushed his tool home. Marta was moaning softly. She was moving as she moaned.

Bernado kept holding her back from her climax.

After an hour, they climaxed together. His arm felt like it was being screwed tight in a vice.

They both got down from the bed. Marta started to dress, Bernado stood up. She was standing behind him. He had just finished dressing, having difficulty in putting his heavy plaster covered arm through the sleeves of his vest and jacket.

There was a loud crashing noise. the door ripped open on the caravan as the lock tore through the wood of the door surround.

Strombolo stood outlined against the watery moon, as he stood on the top step each hand holding the sides of the damaged doorway.

He was peering into the dark with his small beady eyes.

Almost without thinking Bernado dropped his head and charged Strombolo hitting him with his head in the gut. Strombolo toppled back out of the doorway. Bernado fell to the floor on the landing and ladder. This hurt his arm.

Strombolo tried to save himself he threw out his arm to try to grab onto the ladder to stop himself from falling, it got caught in the side of the ladder and one of the timber risers. Bernado heard his forearm crack as the bone was broken. He then swung back as he was held by his broken arm which was still wedged in the ladder. He hit his head on the corner of the truck tray with a sickening thud. He was knocked out cold. He hung in mid-air by his now broken arm. His feet were just touching the ground.

They carefully climbed over Strombolo's still body. They were afraid he may wake as they stepped over him. They both negotiated their way to the ground. Strombolo was snoring with his duck-like squeaky voice.

"I think we should go to the office and get the money and coins stolen from me. You will have to come with me. I do not want to be around when he wakes up."

"Nor do I. I gave Stefano about four large shots of strong Polish vodka for the pain in his leg. He should not wake up."

The two of them carefully walked to Stefano's caravan. He waited while she found the keys. After a short wait, Marta exited the caravan and came back with the sheaf of keys.

"He is sleeping like a log and snoring loudly."

They went to the office, then unlocked the office door, then found a small torch hanging on the wall near the door of the office. The weak torchlight showed the desk with the papers strewn across the top of it, as it had been when he had left the office before he met with Marta.

Bernado lifted the sheaf of papers; there were the nine coins and jewelry he had found when working cleaning up the bombed houses.

The strongbox was tucked in behind the desk and was open. The padlock had been cut through with bolt cutters.

The cutters lay next to the box. The money and other jewelry were still inside.

This was cleaned out into a large hessian grain sack which was crumpled up on the floor in the corner of the office.

Marta once again took the keys. She opened the safe in front of the office van. She took a bag out of the safe and searched through the money with the torch. She took some money from the bag but left most of it. She returned the bag to the safe, then relocked the safe.

He picked up the sack with his jewelry and money in it with his good arm and then sneaked to get the dogs.

Strombolo was still hanging by his broken arm, his feet were on the ground. He was still snoring loudly with a squeaky snore. Bernado kept listening to the snoring intently as he untied the dogs. Letting the dogs loose from the caravan was very difficult with his one arm.

The other arm was extremely painful.

All of the props were left behind as was the cart.

Bernado and the dogs wended their way through the caravans to where Marta had one of the circus cars waiting; he could see the car lights shining through the caravans. Bernado had not trusted her to wait with his money as well.

Marta helped him load the dogs into the rear of the car; she started the car, and then drove out of the gate of the small field, she then turned into the town.

She explained about leaving most of the money behind. "I was not greedy. I did not want to take what was not mine, and shut this circus down, and lose all of my friend's jobs for them. Stefano was not that bad a man. I have met some men many times worse in my time."

On the other side of the city, they stopped at a nice-looking hotel. After waking the old tired looking all night receptionist. They booked a room for the night.

The receptionist stared at the two people in the unusual Circus clothes. A customer was an extra piece of income. He just shrugged his shoulders as he handed them the room key

Marta drove the car around the back of the establishment into a lean-to shed, she then tied the dogs to the bumper bars of the car.

When this was finished, they walked up the rear stairs to their room; Bernado carried the money bag in his good hand. His other arm felt as if it were on fire.

The birds were tweeting in the large tree just outside their window; Marta was asleep but was holding his Bierwurst in her hand. When he tried to move she woke up.

"How is your arm this morning?"

" not as sore as it was last night."

"You were very brave to take on Strombolo."

" I did not have much choice he would probably beaten up both of us to within an inch of our lives, or killed us."

"I have been thinking of leaving for some time. Stefano has beaten me up many times. He was so jealous."

“I can see why. You seem to have been chasing the hired help.” She laughed and snuggled back into the soft mattress.

“Would it hurt if I could make love to you again? Lay on your back. I will be very careful.”

Bernado lay back on the bed, and Marta loosened his underwear to let the Bierwurst stick out.

She carefully climbed on him, making sure to be careful of his broken arm. She reached between his legs and lifted his weapon. She then slowly slid her body onto it until it was fully buried. She kept it the full depth and slowly moved her hips from side to side, so it moved against the bottom of her vagina, she moaned softly as she did so, she would gently climax then restart the procedure again. She did this for almost an hour until the urge got too great. Bernado was filled with desire by this time.

“This sure beat being in the horrible dirty orphanage being raped by a dirty priest,” he said, as Marta carefully dismounted from him.

Afterward, Marta raised her eyebrows and realized there was a lot to get to know about this young man. It would be a very interesting task to find the truth.

CHAPTER 9

As they sat at the small table eating their breakfast, Marta suggested that they should find some way to get the car back to the circus. It was not hers. There was a possibility that Stefano would report it as having been stolen, it was very conspicuous with the advertising writing on it. She did not want to meet up with Stefano again. Strombolo would be no more of a problem for a long time.

They spent most of the day inside the hotel. Bernado did not feel very well with the pain in his arm causing him to feel nauseous.

That evening Marta drove the car to the small bar where Julio and he used to spend nearly every night after work. The car was parked around the corner, so it could not be seen.

Julio was seen walking down the road. Bernado gave him enough time to enter and settle down for his first drink. No other circus people were seen coming. Bernado walked in, Julio spotted him and waved him to come and sit.

"You caused a stir last night before you left. The news is that you cleaned out the safe."

"Well, that's a lie for the start. Marta only took a small amount of cash she thought she was owed. That rotten thief had all of my money and other valuables in his office. He or Strombolo must have stolen it when I was in the hospital."

“Strombolo has got a nasty bruise on his head and a broken arm. He was in a bad way when we found him in the morning. Lucky for him the timber rail of the stairs had broken dropping him to the ground. The doctor said if it had not, he would have lost his arm.

How the hell did you do that? “

“I was extremely angry when I realized that he and Stefano had stolen my money. I noticed one of the gold coins I had found when I was working cleaning up bombed building sites. It was half-covered by some newspaper. I knew then that one of them had stolen all of my money.

Marta made an offer to have sex so I took her to my caravan. This was for a payback. We were just finished dressing when Strombolo broke the door of the caravan; he must have been looking for Marta. I thought he would probably kill Marta and me; I charged him with my head down and hit him in the gut. He fell out of the caravan and tumbled down the stairs backward. He got hooked up, I heard his arm crack, and then he hit his head on the truck tray. Payback I reckon.”

” This is different from the story he told.”

“I would bet it was.”

Bernado accepted a drink Julio had ordered.

“The boss has had the police around about the stolen car. It will be easy to find with the advertising for the circus painted on it.” Bernado took a sip of vodka. “This is what I am here for. We only borrowed it to getaway. I had the dogs and did not want Strombolo waking up and chasing me. I would not even like to have him near me with only one arm."

Julio agreed to drive them into the middle of the town, and then return to the circus with the car. They walked out of the bar and went to the car.

The dogs in the car wagged their tails as Julio appeared, they had always liked him.

Marta moved to the passenger side of the car. Julio started to drive.

"Where are you going?"

" Just to the middle of the town," she said.

Bernado was a bit of a tight fit in the rear with the four dogs.

Esmerelda was the smallest one. She moved and sat on his lap.

"What are you going to do now?" Julio asked.

"We have no idea at present; possibly get some sort of act together with the dogs"

"This will do just here."

Julio stopped at the curbside. They opened the doors and got out, taking the four dogs and the bag with the money and jewelry. Marta went around to the driver's door, opened it, and gave Julio a large sloppy kiss on the lips.

"Thank you, Julio, we will walk to the train station in the street not too far away and see if there is a train out of town."

Bernado shook Julio's hand. He shut the car door. Julio drove off, waving out of the open window as he did.

They did not go to the train station but went to a small hotel some distance from where Julio had dropped them off. Marta told the clerk that he had four dogs which he wanted to be able to keep under cover out of the cold. Bernado was with them just outside of the main doorway

"There were old unused stables at the rear of the hotel; these were from the horse and cart days. Just go down the passage to the rear

door. They are across the yard on your left side."

He paused then spoke again

"You can bring the dogs through with you if you like," Said the clerk.

The dogs were taken outside and put into a secure horse stall Marta then bolted the door. The sides of the stall were quite high.

The room had a large soft feather bed. They could not wait to finally get some sleep. Marta said she was too tired to make love, Bernado was thankful for this as his arm was aching by this time. If he left it to hang down it started to throb.

The next morning Bernado wanted to go to a doctor and have his arm checked. The concierge gave them directions; they set off with the dogs to a clinic not too far from the hotel. Marta sat with the dogs at a small outside café while he visited with the doctor in his room.

The doctor admonished Bernado for not resting the arm more. "You should be sitting around inside a house doing very light duties until the plaster is ready to take off. This will be in three weeks."

Bernado did not have the heart to tell him what had transpired since Strombolo had broken his arm. He was given some tablets for the pain.

People were giving Marta very funny looks as to the clothes she was wearing. The two-piece harem suit and the cape was not the normal dress in the city. She was just about freezing. Bernado's clothes were also out of place.

They walked along the road to some shops.

Marta took the small bag with her money out of the hessian bag. Then went into the emporium and found a woman's clothes shop. Bernado sat with the dogs at an outside table of a small café. After a short while, she came out with some parcels and boxes. She had changed into some woman's slacks blouse and a warm coat and new shoes. She had thrown away the circus clothes. Bernado had his turn in the Men's-wear shop.

He had to parade outside in the clothes he chose for her approval. Each time he changed clothes his arm felt extremely painful. She was minding the four dogs.

Finally, she agreed to the choice of attire.

They visited another shop that sold general merchandise. The hessian bag was discarded for a small suitcase purchased from this store. The new clothes and money and jewelry were changed over to the case as they were sitting in a corner of the emporium where they were alone.

As the money was transferred Marta's eyes opened wide when she realized how much money was being placed in the new case. "Where did you get all of the money?" Bernado felt guilty.

"I taught Shandor and Esmerelda to steal people's cases and handbags. I did this during the night in the German towns when we were on tour." "You have been a naughty man then." She smiled up at him.

"I think we should buy a delivery van so we can travel with your dogs in the box on the back."

"I can't drive."

" That's ok, as you could see, I can. We should get out of this area so there is no chance of being seen by any of the circus people. I have some ideas of what we could do to set ourselves up in business."

They walked inside one of the shops and asked then asked the assistant if there were any car dealers nearby.

"There is an old warehouse about two hundred meters down the road from here. The man there has many different cars and vans inside."

The man gave directions and also drew a map on a small piece of paper. As the building was only a short distance away. They walked off with the dogs in the direction toward the dealer's premises.

There motor car dealership was a ramshackle old building with windows along the front. The building looked as if it had been an old warehouse or factory; inside the building on the floor space, there was a large selection of cars, busses, and vans.

After half an hour of walking around, there was the choice of three vehicles they had found. There was one Citroen van with a clean box on the rear with ventilation and windows, and a smaller Renault van and a Skoda bus. The Citroen was the best looking of the three. Bernado sat on the rear of the tray with the rear door open while Marta talked to the salesman.

The man was not happy at having the four dogs on his premises. “I do not want to have to clean up dog crap.” He said tersely.

“Do you want me to go somewhere else to look for a car? We will be able to find some other people who want to sell a car.”

The salesman wanted the sale, so he reluctantly agreed the dogs could stay. Bernado counted the money out of the small case. He held the lid up so the salesman could not see the interior. Marta signed all of the papers and paid the man. They now had some transport.

As they drove along the road Marta turned off the road and turned into a car parking space in front of a second-hand shop. “What do you want in this shop.” “You will soon find out.” Said Marta.

They walked inside. She asked the old man who was running the business if he had some old heavy storage trunks. The old man took them to the rear of the large building where there were four different trunks to choose from.

She purchased a large solid trunk which was carried out of the shop on a sack truck to the car. The trunk was difficult to find its way through the mountains of stock in the shop.

When they arrived at the van, she smiled at the man and asked him if he could screw the trunk to the floor of the van. The old man agreed to do this.

He walked away and came back with some screws and a large screwdriver. Bernado noticed that he had been having lustful looks at Marta when he was working.

The box was to store their clothes and cases to keep them away from the dogs.

Some old rugs and carpet were also bought from the shop; they were tossed on the floor for the dogs.

"Now I want to get out of this town before we are caught by one of Stefano's stooges. "Bernado said

Marta thought for a while,

"I think that would be a very good idea. Let's go."

"Where shall we go?" Said Bernado,

"I am tired of being cold all of the time; let's head down to the Mediterranean."

They took their time traveling. They traveled through Czechoslovakia. Some mornings the roads were covered in snow and ice. This was a good time to stay and look around the small town where they had stopped for the night. In the early afternoon when the air usually cooled to an icy feel, they would go back to the hotel and have a meal, then adjourn to the bedroom to have fun with Bernado's Bierwurst sausage.

Marta had many different ways of using this large sausage; she was very skilled in the art of lovemaking. Bernado's arm was beginning to feel better; He was now having a problem with a very annoying itch under the plaster cast. He had bought a thin wooden ruler which he used to try to scratch the itch. It did help somewhat. After one particularly spectacular love-making session she was relaxed in a cuddle and started to reminisce.

"During the war, my parent's house was bombed. My father had been a town official in Poland. He had a very good job and was well paid. When the Germans came, we almost starved. My father was lucky he had not been shot. Many of the officials in the towns were. I was sixteen at this time."

Marta stopped talking with a sad look on her face.

"One evening when I was coming home from getting some food, I was dragged into a dark alley by a German soldier and raped. I told my father and mother. There was nothing we could do about this. If we were to report this to the authorities, we may all have been shot." Marta got out of bed and sat on the side next to Bernado, she held his hand.

She continued her story.

"I then decided the only way to provide for my family was to sell myself to the Nazi soldiers. Not the normal dirty soldiers from the field but the officers. They would have some sort of protection for me and my parents. I have always felt ashamed of doing this." She thought with a worried look on her brow.

"I could never tell my parents about this. I told them I had a good job working in a large restaurant. This was partially true. There was some rebellion with some partisans shooting some German soldiers in our town." She shuddered then went on with the story. "The next day the German SS in our town herded up thirty people on the street and took them away. My parents were caught up in this crowd. All of these people were shot in retaliation to the partisans shooting four soldiers”

Marta had tears streaming down her face as she thought of what had happened to her friends and parents.

Bernado sat up and put his good arm around her shoulder.

“We did a lot of things to survive in those bad times. I watched as a Nazi Officer directed soldiers and young boys to kill my parents and relatives. They then burned our caravans and shot our horses. I was hiding in a thick bush. I saw the commander of the soldiers laughing after he had done this when they had buried all of our people in the ground.”

He stopped and shuddered at having recalled this horrible story.

“I then found a small town nearby and was lucky to meet an old Gypsy lady who took me in to teach me how to tell fortunes and heal people. She was shot at her house a few months later by some German soldiers looking for food.”

He gave her an extra squeeze with his arm. “I discovered this commander of this murdering crew when I was performing at the circus one night. I took Shandor and followed him. When we were in a very secluded part of town with no houses, I sent Shandor to kill him. As he was dying I told him why. “

He caressed her warm body; rubbing her warm breasts and making the nipples rise with her desire.

“As I said we all have a lot of things we did to survive we are not proud of. I have no regrets about killing this man though.”

The weather was starting to warm as spring had just started to show its presence. The trees were starting to show the first of the green leaves. The new adventure had just started. There was a trip to travel down through Italy chasing the warm weather, and a new life to look forward to.

CHAPTER 10

The steep rugged mountain country slowly gave way to farming land. The freezing nights started to warm.

In a medium-size town not far from Rome, they decided to stop traveling.

That night as they had finished making love, Bernado sat up and thought for a short while.

"What would you like to do for the rest of your life?" Marta pondered the question for a short while.

"I would like to find a city next to the sea where the tourist trade is and run a bar and strip show each night. Tourists like this type of entertainment. I mean a high-class show. Not the ugly women just wiggling and gyrating with their smelly bodies and then selling themselves to the dirty customers. The selling themselves could be part of the business, but it would be too rich businessmen." Bernado nodded approval.

"Our money is not going to last forever. I realize this. I think you have a very good idea."

That afternoon Bernado found a doctor and had his plaster cast removed from his arm. His arm still felt tender. He was relieved to have the weight of the plaster cast taken away.

The itching stopped almost within minutes of the cast being cut off with the snippers. He scratched all of the dry skin off when he came out to the street.

Bernado and Marta would take the dogs walking. When there were people and children together, he would run through the routine they played in the circus. He had a large hat he would lay on the ground for donations. Marta had protested. He replied, “People who watch these acts are more likely to enjoy the show if they can show their appreciation by giving some money.” Marta had to agree.

The people of this Italian town were very happy laughing people. The whole ambiance was different from the up-tight attitude of the Poles, Russians, and Germans, Bernado liked the people.

After a week in the town, they drove through Rome to a beautiful city, fifty kilometers further on.

Anzio, this city had been an invasion point for the allies during World War 2. The city still showed the deep scars of the bombardment.

“What do you think of this place?” asked Marta, as they drove along the esplanade above the beach.

“I have never seen the ocean before. It is beautiful. Does the temperature get very hot in the summer?” We shall ask when we have lunch” she said.

Bernado let the dogs out to stretch themselves and have some food and drink. He walked down to the sandy beach with them, the dogs tried to drink the water. Bernado tasted it also. It tasted terrible. Marta waited by the van. She smiled. When they returned, she asked, “What did the water taste like?” It was terrible it tasted like salt.” She laughed.

“All seawater tastes like this.”

They walked together to a small café. They took the nooses in the dog's leashes and put them under the chair legs so the dogs did not wander. She asked the waiter about the climate. She spoke in Italian. The waiter gave her some details as he gestured with his hands.

Bernado could see that he was also ogling Marta with his brown eyes. As she turned, he kissed his fingers in a gesture of approval. Bernado smiled.

The tasty food and wine were so different from any other food Bernado had seen or tasted before.

"I think I could spend my time in this beautiful city. Look at the tourists walking around. Big fat geese ready for plucking and supping" he smiled at Marta.

"We should look at some real-estate. See the areas along the seaside which have been damaged. They should be worth a fortune when they are restored. Do you fancy doing some work?"

After lunch, they walked the esplanade. One damaged building seemed to speak to them.

" Please help me." It seemed to cry.

This building had an ornate façade that had been damaged by shell fire during the invasion. A sign in Italian offered it for sale. There were a phone number and address.

A short distance along the road was another café. They stopped for coffee. The dogs were tied up to a post next to a large tree. Marta asked the owner if she could get some water for the dogs. The man found a large pan and walked off to fill it with water. She thanked him then walked to the dogs and gave them the water to drink. They greedily lapped it up.

When she returned, she asked the man for two cups of coffee. She then asked about the old damaged building. She was told by the concierge that the owner of the building was an old lady who lived close by. The man knew her. He told them the building had once been a casino. He drew a map on a scrap of paper. The owner lived in a large house directly behind the casino.

She paid and thanked the man. The Concierge also had the look of approval for the beautiful Marta.

They walked up a small street past the Café onto the back street to the rear of the old casino. The damage to the building the old lady lived in on the back street was far less than it was along the esplanade. Marta pulled the bell in the wall next to the door of the old large building which had a small court-yard out front with some magnificent statues in it.

A pretty young girl answered the door. She was dressed as a maid. Marta asked to talk to the lady who owned the building in front of her house.

She told her they were interested in buying the damaged building.

The girl smiled.

"You may come inside and sit down please while I get Donna Gabriella."

They followed the maid into the house.

The girl turned then walked up the curved staircase to get her. Bernado watched her tight rump moving under the uniform as she walked up the stairs.

They looked around the room, all of the furniture, paintings on the walls, and other fittings all showed the signs of wealth.

A small old grey-haired lady with a stick hobbled down the stairs, she looked down on them and smiled as she negotiated the stairs.

Marta spoke to her for some time in Italian about the building. The lady then told the maid to take them to see the property. The maid then left them to find the keys. When she returned, they set off back toward the front of the damaged building.

As they walked Marta explained the conversation.

"The lady is a widow. The building was run as a casino by her family, then her and her husband for many years ago, and has lain empty since her husband had died five years before the war.

The damage done during the occupation was worrying her. She is worried about the building being taken over by the vandals and dirty pigeons. She gave me a price. It is very cheap. I have done a quick calculation for the currency. We can afford it with plenty to spare if you sell the coins and jewelry."

The threesome walked down a narrow walkway to the esplanade in front of the building. The young maid unlocked the heavy ornate doors; they creaked as they were opened. She then produced a torch from her pocket.

Inside was a huge marble tiled floor area, doors were leading off to the side.

As they walked they found a large commercial kitchen that was at the rear with all other amenities. Old furniture lay strewn around. some roulette wheels and moth-eaten gambling tables showed traces of the now moth-eaten green felt tops. A large spinning numbers wheel had spider webs hanging from it. The furniture all still looked solid, it just needed restoring.

Two curved marble staircases led from the rear of the room. The walls of the room were covered in different colored marble to waist height. Dust covered paintings still hung on the walls.

The trio walked up the staircase to the second floor. Both staircases ended at a marble floor landing with rooms leading off. They then explored the rooms. Most were still furnished. The furniture and beds were covered in dust.

At the top of the stairs on the third floor, there was a group of four rooms which was the manager's suite. These rooms commanded a beautiful view of the beach and ocean. There was a large breakwater out from the shoreline of the ocean with a rotunda at the end. There were two ornate towers on each side of the main building

The balustrade of the balcony was badly damaged by the fighting, plus some of the façade. These were all things which could be repaired. There did not seem to be any major structural damage. Some of the rooms had shattered windows. The dirty pigeons had made a mess in them. The smell of the birds was not pleasant as the doors were opened, then quickly shut again.

The price of this building sounded very cheap.

"I think we should buy this. Just think what it would look like when repaired,"

Bernado agreed,

"We could live here ourselves and do a lot of the cleaning and small jobs. It is a good thing you can speak Italian."

"I told you before, my parents were wealthy, I was taught Italian when I was at school."

As they returned to the old lady's house, Marta had a real brainwave.

"Just think Bernado we will be buying a casino. All three businesses can meld in together. I can see this being a beautiful building once more. I think you will have to learn to speak Italian."

They walked across the road; they entered the old ladies' large house behind the Casino with Lola.

Marta spoke some time with Donna Gabriella. She talked about the times when the Casino had been running. After some coffee and biscuits, a deal was struck with the lady. They were to find a notary to work the paperwork and see a bank to transfer their money to Liras.

They were staying at a small hotel on the esplanade not far from the old Casino. The front rooms of this hotel were boarded up on the outside to cover up the damage from the invasion. As they left for the Casino in the morning, they stopped to appreciate the view of the ocean.

They drove around the business sector of the city and found a large bank in the city in the morning,

After Marta enquired at the counter, a young girl took them to see one of the bank officers in his office.

Marta explained to the man that they had offered to buy a property in Anzio and would like one of the bank officers to come and see them the next day.

She asked for a sheet of paper from the man and wrote down the address of the casino.

The man from the bank was to come and inspect the building at noon the next day and advised them of the procedure involved in paying for the property and other title transfers.

The door of the Casino was opened, while they waited inside for the man from the bank to arrive, two old people who were walking by knocked on the open door and then tentatively walked in. They went to meet them. These people introduced themselves. They had been regular visitors to the Casino many years before. They were interested to see the doors finally open again. Bernado and Rina let them walk around the large room to have a look. The people spoke to Marta about the wonderful times they had enjoyed with friends when visiting the casino. They had seen shows with some of the old movie stars and cabaret performers acting and singing. Bernado felt left out as he could not understand the conversation as Marta was laughing and talking to the old couple.

The man from the bank arrived. The old people left. They thanked them very much for showing them the old building. They wished them good luck as they left. The old man shook Bernado's hand vigorously as they departed.

The man from the bank had a quick look around the Casino and made some comments about the building.

They sat down at one of the dusty tables after they had dusted off three chairs.

He explained to Marta. The transferring of titles and other works were expensive. It appeared that every transaction had some kickback or bribe for some official. The bank employee left the building and headed back to the bank.

The biggest problem looming was to have the Casino license reinstated. Marta and Bernado drove to the Anzio City Hall and asked at the counter to speak to the man responsible.

They were taken upstairs and ushered into an office. A small dark sinister-looking man rose from his large desk and bade them sit down.

Marta explained that they were negotiating to purchase the old Casino on the foreshore, and said what they wanted to do with the old casino.

"We are going to buy this building and restore it if we would be able to reinstate the casino license."

The man said, "This would cost a lot of money. We have to contact the government in Rome and many other things before this could happen," He quoted a figure. It was expensive.

Marta explained to the official that this business would create many jobs for the city, where there were now many people out of work and poor. "I think this man is trying to rob us." She said to Bernado in Polish.

The man pricked his ears up and smiled. They had been caught out. "I can speak Polish if you would want to. My mother was Polish."

After that the language changed to Polish, the deal progressed at an easier pace. The main thing to do was to barter with this man. Bernado was very good at this. It was part of his heritage. Finally, after a half-day marathon, the official agreed to reinstate the license for almost half the original figure.

The dogs had been tied to the van under a shady tree; they had food and water with them.

That evening Marta and Bernado went to visit Donna Gabriella the old lady. As they entered the house Marta asked Lola the maid if she knew of any good tradesmen that would be interested in working with them.

Lola smiled broadly; she was pleased to hear of this, as she had four brothers who were good building workers.

Marta explained to Gabriella that they had been able to reinstate the license for the Casino. She clapped her hands and smiled widely. "Oh, this is good news. My family casino will be running again. My family has owned the casino for three generations." She then reached over and kissed her on the cheek. Lola returned to the room with some small coffee cups and delicate almond biscuits. Bernado was sad that he could not understand the conversation. Marta asked if they could move into the building to start work. Gabriella agreed.

The building had a rear laneway that led to the goods entrance and workers' quarters. A small yard was located behind a tall wall that had a large stout wooden gate. Bernado opened the gate from inside while Marta waited to enter with the van.

After shutting the gate, they searched the rooms. The rooms all had large padlocks on the doors. It took a lot of searching through the keys on the large keyring to finally open the doors.

Outbuildings lined one wall of the courtyard, these held tools and other goods like broken chairs and other furniture waiting to be repaired.

One of the small rooms was selected for the dogs to live in. Musty blankets were taken from one of the repair rooms and laid on the floor for them to sleep.

There was one room with two wide high doors on it. There was a smaller door set into the wide door on one side. After some effort, the rusty lock yielded.

They opened the door of what was a large garage.

In the front of them stood a huge car covered with some light canvas sheeting. The sheeting was carefully removed to show a huge dark green car with black mudguards. All four tires were flat and perished. Marta had never seen a car like this before, nor had Bernado. He rubbed the dust off the badge on the large radiator. The name said 'Avions Voisin'.

This huge low car had a silver mascot on the radiator cap, shaped like a tall winged bird. This was one of the most spectacular looking cars that either of them had ever seen. Bernado searched and found a key for the car door; the car was finished with top quality fittings inside,

Marta lifted the huge bonnet with effort; there was a huge engine under it. The engine was leaning to one side. Twelve wires were leading to the spark plugs on the cylinder heads. The car was a beautiful object, similar to a classic work of art.

The garage doors were closed. Both Bernado and Marta felt as if they had just found a priceless painting or some other work of art.

As they walked through the building to the front Bernado noticed four men looking into one of the dirty windows. Bernado opened the front door. The men were all strong good-looking men. They looked like brothers. The men came through the door and walked up to him. Each one shook his hand and smiled.

" Enzo, "said the first man,

" Antonio, Tony," said the second man.

"Francisco, Frank", said the third man.

"Roberto, Bobby," said the fourth man.

Bernado was a little bewildered.

"Our sister is Lola, who works for Gabriella."

Bernado understood enough of this conversation to realize who the men were. Marta walked over. She spoke to the men.

The men followed Marta and Bernado around the huge building. They pointed and explained in Italian to Marta about jobs that needed doing. After three hours, they left.

"I think we have some helpers. They do seem to know what they are talking about. They were building together and doing repairs before the war, working with their father. They have children who could also help. They will be here at 7.00 in the morning to start." "We should look around in the back buildings to find brooms and other cleaning tools if we are going to clean one of the top rooms to sleep in". Said Bernado

The many years of dust swirled around the room, most of it finally found its way out of the opened window. The blankets were taken from the room and shaken out on the balcony. Finally, the room was fit to sleep in.

They walked out of the building along the esplanade to the small café where they had been before. The concierge at Donaldo's recognized them. "Did you see Donna Gabriella about the old Casino?" Marta explained that they were the new owners.

Donaldo offered them a free meal and wine to celebrate.

The room was still very musty; this was the first night in their new life. Bernado ruffled up some dust that they had not beaten out of the bedding, during the night when he was driving his Bierwurst inside Marta. She moaned contentedly as it moved around.

Marta and Bernado left the casino in the morning and drove o the business part of town. They searched for jewelry shops. After being told the jewelry was just paste and plated gold by some of the unscrupulous jewelers they finally found an honest man in a large shop.

He had books on coins and looked up the prices and then discussed the condition of each coin. Stefan had been right these nine coins were quite rare. When he was told the price of each coin Bernado realized that Stefan would not have to pull the heavy cart to find enough money to survive. He felt pleased for him. The rings and other jewelry were appraised. The man asked where the jewelry had come from, Bernado explained that he had been working at cleaning up bombed buildings in Poland just after the war, and had found all of these items in the bombed houses.

"You have been very lucky to find such beautiful pieces. The Germans stole so much art and jewelry from the Jews. Many of these items have never been found."

As they left the store with a large bag filled with cash, Marta commented on the large prices paid for the rare coins. "I gave one of them to a friend who helped me when I escaped from the orphanage. I hope this changed his life as he was just earning enough to keep himself alive."

During the next week, the building was paid for. The power and other services were restored.

Even with the years of dust clinging to them, the large crystal chandeliers looked spectacular, when turned on the first time for many years.

Lola's brothers had bought their wives and children to help remove all of the dust off the walls and floors. Scaffolding was erected to reach the ceiling. The smaller children livened up the rooms with their laughter and antics,

The children were trying to help Bernado to speak Italian; they would point and then say the name of the object in Italian. The children were patient and quite often laughed when he first tried to pronounce a new word.

Donna Gabriella and Lola came to visit. She spoke to Marta for a long time about the parties and dignitaries which had happened and had visited many years before.

“Have you found the old car in the garage? “

“Yes, what a beautiful work of art it is,” Marta said.

“This car was purchased by my husband a year before he died; He became ill not long after he bought it. It was a very expensive car.” She hobbled around then pointed with her stick as she explained about the room when she was younger, and helping her husband work in the Casino.

After some of the smaller rooms had been cleaned, old rugs were placed on the floor. Furniture was taken first to one room and carefully sanded down then it was taken to a clean room without dust, and polished with new coatings of varnish. Some of the older children were very good at this job. When the varnish on the furniture had dried it was carefully stored in a safe place. During the month, the card tables were polished then re-felted, all of the beds, chairs, and tables from the rooms were varnished.

The damaged façade was repaired and the dirty pigeons evicted. The façade of the building was then whitewashed. The building stood out from all of the other damaged and half repaired buildings in the street.

One-day Bernado asked Frank about getting a mechanic to fit new tires and to see if the car could be made run again.

“I think this car could be a very good advertisement for the Casino.

I have never seen anything as beautiful before.”

Frank agreed and knew just the man for the job. This man had worked at Alfa Romeo for many years in the nineteen-thirties.

There was a phone call one morning from the Anzio council, a delegation from the city administrators and the mayor were wishing to look at the progress. They wanted to arrive at 10.30 am. The council employees filed through the front door. They were very impressed as Marta showed them through the refurbished rooms.

The short plump official who had tried to overcharge them was with the group. He was trying to take the accolades for the project. The man was looking down at Marta's cleavage every time she bent over to open a door. He looked at her behind as she walked; he was undressing her with his brown eyes. Marta kept the mouth shut as she did not want enemies at this time.

"Did you notice that little fat crook perving on you as you bent over? He was undressing you in his mind." Marta laughed and shook her head.

"I knew that I was teasing the little pervert. I think he even got a look at my nipples on one occasion. He nearly fell over on top of me."

She was still laughing,

"All of these things help when you are dealing with dishonest people."

Their finances were disappearing rapidly. The deal with Marta was on an eighty twenty basis. This deal had been written on the title of the Casino. Bernado had put all of his money into buying the property and paying the wages. They did not want any other partnership deals with other parties; He was to go to the bank then the city council to raise a loan and try to get a Government grant. This building was classed as a heritage building; it was very old and significant in Anzio city.

On Thursday morning when they were in their dirty clothes working. A pompous looking man, from the Government administration, arrived unannounced. Bernado and Marta met him after he walked through the door.

This man looked like trouble. The man reached into his pocket and produced a business card. He handed this to Bernado.

The children and others had been working hard and had done a very good job of teaching Bernado to speak Italian. With the many different jobs and other everyday occurrences, they had drilled into him the right way to pronounce and formulate words and sentences in Italian. He was far from fluent but was trying hard.

The pompous man introduced himself as Antoni Riccotelli. He was the minister for antiquities from the Italian Government in Rome. His job was to inspect the property to make sure no changes had been made to the building.

"I have here a book about this property when it was being used before as the city casino. This building has to be as it was before you started to do your work."

"It would have been nice if you had arrived as we were starting to restore the building," said Marta.

"I am not from the city. I am from the Italian Government. The city council from Anzio has only just informed me that this project is happening. This came about when you asked for a grant to finish the job."

This bought a worried look from Marta and Bernado. They followed the man as he walked from room to room checking with the book with illustrations and text describing the old building.

"Hmmm. "

He would say as he checked the page off then turned to another page.

They both followed and kept quiet as he finally walked back to the main marble room.

He took his briefcase and placed it on a large table, then selected a sheaf of papers from it. He then sat at a table and fanned them out. "Please take a seat so we can talk about your project." They both sat across the table from the man.

"I can see you are using good Italian craftsmen to do this job. This is good as it is giving work and money for the people and the city."

He then took a piece of paper and scribbled on it for a few seconds. "When you need the employees to run the casino, will you be hiring in the city? "

"Yes, that was our idea; we may have to get one or two other people who have had casino experience to teach the people."

He thought for a short while, he then scribbled again.

"Yes, I can understand this."

He shuffled some papers in front of himself.

"Now, let us talk about the building! I can see that the building is very similar to as it was many years ago. Only the kitchen and bathrooms and toilets seem to have been upgraded. As this is a significant building in Anzio, I can almost guarantee the government would consider a significant grant for this project." He mentioned a sum of money Both Bernado and Marta kept a straight face. This was a seriously large grant.

The man took another form from his brief-case and as he asked questions, he filled in their answers. This process is going to take a lot of work from me on your behalf to get this grant. I can not do this work for free. He wrote a figure in a box on the bottom of the form.

His fees were also very expensive.

"Are we guaranteed to get this grant?"

"Yes, this is government policy now to bring our cities back to their former glory."

Marta walked to the office and returned with a checkbook. She filled out the cheque and then asked for a receipt. The two forms were exchanged.

The official then restored all of the forms to his case and bid them farewell. They followed him outside and noticed he had an expensive government car with a chauffeur.

"This makes our stash of cash look slim. I hope he is not a crook."

The work on the building was scaled back due to the lack of funds. In the beginning, the project seemed to be just cleaning up an old building. This had been an understatement on their behalf as when the carpets had to be replaced and new bedding for the rooms, plus when the kitchen and other amenities were added the figure had ballooned enormously.

Lola and Donna Gabriella visited one morning; she was given the grand tour of the building.

"I am so pleased to see our lovely old casino coming back to life once more. What has happened to the workers? Is there not more work to be done?"

Marta sat next to her at the table. She had left to make coffee and had just returned. "We have underestimated as to how much money was needed to finish the job."

Donna Gabriella sipped her coffee.

"I can understand how this would have happened. You are restoring a masterpiece not building a tin shed."

She pondered for a short while as she sipped her coffee. "I did not have children. I have a sister who married a man who was a fool. They have lost almost all of her part of the family inheritance. I do not like their children; they are of the same stamp as the father." She sipped her coffee.

"I have a request for you. I would like my name on the casino if this does not offend you. 'Casino Donna Gabriella'", Both Bernado and Marta smiled.

"What a marvelous name. "Marta said, Bernado agreed.

"I possibly sound like a vain silly old woman, but this casino was in my family for three generations. I would like some sort of remembrance for me and my family. "

She sipped her coffee once more.

“I have a lot of money that is not going to be used. I shudder to think my sister’s family getting it and wasting the money as their father did. I would like you to consider me a part of the family. I would like to put money into the casino to finally bring it to a new beginning. This casino would bring many tourists and give work to many people in Anzio.”

Marta kissed Donna Gabriella on the cheek and thanked her very much. Bernado was lost for words, as the disappointing part was that the work had ceased as the casino had almost regained the former beauty of the building. “Welcome to our family Nonna.” Donna Gabriella laughed.

“Thank you, my grandson.”

“We will celebrate at Donaldo’s tonight,” added Marta.

Donaldo’s was filled to overflowing from all of the workers and their families. Some of the children helped Donaldo and his cook; three others went to find more food to cook.

Lola’s Father bought his accordion while her uncle had a violin. The music flowed out into the street. Passing people joined in the drinking and dancing. Some put money on the bar to help pay for the wine and food.

Donna Gabriella was dressed like a princess with her diamonds and beautiful clothes. She was laughing and talking to all who came near her.

“It is just as well I have not gotten fat, I have not worn these clothes for thirty years,” she said to the crowd.

"This is just like the old times when everyone was happy."

The dancing spilled out onto the pavement.

"Donna you will come to the casino every night dressed like this and be the Queen of Donna Gabriella's Casino," Said Bernado.

The next day was a day of rest for all. The party had continued to almost dawn, Bernado and Marta had found some very nice wine which Donaldo kept for special occasions. They had a wobbly walk back to the casino as the first rays of sunshine peaked over the horizon.

It was almost noon when they woke.

"My head feels as if it has a swarm of bees inside it, Wow the room is starting to spin."

"Keep your voice down," grumbled Marta.

"What about Donna Gabriella, she looked twenty years younger."

"Be quiet. I feel twenty years older."

The rest of the day was spent sitting around in the almost restored casino.

Late in the afternoon, Lola knocked on the door. Bernado opened it slowly.

"I think I have a hangover."

Lola smiled broadly, then laughed.

"Yes, I noticed that you took a liking to some of the wine last night. Donna Gabriella would like you to come for dinner in an hour if this is OK with you." "Yes, we will be there" called Marta from inside the room. The food and wine affected hangover benefitted from the cheesy pasta helped coat their insides against the alcohol.

"We will have to look to start to interview some employees for the casino. We will need a manager with experience in running a casino. This man would not come cheap, as we will have to get a person who is already doing this type of work." Bernado pondered for a few seconds.

"I have also been thinking about this. Most people with the skills we would need to run the casino would be in great demand. If they were not working, there would possibly be a good reason. There will also have to be a very tight security crew as well. Where there is money there is always someone trying to help themselves."

The discussion went on for three hours. Donna Gabriella's previous experience was going to be a godsend. Her manner had changed from a little old lady to an astute businesswoman.

"My children, this has started to change my life. I feel like I have shed the little old woman waiting to die image, to be some use to society again. Heaven helps us Anzio needs a helping hand now."

"Thank you very much, Nonna. I think we had bitten off more than we could chew with this project. You have had experience in running this casino. You know much more than we would ever know."

"Thank you, Marta. Have you asked the workers to return yet?" "They will start tomorrow morning. I spoke to them last night before I started to drink the lovely wine." Bernado shuddered at the thought of wine again.

“I have not enjoyed myself so much for so many years. This was like the old days before the war. Good friends, good food, good wine. Ay, Bernado”

She smiled at Bernado.

Lola walked outside with them as they were leaving. “I have not seen her so happy for many years. She has a fire in her belly now and talks only about the new casino.” Marta kissed her on the cheek.

“This makes us happy as well; both of our parents were murdered by the Nazis during the war. We do not have any other relatives left we know about. We only have each other.”

CHAPTER 11

The Casino was filled with laughter as the people and children returned and began working one more. The building was coming back to life.

People from the city would sometimes enter the building and ask if they could just have a look at the restoration.

Some of the older people could remember visiting the casino when it had been running. They described the good times they had experienced all of those years before.

Some mentioned meeting movie stars and other dignitaries and statesmen from the years before the war.

After many months of working the project was finally melding together. Donna Gabriella had placed some large advertisements in some of the daily papers throughout Europe, for experienced management staff. The job offered above-average remuneration and a bonus package as well.

There was now a waiting game for written submissions from prospective employees.

Bernado had an idea and had scoured the second-hand, and antique shops in Anzio.

He had Marta drive him around in the van.

"What are you looking for," asked Marta,

"I will tell you when I see one." After a lot of walking and looking Bernado found what he wanted. It was tucked away in the rear of an old musty shop. It was a large ornate chair with a rich brocade seat. It was not too high and looked like a king's throne.

"You cunning devil I see what you are looking for now, what a good idea, a throne for Donna Gabriella." She thought for a while.

"This could go just inside the door in the niche where we were going to put the large statue."

"You're right, that is just where I thought this should go. It is a throne for the Queen of the casino."

The throne was removed from the rear door of the second-hand shop with difficulty and loaded into the rear of the van. It was then taken back to the casino and taken through the rear gate to one of the outside rooms where Donna Gabriella did not usually go. Enzo, Tony, Frank, and Bob were let into the secret. No word of this was to get to Donna Gabriella.

"I would like you to clean this up and paint it gold".

Enzo studied the chair. He pointed to the middle of the rosettes. "I could set some fake jewels into some of the large ornate top pieces of the throne, "said Enzo.

"What a good idea. I will leave it in your hands, but if she hears of this, I will kick your backsides".

The men all laughed.

The day arrived when interviews were to be had with the potential manager and security heads for the casino. Donna Gabriella sat in the middle of the table. She was dressed like a businesswoman with a felt hat on her head. She asked most of the questions.

This was to be a head-hunting expedition. She was interviewing people who were already working in the industry.

She had offered a very good package of wages and conditions.

"If you spend peanuts you get monkeys" She had said before the prospective employees arrived.

'Where had all of these people come from' thought Bernado as each person had filed through during the day?

Each interview took nearly fifteen minutes. A series of questions were asked from a list each interviewer had on the table in front of them. Not all questions were asked of every person being interviewed. Some stood out as being unsuitable and some were classed as very suitable.

"Phew. What a long day. I have not had so much fun for years. What did both of you think of our potential new employees?" I think we could cut out half of them for the beginning. Some appear arrogant and others seem to be the opposite". Donna Gabriella placed a list of names and photos which the men and women had posted with their résumés.

"You take out the first run of people you would not like. I will reserve my judgment."

Marta and Bernado studied the photos and resumes once more as they did so they removed over half of the photos.

"I agree with that except for this man, Shall I put him back?" The photo was restored to the potential manager's pile. The resumes were read and discussed. More photos and resumes were taken from the potentials. Finally, three people were selected from the forty applicants. The process was repeated for the head of security. Letters were to be sent to the top three men of every job to ask them to return for further evaluation.

The next morning Enzo, Tony, Frank, and Bob approached Bernado about jobs at the casino after the grand opening.

“What would you like to do?” asked Bernado.

” I think two of us could do the running around and maintenance. We also think we should teach you to drive. You could pick up all of the dignitaries from the airport or railway station in the Mercedes.”

“Your game, I have only ever driven a gypsy wagon when I was a kid.”

“Ah boys that is where he gets his black curly hair, and his way with the women,” Frank said jokingly.

“I will teach you to drive.”

“If you would like to alternate jobs and help inside as well when or if we ever get busy you all have permanent jobs. What about some of your older kids who have left school? They will be looking for work soon.”

Bernado had discussed this with Marta. Having good hardworking friends working and keeping their eyes on the other staff could be a very good idea.

After working together for so long Bernado had great respect for the four men and their families.

The finishing touches were taking place. During the last three weeks, the staff was being trained to take their new jobs. In all there was fifty staff, ten were the four workers and other family members.

Luigi Perini was employed as the manager. Luigi was a very studious looking man with thin steel-rimmed glasses. He gave the impression of being a very intelligent man. Luigi had worked at Monte Carlo and Las Vegas in the casino management areas.

Pierre Bouton was security head. He had worked at casino

security after leaving the French police. Pierre had the look of a man not to be trifled with. He still held the distrust of fools from when he was a police officer.

Donna Gabriella had called a few late favors from some of the older people she had known years before; both men had their past checked extensively.

The other main spoke to the wheel was a brilliant Chef to manage the kitchen; Anton Bouvierre had been the chef for the president of France. Anton was a typical chef. He had a small mustache and an amply proportioned heavy build. He was a smiling man who liked his food.

The general casino staff was being well trained by three lesser managers appointed by Luigi Perini; they had been working in other casinos before.

The day before the grand reopening of Casino Donna Gabriella, the throne was smuggled through the complex hidden under some drop sheets. It was installed in the niche inside the entrance. A curtain was placed across the entrance to the niche. Donna Gabriella commented on this as she walked by.

"This is a surprise for Marta, and I do not want any person telling her," they walked on past.

Invitations had been sent to many dignitaries and movie stars; the opening was extensively advertised. The city mayor Silvio Fiori and his family were guests of honor. Silvio was to open the refurbished casino.

Just before the doors were to be opened to the public a special announcement was made for Donna Gabriella to come to the main entrance. The crowd of workers was asked to come to the entrance to be part of the ceremony

She was to cut a ribbon to open the curtains for a special event. She came to the entrance and was handed a pair of gilded scissors which were going to be used by the Mayor for the official opening. Donna Gabriella with some pomp sliced through the ribbon holding the curtains closed. They were pulled aside to show the golden bejeweled throne. The staff clapped their hands.

"What is this for," she asked slightly bewildered.

"We have built a throne for the Queen of the casino to welcome guests when she feels the urge. This is your special place if you would like it."

"Donna Gabriella reddened with a blush.

"What a wonderful place you have built for me. Thank you so much."

She walked into the niche and took to the throne. Everyone clapped and cheered once more.

Finally, at eleven o'clock the door was opened for the mayor to cut the ribbon. The mayor in his gold chain of office and other regalia and robes strode to the ribbon across the entrance and with some pizazz cut it through with the gilded scissors.

He walked to Donna Gabriella on her throne and bent and kissed her hand. His family followed and did a similar greeting.

The town dignitaries did the same. Donna Gabriella wore a diamond tiara and did look the part of a Queen.

The large room was filled with visitors. The roulette and other games of chance started up for the first time in thirty years.

Marta was explaining some of the names of people who were prominently featured in the newspapers to Bernado; many were in the movie and fashion business. Photographers followed the crowd like hungry wolves following a mob of sheep. The room sparkled with the flashes of the many cameras, causing the crystals of the chandeliers to glitter like diamonds.

The mayor took the stage and made a speech to Donna Gabriella, Bernado and Marta were at her side on the stage. The mayor turned to the crowd, then waved his hand toward the refurbished casino, then offered his congratulations for the job achieved in the restoration of the casino.

Bernado responded with thanks to Donna Gabriella and Enzo, Frank, Tony, and Bob and their families. He pointed to the paintings and all of the furniture. He extolled the skills his helpers had shown in such a large restoration.

He thanked his new Nonna, Donna Gabriella for her assistance in setting things in the casino as they were before and helping to hire the staff.

As he gave his thanks to all of the helpers, he just then fully realized that there were hundreds of people in the Casino, evidently people from all over Europe by the different languages spoken and the mode of dress.

The sound of the crowds at the roulette, blackjack, poker, and other games was nearly deafening. Large amounts of money were changing hands.

The bar was crowded. Further afield in the large dining room patrons were ordering lunch.

People were climbing the marble staircase, standing on the landing, and then looking down onto the crowd.

The Mayor and his family were now evidently giving the city council's finances somewhat of overspending on the tables.

Bernado and Marta were on hand until the last patrons were politely asked to leave. This was four am in the morning.

The newly trained cleaning staff comprising of the Italian workers older children and some other new local people started Vacuuming the carpets and sweeping. The kitchen was abuzz with the noise of dishes and pans being washed.

Donna Gabriella had excused herself at midnight. Her smile was starting to fade.

"I think you and Marta have done a good thing for Anzio. Look at the tourists and locals who are here.

Think of the work we have created for some of the poorer families."

"You had a large part of finally bringing this lovely building to life once more. Without your help, this would not have happened. You looked truly regal sitting on your throne greeting the people."

"I did feel that way at the beginning, but now the noise and banter have started to jade my nerves. I will bid you good luck and good night."

Lola walked out with Nonna and took her home.

Marta had looked sensational in her new designer clothes, Bernado was dressed in a dinner suit Tuxedo and bow tie. He had remarked as he dressed that he looked like a penguin.

"You had better get used to looking like a penguin as you have to wear this suit for a badge of authority. This penguin is here to make some money."

They watched over the staff as the chips were all taken back to the strong room with the large safe. Counting the proceeds would take place in the morning.

As he woke in the morning at nine am, he thought of the success of the opening night and the huge crowds playing the games. He quickly dressed in casual clothes, he then walked downstairs. He was eating his breakfast in the dining room when Frank came in with an arm filled with newspapers. "Looks like you and Marta have made front-page news all over Europe."

The Anzio paper had the Mayor shaking hands with Bernado as Donna Gabriella as Marta watched on. Other papers had smaller photos on the bottom of the newspaper front page with similar photos of them with dignitaries from their respective countries. This was good publicity, but there might be a few people that Bernado did not want to know what he was doing, Stefano and Strombolo at the circus for instance.

People were working inside tidying and cleaning. The kitchen was abuzz with people being instructed by Chef Anton in the fine arts of pastry making. The ovens were filled with delicate tartlets and cakes. Bernado and Marta sat at a table. Chef Anton came to their table,

"Congratulations we had an excellent opening night last night. We almost ran out of food." Chef Anton looked down at them. "What would you like for breakfast?" They both ordered and thanked him.

After they finished the meal they went to the strong room. Bernado opened the large safe and started to remove the chips, then the proceeds from the night. This was piled onto a large table. The chips in their value boxes and the money in the calico bags it was stored in from last night. Luigi and Pierre oversaw the proceedings. The money was sorted into values and nationalities. Some tourists and visitors from other countries had not changed enough of their money into Liras; the new office employees were well-schooled on the exchange rates for many countries.

When the final figure was totaled up and a rough estimate of expenses for food alcohol and wages was deducted, Bernado and Marta were amazed.

"This is much more than we paid for the building".

Bernado whispered to Marta. A sum was taken from the counted money to cover the days coming food costs as well as change for the customers.

Bernado accompanied Pierre to the bank in the new car which had been purchased to ferry customers from their hotels and other locations to the casino. The car was a large black Mercedes Benz. "I think you should be happy with last night's takings." offered Pierre as he drove toward the large bank building in the center of Anzio.

"I had no idea as to what we should expect. This is way above what I ever dreamed it would be."

"Of course, this was the grand reopening and you had all of the city and other officials probably spending the government's money." Pierre Laughed.

They were taken to a secure room where the night's takings were counted by two bank employees. They signed off on the figure which then was taken to be deposited.

On the trip, back to the Casino Pierre talked of being in France during the war. His family had all survived the war. They had some other nasty experiences with relatives going missing. Bernado kept his past to himself. He did not want the details broadcast to the casino staff.

When they returned to the Casino, taxis, and cars were lining up with new customers for the day. As they entered, the patrons were starting to play the tables.

When Bernado and Marta were alone he discussed taking the dogs out of retirement for a show in the early afternoon twice a week. He would have to purchase some costumes.

"You had better have more room in the crotch than you had in the circus costume or you will distract the customers."

"I wonder how many people we will attract to our business today."

Donna Gabriella arrived at three-thirty pm to sit on the throne to greet people. Bernado left to purchase the costume for the dog act just after she had arrived. At six pm he entered the room with the stage for performers with his dogs, Donna Gabriella was taken to a front-row seat.

The dogs had not forgotten their teaching and performed their acts flawlessly. Bernado had given them some training in the short periods of spare time he had during the renovations. The children working with their parents had enjoyed these impromptu performances.

As the act proceeded, more people came to watch, lured by the laughing and clapping of the audience. The dogs were proud to be performing to a large audience once more, Donna Gabriella was amazed and stood and clapped at every new act. Bernado had sad thoughts of Shandor being missing from the troupe.

During the next weeks, the crowd had not diminished. Other buildings along the esplanade were being restored to take advantage of the crowd the casino was attracting.

Some well-known singers and musicians were booked to play for the crowds. In one room Poker machines were installed. This was a large cost that had been covered by the grant which had been offered by the government official Antonio Riccotelli, the business was now running like a well- oiled machine.

One morning when walking through the casino as the customers were just starting to enter, a familiar voice called to him from behind. Bernado turned, Rina stood before him. She was heavily pregnant.

"You look like you have landed on your feet."

"Hi, Rina it is great to see you. Did you hear what happened at the circus?"

"I only heard their story."

"Come into the dining room and have some coffee, we will talk of the past."

They both walked through the crowd to the dining room and sat in a deserted corner. A waiter arrived at the table Bernado ordered." What did you hear from the circus?" Bernado listened to the story. This was Stefano's version which Julio had told them.

"Ok, I will tell you all of the truth."

He recounted the whipping of the poor young horse and how

Shandor had attacked Stefano. Then he told of the beating and broken arm by Strombolo and then finding all of his money stolen when he returned from the hospital.

" Much of the money and jewelry was stolen from people when I trained Shandor and Esmerelda to steal from people in the street. This is one of the main reasons I could not leave the dogs with some other person to mind. The dogs may have gotten away and shown my robbing scheme" He looked up at Rina.

"When I returned to the circus from the hospital, I went to see Stefano about the severance pay he offered. I noticed one of the gold coins I had taken when I was working cleaning the bombed buildings. It was poking out from under some papers on his desk, I knew then he and Strombolo had been tied to the robbery. I was too frightened of Strombolo to do anything about it."

They both sipped their coffee and nibbled on a biscuit.

"What happened between you and Marta?"

"Marta had offered herself to me on some other occasions. I talked my way out of it. I did not want to be tangling with Strombolo. He had warned me once before when Marta was seen talking to me."

He reached and held Rina's hand

"On that night, when I left his office with a meager amount of money, Marta confronted me again. I told her about the robbery, and who had done it. How I had seen one of my coins in his office. I was angry and decided to take her to my caravan and give her the slow treatment so she would not forget, and Stefano would not compare. I was very angry."

They sipped the coffee once more.

"I had just finished giving her the treatment when Strombolo ripped the door off the hinges and was looking into the dark caravan. I thought he was possibly going to kill me, so I charged him and hit him with my head in the gut. He was tangled in the ladder of the caravan and broke his arm as he fell back. Luckily, he knocked himself out on the tray of the truck. We knew Marta could not stay; Stefano was already beating her before this happened. We took my money and jewelry and Marta took what she figured she was owed. We did not clean out the safe."

"This is different from the story Stefano and Strombolo told everyone."

"He killed Shandor after he had starved him for a week in the cold before he did so. Shandor did get some revenge before being shot. He had bitten Stefano once more" said Bernado Rina patted her bulging tummy.

"You know where this came from don't you." Bernado smiled.

"I have a pretty good idea. It would be something to do with a Bierwurst stick" They both laughed.

Bernado took Rina with him while they went to find Marta. Marta was overseeing a new game table being installed in the main gambling hall.

She looked up as Rina arrived and smiled, raising her eyebrows as she did so as she then looked down at the bulge of her tummy. "It looks like the Bierwurst has done some damage. I also have some news I was holding back on. I have just found I have the same affliction".

She laughed.

"I wonder if any of the other girls at the circus have the same problem."

Bernado did not know how to react to this news. "I think we had all go up to our apartment and discuss the situation."

As they climbed the stairs, they discussed the circus and whether it was on tour.

Rina assured them it certainly was.

“Stefano had a new woman, a strong Russian woman weightlifter.” “Good, if he tries to beat her up she will probably kill him,” said Marta.

“Strombolo took a long time to heal and has a bend in his arm from a botched job.”

” That serves him right.” said Bernado.

After an amicable discussion, it appeared that Bernado was to look after the two women. Rina would stay at the casino.

“We have all been friends and have shared the circus life. I see no reason for animosity now. I think our Bernado would have enough Bierwurst to go around.” Marta said.

“Yes, I think the war should have taught us about kinship and friends. So many good people we have known disappeared forever.” “I had better have a roster so you girls know which night is your turn,” Said Bernado with a giant smirk on his face.

“I think he may get too big for his boots. What do you think about helping me to do the roster, Rina? Maybe we should also include the ugly old lady in the kitchen who washes the dishes. He sounds like some Arab Sheik.”

CHAPTER 12

Donna Gabriella laughed at the news, "The Lord said, what thou shall sew, thou shall reap. You have been a naughty boy Bernado, now your harvest is nearly ready to reap." she winked at him with a mischievous smile.

A week after this eventful happening Bernado was walking through the gambling room talking to the gamblers and other people when he was approached by a man and woman.

"I would like to talk to you" demanded the man. "What do you want to talk about?" "Can we go somewhere private?" "Ok come to my office".

They followed Bernado to the small room which he escaped from the crowd sometimes when he wished to be alone. He sat behind the desk piled with papers.

"Take a Seat." He offered.

" No thank you." they both said in unison.

"What is your problem?"

The small sour-looking woman spoke with a vinegary whine. "It appears that you have worked some scam with our auntie, and have stolen a large sum of money from her,"

Bernado now worked out who he was talking to; he was not letting them know. "Who are you talking about?"

"Our auntie Gabriella, you have taken a fortune from her, and you robbed her when you bought this magnificent building." "I will have you know we paid exactly what she asked for in this building. If you had looked at the building before, we purchased it you would have found it far from magnificent when we took over, it had holes in the walls and half of the façade was blown away during the invasion of Anzio by the Americans during the war. Pigeons were living in half of the rooms upstairs." This seemed to take the wind out of the nasty pair's sails somewhat.

"You will be hearing from my lawyers."

"I will look forward to it. Donna Gabriella is now a partner in this business, and has taken to her job as an adviser."

Bernado followed them to the door.

" I will not tell Donna Gabriella about this conversation. She has confided in me and told me that you are very prominent in her last will as her only close living relatives if she were to hear what you said here today. I would say she would almost surely change her mind and cut you out altogether."

Both the man and woman had a shocked look on their faces. They turned and hurried across the floor of the casino, they quickly left for the street.

Bernado felt smug at the way he had handled the pair. The lawyer was only a bluff on their part and he did not know anything about Donna Gabriella's last wishes at all, nor did he care. In the eyes of the law, she was not a mother only an auntie, who had enough sense to invest her money wisely.

Rina and Marta got along together extremely well. Rina was helping around the casino until she was almost ready to have her baby. Bernado had been worried that there may have been some infighting.

The experience of the war and what they had to do to survive was a factor. The girls acted like two sisters more than rivals for Bernado. He felt proud to think he was soon to be a father.

Bernado was watching some of the punters playing the poker machines one day and thought that they would almost be silly enough to sit in front of a covered bucket with a coin slot in the top. These machines had been extremely lucrative in boosting the Casino's income.

The crowds had not dropped off at all. The quality floor shows and the occasional dog act all helped to keep the people coming through the doors. Chef Anton had a huge following. The dining room had a far-reaching reputation. Many people came just for the food and good wine. Not many of the diners ever left without playing the poker machines or one of the table games. The meal prices were kept to a very low price as they drew the crowd for the gambling.

The day had come. Rina had been collecting baby regalia like a crib, nappies, and other essentials for her newborn baby. Rina called Marta. She was starting to have contractions. Marta phoned the casino. Bernado came running to the room. Marta drove her and Bernado to the hospital.

Sitting in the waiting room of the large hospital was extremely stressful for both Bernado and Marta. The time seemed to be moving at a snail's pace. Finally, a young nurse appeared in the waiting room.

"Mr. Rominski you are the father of a baby boy"

Bernado and Marta jumped up from their seats. After the three long hours of waiting a large baby boy was born. They moved from the waiting room to the window of the crèche where the newborn babies were kept in their cribs. The nurse who had called them walked into the crèche. The baby had been cleaned up. He was held up naked by the young nurse for them to see.

"He is definitely yours,"

Marta remarked as she noted the mini Bierwurst the baby displayed.

A week had passed since Rina had given birth. Bernado and Marta went to the hospital and picked Rina and the yet to be named baby, they then bought them back to the apartment in the casino.

Marta had just started to bulge in the tummy region slightly.

Bernado was so pleased that the two girls were such good friends. Under similar circumstances, a lot of women would not be and would conspire against each other.

On many nights, a man with a mob of evident bodyguards with him would come for dinner and to gamble. This man was a big gambler. He had only three fingers on his left hand.

One-night Bernado asked Pierre who he was.

“You would not want to tangle with him. He was head of one of the mobs of Mafia gangsters in the USA and was deported back to Italy. Three Fingers Frankie had run a sizeable part of the US drug trade. He lost his fingers when he was in the US. A rival gang of the Mafia caught him when he was only young. They cut his fingers off with garden shears. He now runs some large farms near Rome. These guys are tied up with corrupt officials and part of the Mafia. They get preferential treatment for a large slice of the civil projects in Italy.”

One evening Bernado had been casually talking to Frankie about the local politics and the casino.

“I am having some friends over for dinner tomorrow night. Would you and Marta like to come along and meet the family? Just bring yourself; if you would like to come I have plenty of wine and good food.”

Bernado felt he was obliged to accept. He did not want to make enemies with these people for at least two reasons. Number one was they spent a lot of money in the casino. The second was that a refusal may be construed to be an insult.

Marta drove the car to the so-called farm. The house was like a Roman palace surrounded by beautifully manicured gardens. Bouncers wandered around outside the home being vigilant. One came to the car and looked inside; he was a regular at the casino. “OK, Bernado you can pass. Park your car over there” He indicated a parking place. Marta drove across and parked the car. They then walked a short distance to the large house.

A frowsy blonde woman came to the door. “Hey Franky, the guy from the Casino is here with the woman", she yelled in a raucous voice. Frankie came across and shook their hands. "Welcome to my humble house ". He sneezed then blew his large nose on a red-checked handkerchief. "Please excuse the sneeze, I have been getting hay-fever from the garden lately, Dinner will be served in about half an hour."

Giorgio at the bar will fix you up with a drink." He waved his three-fingered hand toward the large bar.

Bernado recognized some of the guests as being city officials. Silvio Fiori the city mayor and his family were present.

The afternoon was spent socializing with the other guests and talking to the host and hostess. Mildred had been a bar hostess in the US before Frankie had been asked to leave by the government. She did not appear to be too heavy on the bright side. "She must have hidden talents," Marta whispered in his ear.

As they were about to leave, Frankie came to Bernado.

"I hear you may be going to have some trouble soon from one of our rival families. The man is a creep, I like coming to your place and have fun at the tables. Just mention my name if something funny happens"?

"Thanks, I'll keep my eyes open."

He had no idea as to what Frankie was talking about.

A fortnight after the meeting all was going well with the casino.

Rina had talked about a name for the baby with Bernado and Marta.

Johan was chosen. This had been her late father's name. Johan had inherited a very good pair of lungs from someone. Rina and Marta took turns in looking after him.

Bernado had no doubts as to his being his father. The facial features were similar and the small Bierwurst took any doubts away. Marta still had three months to go before she was due to have her child.

One afternoon an ugly rough-looking small plump man dressed in a grubby black poorly fitted suit entered the foyer of the casino. He had a pockmarked face; he was followed by four dopey looking goons. The men started asking questions from a staff member. He pointed to where Bernado was talking to a man

Bernado had been talking to one of the bar staff when they entered. The group stood out from the usual patrons of the casino. One of the goons came to Bernado. "Hey, are you the boss here"?

Bernado looked at the grubby man.

"Yes. What do you want"?

Mr. Corrigano wants to talk to you."

"Tell him to come to my office."

Bernado waved to Pierre in an underhand way as he passed by. Pierre nodded slightly in assent, and then followed at a distance. The rough-looking man joined Bernado at the office door. As they entered, he held out his hand.

"Vince Corrigano is my name. I run things around here."

"What sort of things Vince?"

"Oh, just a bit of this and a bit of that. I make sure no one tries to muscle in on your patch. Looks like a good business you are running here. You would not want the building to catch fire. We have people that make sure that this doesn't happen."

Bernado felt a rage of cold hatred for this man but did not show it. "You Know Vince I already have some men who also have this worry about the casino. They are also watching out for me. I pay for them every month. Do you know my friend Frankie with the three fingers?" Vince's demeanor of being cocky changed considerably. "It's good to know that you have the right protection, I was just trying to be helpful."

He turned toward the door.

"You should look out for yourself now. Goodbye".

He waved to his goons and quickly left.

After they had left Pierre entered the office.

"Wow, what a nasty looking character he was. I think I have seen him before, A Vince Cogano or something like that."

"You are nearly right Corrigano was his name. I think he was offering to burn the casino down if I did not pay up." Bernado sat down.

"Hopefully we will not have any-more problems with him again. I said I was already paying three-fingered Frankie. This changed his mind. Frankie told me I was about to have some trouble three weeks ago."

That evening Frankie and Mildred came to play the tables. He sidled up to Bernado.

"I hear you had an unwelcome visitor called Vince to see you today."

"Yes, I did. How did you get to find out?"

"I have friends all over the place; they all have very good eyes and ears."

"Thanks very much, I did mention your name."

"Hey, that's ok. That's why I told you about the trouble the other week at the farmhouse. A little birdie told me that Donna Gabriella's niece and nephew may have whispered into his ears. Do you want me to do something about this?"

"I think they have had their try. Let the bastards alone to stew. You don't need to touch them."

'Life is cheap to some people.' thought Bernado.

The casino was starting to attract some very heavy gamblers.

Bernado had suspicions that they may have been sent by Frankie. Gambling was an easy and legal method of laundering illegally obtained money. No records were kept of what was spent to get the large payouts. Frankie often talked to these people. It appeared that he knew them.

One evening Bernado was eating dinner with Rina and Marta. A daughter of Enzo's was minding Johan.

Bernado had a compulsion to look behind over his shoulder. Lilly walked through the door of the dining room. Bernado rose and invited her to his table.

He had a feeling of dread; did she have another bouncing crying surprise. The girls started to talk,

Bernado listened intently. He was relieved to hear she was still in the circus and did not have any more crying surprises for them.

The Circus was doing the Mediterranean circuit this year to avoid the winter. The circus was setting up in a town nearby.

“I have kept the photos of you at the casino opening. Wow-what a good job. I bet you are both proud.” “What has happened to the circus?”

“Oh, it is just the same, some different acts of course. Stefano and Strombolo are here in the casino. I came with them.”’

A cold shiver ran down Bernado’s spine, he would not like to meet up with Strombolo again.

“I hope they are not here looking for me”

“No, silly they are circus people they do not hold a grudge. I will go and get them if you like.” Bernado reluctantly agreed.

Lilly walked off and after a short while returned with Stefano and Strombolo. They were both smiling. Stefano had a very attractive ash-blonde woman with him. She looked like a very strong lady. Stefano and Strombolo shook hands with Bernado. Bernado had the feeling that the vicelike grip of Strombolo may have had a bit of double meaning; Bernado noticed that he had a crooked arm. Stefano introduced Annatalia the Russian weightlifter.

“I have a strong woman act in the circus.” She said with a heavy Russian accent.

Bernado had visions of her lifting the elephant.

There were a lot of small talks. No mention was made about the robbery of money by Marta and Bernado.

They all had a sumptuous meal and some wine which Bernado would not take payment for. When they were at the door Stefano congratulated Bernado and Marta on the business they had created and were running.

When they had left the building, Bernado had a sense of relief. He had a dread of ever meeting up with Stefano or Strombolo after leaving the circus. He had a feeling that these fears had been set to rest.

CHAPTER 13

Marta sent Lola to get Rina from the Casino, She had started having contractions from the new baby. It was telling her it was ready to come out into the world.

Rina hurried to the house. She then drove her to the clinic in the casino car; Johan was left with a babysitter at the casino. Bernado was at an important conference with Donna Gabriella, Luigi, and Pierre.

The office was filled with boxes of papers and accounts. There seemed to be a serious problem with the income at this time.

Someone seemed to be skimming the profits from the top.

The new accountant Julio Chassa was recently hired, when the previous accountant Alfonso Cherini had suddenly left for health reasons. His reason for leaving was that his parents were both involved in a car accident in Genoa. They needed his assistance to recover. When the discrepancies were found Bernado checked to see if this story was legitimate. It was.

Julio had started to have a mini audit of accounts and had found some discrepancies in the more recent accounts. Donna Gabriella spoke of a previous experience.

"When my husband and I were running the Casino, we had a similar problem. One rotten apple seems to bring out more. Like cancer, it keeps growing through the staff.

We had to check many of people in the casino at this time."

Donna Gabriella thought deeply of the time years ago

"We hired a young German private detective called Hans Strauss. He was a very devious man and set traps for many people who were thought to be involved."

Julio asked whether she knew if this man still practiced.

"The last I heard was that he owned a detective agency in Rome. That was over ten years ago. I called him about some trouble my niece and nephew were trying to stir up regarding my money."

Bernado pondered the problem,

"I think we should try to find if this man is still available".

The next morning Bernado phoned the police station and asked for an appointment to see Frank Brazzi.

As he drove to the Anzio Police Station, his head was filled with thoughts of how such a scheme may have been instigated. The head of the police Frank Brazzi was an occasional visitor to the casino. Frank rose from his chair and shook Bernado's hand as he entered the office.

"Hi, Bernado what can we do for you?"

He asked,

"We seem to have problems with one or some of the staff skimming off cash. I do not want a police presence which will possibly scare off some of our customers. Donna Gabriella had a similar problem some years ago and had used a private detective called Hans Strauss." "I know of this man he has a private detective agency in Rome called Strauss and Co., I think I have his number here somewhere."

Frank took a large book out of one of the desk drawers and opened the alphabetical index. "Here is the address and phone number you need." He wrote the details on a piece of paper.

"As soon as someone starts a new business and begins to make money the thieves and other vermin seem to come out of the woodwork and start gnawing like a sewer rat at your profits. I have seen this many times. Sometimes they are easily caught, other times they have been very difficult to find. Many times, we have found them to be family members trying to pad their pockets. Good luck!"

As he returned to the casino Enzo met him outside the door.

"I think you had better go to the hospital, you have just become the father of a little girl."

Bernado returned to the van and then sped off to the hospital.

A nurse ushered Bernado along a corridor. Rina and Donna Gabriella were waiting for him in the room. Marta lay in the bed with a small bundle in her arms; Bernado looked down to see the beautiful face of the small baby girl. There was a lot of clucking from the three women in the room.

"Well, Bernado, it looks like you have got your hands full now with two babies. I wonder if there are any other little Bernado's running around that we do not know about." Donna Gabriella said, with a mischievous smile, she gave him a long wink.

When Bernado finally returned to the casino he phoned the Strauss detective agency. The receptionist connected Bernado to Hans. After introducing himself to Hans, he told him what they thought had been happening in the casino. Hans offered to call in in a week for a conference and to look through the security systems in place in the casino.

One thing that had been on Bernado's mind was the mafia crook Vince Corrigano had been frequenting the casino during the last month. He seemed to have a preference with some of the dealers on some tables.

A man knocked on the office door. Bernado opened the door and then stepped back then stood as the man approached the desk. He sat down once more. Bernado felt as if he may be another problem.

The small dark-skinned ferrety looking man was holding his hat in his hand. He looked at Bernado then spoke.

"Antonio is my name. I used to work at Alfa Romeo many years ago."

Bernado stood up and walked around from the desk. The two men shook hands.

"I am sorry to have taken so long to come and see you. I understand that you have a Voisin car you would like me to look at. I have been very busy lately restoring another car." Bernado was relieved to find that he was not another ticklish problem he had to solve.

Bernado walked from behind the desk

“You had better follow me to the garage.”

He had been thinking of this rare car on occasions and believed this car could be a draw-card and talking point about the casino.

As they walked out to the garage Bernado talked about finding the Voisin in the shed after they had purchased the casino. The small door was opened Antonio followed Bernado into the dim room, Bernado turned the lights on. Antonio walked reverently toward the car. He opened the door and checked the kilometers on the speedometer dial,

“This car has only traveled two thousand kilometers. It is almost as new. These were some of the very innovative cars of their time. I think this one would be around the nineteen thirty-two years.”

Antonio lifted the bonnet, the leaning twelve-cylinder motor made him gasp.

” Look at the bird mascot on the radiator. This is one of the most impressive mascots I have ever seen.”

He walked around the perimeter of the car checking,

“I will bring new tires and a battery. We will have to take all of the spark plugs out and lubricate the bore of the motor before I try to start the motor.”

Bernado did not understand most of what Antonio said.

“The paintwork is as new, it just needs the grime and dust washing off and the chrome fittings polished. What are you going to do with the car when it is running?”

"I thought we would have a position in front of the casino and have the car taken out there every morning as a draw-card for customers."

"The car is very different."

Antonio ran his hand along the front mudguard reverently. "Have you any room inside the foyer of the casino?" Bernado thought for a short while.

"This is a good idea; I had not thought of this, it may be possible to get the car inside the double doors."

"I would not like to drive this car and leave it out in the weather every day. This car is a work of art. This would be like having one of Rueben's painting left in the rain."

As the garage door was closed Antonio said that he would return with the tires and battery in three days.

Antonio returned with the tires and a small electric air compressor to re-inflate the new tires. Bernado watched as he removed each spark plug and squirted some atomized thin oil into each hole. The plugs were left out for tomorrow when the battery would be fitted. He also siphoned all of the old petrol from the tank into a large oil drum and then poured twenty liters of new fuel back into the tank from a steel Jerry-Can. The oil was checked and the radiator filled in readiness for the next day. The old perished tires were then changed one by one.

The car looked even more impressive with the new tires pumped up. The body was washed with soapy water and rinsed off, then had a chamois rubbed over to take away any smears. The chrome was polished. The winged mascot looked spectacular shining in the light.

The old car looked in showroom condition. Bernado was impressed.

He had measured the doorway of the casino when fully opened. The car would just fit inside.

Antonio arrived early the next morning; He tooted the horn of the small van. Bernado opened the rear gates to the Casino to accommodate him.

The battery was fitted and then Antonio tentatively pressed the starter to see if the motor was not seized from being left for so long. The motor turned over easily. The carburetor was primed and then drained to remove any wax from the old evaporated fuel.

The spark plugs were refitted. Antonio turned the ignition key then pressed the starter. The old motor sputtered to life letting a white cloud from the exhaust. This had been from the thin oil used to lubricate the cylinders. The motor settled down to a purr as the large seven-and a half-liter engine ran for a few minutes, for the first time in over thirty years.

Antonio was impressed.

"I would love to take this car for a run down the main street in the center of the city; we would get some amazing comments from the people."

He thought for a few seconds.

"If you would like I will drive her into the doors of the casino tomorrow morning. Do you want me to reverse her in?" "Yes, I think the front image with the huge headlights would look spectacular, I will have a photographer from the Anzio newspaper be present for the first showing". Antonio shook Bernado's hand and left the Garage

Bernado had a member of the staff knock on the office door. He rose from the desk then opened it. A man stood with the young waiter. The man held out his hand

"Hans Strauss is my name"

Bernado took the man's outstretched hand.

Hans was a heavy man with pepper grey hair and a bushy mustache. He was a tough-looking man, a man who one would like to have accompanied him if there was any trouble.

"I remember coming here twenty-five years or so ago when I first started my agency. It appears that you have a similar problem." Bernado asked the waiter to find Donna Gabriella. Luigi and Paul and ask them to come to the office.

"Would you care for a coffee while we wait for the others to arrive?"

The two men both sat down at the office desk. Bernado Phoned for two coffees to be bought to the office.

While they were waiting Hans spoke of previous problems such as the casino was experiencing.

"I will set some traps for the obvious type of thief. I will mark some banknotes and play them through the dealers. We will see what comes back when we check the money each night. I can do this with some ink that glows under ultraviolet light. The marking is not noticeable to the normal eye. I have a small UV light unit with me in my car to detect the marked notes. This should show who is taking the money if it does not show up in their daily money counting, but not how they are doing it."

"I have a feeling that the mafia may be involved. There is a little shit, Vince Corrigano who tried to shake me down for protection a couple of months ago. I said I was already paying Three Fingers, Frankie, for protection. I am not really; I know Frankie. He warned me that I was going to have a visit from Vince."

For Donna Gabriella's sake, he did want to mention the meeting with her niece and nephew.

"I have had dealings with that nasty devious crook before. He is well down the rungs of command from the real Mafia. He is just a gangster with some dopey goons following him. I do not know why the real Mafia have not tossed him off a wharf with cement boots" Hans said

Hans was going to work around the casino for the next week. He would have no public association with any of the staff. He would just be another punter who played the tables. The money he played with would be marked with a different code for each table on the edge of the banknote. This would show which dealer or dealers were taking the money. The next problem was to work out how so this could be prevented at other times.

Chips for the games could be purchased at the money counter, or bought at the table. The croupier would push the bills through a slot next to the rows of chips with a thin board. The chips themselves could be another problem. If counterfeit chips were bought to the casino there could be a huge racket taking money.

The casino had started with a certain number of chips of all different values. These would have to be counted into piles of each value. Losses were not rare as sometimes people left with some of the lower value chips as a keepsake, or if they had been drinking they forgot that they had them.

Bernado talked about the run-in with Donna Gabriella's niece and nephew.

"Jealous families are one very huge problem. Like the grasshopper and the ants. The grasshopper spends and wastes his money and the ant saves his, then the grasshopper tries to steal the ant's food. I have seen this many times" Hans said.

Donna Gabriella, Luigi, and Paul knocked on the door of the office. Bernado Opened the door. They came to the desk. Bernado introduced them to Hans. After shaking hands, they selected a chair and sat in front of the desk.

"I have a feeling that there is an association with your niece and nephew with Vince Corrigano. Three Fingers Frankie told me this. They said I had robbed you. They were going to get a lawyer to check on this. I had not told you about this, I know you have a very poor opinion of them even now." He turned toward Donna Gabriella.

"I am sorry Nonna I should have told you."

"I have expected as much from them my son. They are like their father. They tried in a very devious way to get some money out of me some years ago. I refused to help them."

Hans thought for a while. "I think this may be all tied together with them and this Vince creep. I will do some checking around some of my sources and should find out for sure. I will do more checking before I return to the casino to check the tables and dealers."

Marta had returned home with Gabriella the new baby. Donna Gabriella was thrilled when she learned the pretty baby had been named after her.

The rooms upstairs began to have a noise problem. There were numerous duets with the bass and soprano taking their turns. Gabriella also had a very good set of lungs. She had a cry not to be ignored also.

Bernado was starting to suffer from a businessman's disease. The stress of the people robbing the casino and the interruptions at night from the two crying babies took a toll on his huge sexual desire. Rina thought she should be ready for her reencounter with the Bierwurst sausage. The sausage had other ideas; it was a large soft grub.

They spent the night together and cuddled up together. The problems were on Bernado's mind. The Bierwurst would not perform.

"Maybe I should start to yodel."

She suggested with a laugh. Bernado laughed with her. The memories of the simple circus life flooded back.

The next morning the huge Voisin car was reversed out of the garage. The car was then driven round to the front of the Casino. Blocks were placed in the gutter along the curb for the car to climb up onto. The car was reversed slowly inside the casino.

The newspaper photographer took many photos of the car as it entered the doorway. The car was placed under one of the huge chandeliers. The light from the myriad of globes sparkled on the gleaming paintwork. The centerpiece in the entrance to the casino was extremely impressive. A long grease tray was laid under the car to protect the marble floor.

Hans walked into the casino just as they finished the job.

He had a look of amazement on his face.

“Where did you find this beauty?”

“This was in a shed out back when we purchased the building from Donna Gabriella.”

Hans opened the door and checked inside.

” This car is still in new condition. This car would be worth a small fortune.”

They walked from the car to Bernado’s office to a meeting and discussion with Luigi, Pierre, and Donna Gabriella. He would start checking on the staff the next morning.

Hans worked the tables through the casino. He particularly tried to check on Vince Corrigano. He watched him from the distance. Vince occasionally took a large denomination chip from his pocket, it was usually under the guise of blowing his nose or some other furtive act, and then played this with one of his selected dealers. He also seemed to be winning more hands with these dealers, especially when he made a large bet. The tables with the dealers Vince played with, all had discrepancies with the marked money when it was checked that night.

The next morning Hans returned. He walked reverently past the Voisin car, the walked to Bernado’s office.

“I have a few men who would help me to hold the goons who protect Vince Corrigano. I have found some counterfeit chips in the casino chips. They are hard to detect but not impossible. I want to shake him down and take any of the chips he has in his pocket. I would not do this if I were not sure. I want Luigi and Pierre on hand when I do this. I have asked Frank Brazzi and some plain-clothed officers to help. Frank has been after the little crook for a few years now. Every time he has caught him, a shyster lawyer gets him off the hook.

Frank Brazzi came to the office and joined the men. Frank was in good spirits about the anticipated catching Vince in the act; “I have been trying to pin something on this creep for a while now; he is a real nasty bit of work. Hopefully, today is the day.”

Vince and four goons had just started to play the tables. Two men isolated each one of the men and marched them to a large room with some chairs. They were frisked by the police officers; they had their guns were taken, as well as some nasty knives and knuckle dusters. There was also a small fortune in counterfeit chips in their pockets.

” Right, you lot sit down,” said Frank with a loud

assertive voice. Vince opened his mouth to protest.

“I would not do that you little creep. You have been caught red-handed. I have been waiting for this day for a long time.“

The four dealers under suspicion were asked to come to this room by one of the floor staff. Replacement dealers were assigned to their tables.

The dealers had a look of fear when they saw Vince and his goons in the room.

“He threatened to hurt my family if I did not help him”.

One of the men said. The three others had similar outbursts. They looked very worried. Vince’s demeanor had suffered greatly. This did not explain how the money had disappeared with the markings on it. This was another problem.

The nine men were taken quietly out of a rear door to the casino to a waiting police van.

“I have been waiting to catch this nasty piece of poop for a long time. He will be having a very long holiday in the state prison. I may even pick the inmate who shares his cell, someone who likes to play sexy games with smelly little nasty men.”

Frank shook Bernardo’s hand as he left. “This has made my day.”

Frank had a large grin on his face as he shook his head in glee. “Caught red-handed. Thank you, God,”, he looked up at the sky. He crossed himself, then followed the men outside.

The next morning the tables the men worked were checked. The daily procedure was for the security staff would take the drawers filled with money from the bottom of the tables. When the complex lock was undone, a spring-loaded lid slid over the top of the drawer, this also locked in place as it covered the square hole the money fell into. Two security staff took each drawer to the large table in the room where the chips and money were locked away in the large safe. After this, the money was counted and sorted each night.

When the drawers were removed Julio lay on the floor and looked into the void above the drawer. Hidden away above the drawer held by a clip which fitted into the ends of the money slot was a device with a tray, when the board pushing the money through the slot, if the board and folded money was pushed at a certain angle this tray was slid under the money. The trays had money in them from the day before.

The dealers picked up the empty drawers to take the money each morning after they had been emptied.

They had emptied the hidden tray when refitting the drawers which locked when pushed in place, very simple, cunning, and effective. All other tables were checked and no other devices were found.

Hans checked out the devices which had been installed on the money slots on the tables.

"I wonder where the little creep got these. He would not have enough brains to make something like this." Bernado paid Hans for the work he had done and thanked him sincerely.

"I hope you never need me again, but if you do you know where to find me. I think you should have a good chance of getting a fair amount of money back that crook stole off you. "He said as he walked through the casino.

He looked lovingly at the large Voisin limo.

"If you ever want to sell your car, phone me".

That night when eating dinner with Donna Gabriella, Marta, and Rina, he felt as if a huge load had been lifted from his shoulders. Lola was minding the two babies.

Bernado had an early night. Before he left the floor of casino the and walked upstairs he had paid attention to the reaction of the customers to the shiny Voisin.

Most people stopped and looked lovingly inside the car and were still talking about it when they were walking away.

Rina was in bed. She had just fed Johan. Lola had taken him back to the children's room. Bernado undressed and slipped in beside her. The Bierwurst stick had lost all of his inhibitions, he was standing to attention.

"Welcome back big boy," said Rina as she turned on to her back in anticipation.

Frank Brazzi phoned in the morning with news about Vince. It appeared that there was an association with Donna Gabriella's niece and nephew. They had been picked up and were being questioned. They were the people who had provided the money skimming machines and counterfeit chips. "I have had Vince's shyster lawyer here all morning telling me he was innocent. I told him they were caught in the act. I am really happy about catching the little crook"

Donna Gabriella had read the morning newspaper. There was a story about the arrests of Vince and his gang.

"My niece and nephew were involved with that little nasty mafia crook from what I have been reading. They are just like their father."

The casino was once again running like a well- oiled watch. The employees were doing a very good job. The Voisin was still a huge conversation piece to new customers. Bernado had some serious offers to sell the car from some rich patrons, he just laughed. "I suppose you would shut it up in a padlocked shed so only you can see it. That would be a shame, just see the people who are enjoying talking about her."

Bernado had been advised to have his accountant submit an estimate as to the amount of money Vince and his men had stolen. This was to be submitted as a claim against Vince Corrigano. Vince and his goons were going to jail for a long time.

The four dealers were placed on good behavior bonds because of the threats made against their families by Vince. They would not work in the casino business again.

CHAPTER 14

Five years had passed since the robbery incident. The casino was running exceedingly well. The tourist trade in the city had exploded. Tourists from all over the world were visiting Italy in large numbers.

Donna Gabriella had just enjoyed her eight- fifth birthday with a huge party at the casino. Bernado offered free wine and spirits for an hour early in the night and a huge floorshow of popular entertainers. There was even a classy strip- show in one of the rear rooms for the men and any interested women to visit.

Donna Gabriel welcomed the guests from her throne. She even had a mock sword and during the early evening knighted some of the prominent guests.

The polished Voisin stood proud as the guests filed past into the main casino area. Since the start of work on her family casino, she had blossomed and turned from a little old lonely lady waiting to die, into the canny businesswoman of today.

“Bernado I would like to have a look at the show you are putting on for the men in the rear room.” Bernado went red.

“You might get offended.”

“I am an old lady; I have never seen a strip show before. I don’t think I will die from shame or envy now.” Bernado reluctantly conducted Donna Gabriella to the rear room show.

As she entered the room the crowd parted and let her through to the front. A man stood up and offered her his chair, another man offered Bernado his chair also.

A small quartet orchestra started to play some haunting music; the haunting sounds of the clarinet led into the tune.

A very classy looking brunette, very well dressed, drifted onto the stage. She started dancing a slow rhythmic dance. She came to one of the front row men and offered for him to take off her glove. She then bent over, with her hand between her legs and asked him to use his teeth to remove it. The man went very red but complied.

The other glove was removed in the same manner by another customer. As the undressing progressed, she became coy and acted as if she did not want the men to see her breasts, she kept a piece of her see-through clothes and kept covering them, just giving the audience a quick glimpse.

After removing all of her clothes except the sheer knickers, she turned toward the stage exit. As she did so she slowly removed her knickers and slid them off one leg at a time over her high-heeled shoes.

The men were cheering and encouraging her to turn around. She bent over and touched her toes, then slid her feet apart to do a perfect splits position. The crowd went wild. They stood and cheered loudly.

When Bernado sat down Donna Gabriella was laughing loudly. “Bernado you should have this sort of act two or three times a week. I don’t think I would qualify as tripper, would I?" She winked at him, then laughed loudly.

He laughed so hard he nearly fell off his chair.

Bernado, Marta, Rina, and the children moved into Donna Gabriella's home. Bernado had resisted the move in the beginning. He did not want to try to take over someone else's home. He had been looking at properties that were for sale nearby. Donna Gabriella became angry when she finally found out that this was happening. The house hunting was to have been a secret. "This is the way we Italians live we have our family with us. You are all my new family now. I certainly do not class the weasels of niece and nephew as a family anymore. I think they are both still in jail. The children all call me Nonna, I am their Nonna." There was nothing more to say, Bernado was secretly very pleased. He had no close family also nor did Marta and Rina.

The staff at the casino almost ran the business without his intervention, Luigi, Aldo, and Pierre were very good friends of the family by now. Enzo, Tony, Frank and Bob, and their family members were a real godsend. They were more like family than friends and workers.

At her insistence, the suggestion by Donna Gabriella the weekly strip show with high-class strippers continued. Donna Gabriella would quite often watch the show.

She would comment on the performance of the girls as they went through their routines. Bernado would listen to a woman's view of the performances with interest.

Bernado's early morning walk to check the casino and grounds always incorporated a visit to the dogs to water and feed them. Most mornings he would put their leashes on and take them all for a walk around the block. He carried a paper bag and scoop to cope with any indiscretions. As he walked, he usually spoke to the dogs about the daily affairs at the casino.

The dog act had been stopped at the casino, as all of the dogs were now showing their age.

Lola came back into the house one afternoon, just as she was to leave for home. She had met her new man who was there to take her home in his car. “I would like to introduce my friend Antonio.” Antonio was possibly aged in his late twenties; he was a tall very good-looking young man dressed in the latest fashion. She introduced him to the family one by one, then with a special introduction to the children. Antonio worked in a bank in Anzio not too far from the casino.

Rina went to make some coffee for them. Antonio sat down next to Lola and started to talk about his job and other small talks while they were waiting for the coffee. Lola kept glancing at Antonio with a look of adoration on her face as he spoke. After an hour, they left for home.

“I think Lola has found herself a very nice man,” Said Donna Gabriella after they had gone. “He is certainly good looking,” commented Marta.

Early one morning three weeks after meeting the young man, Lola walked into the house to start work; she held her left hand out prominently in front of her as she walked through the door. Donna Gabriella was first to notice the flashing diamond engagement ring on her fourth finger. She was to be married in twelve months. The women made a big issue of the large diamond ring.

Silvio Fiori the Mayor approached Bernado one evening in the casino. He started talking about the local government and how difficult it had been in the past to find honest and intelligent people to help run the city. He asked Bernado if he would be prepared to sit on the city's governing council.

"Bernado, your contacts with the huge customer base of the casino could be of great assistance in the city administration. We need people like you to help get the city up and running to cash in on the lucrative tourist business." Bernado thought for a while and agreed to come to see Silvio the next day to talk further about the matter.

The conversation turned to some of the problems which had beset Italy after the war. One huge problem was the orphans left behind.

Some were the result of the parents being killed.

Others were from when the American invaders had landed. Scores of young women had become pregnant with them.

Italy was very poor at this time and food was hard to come by, many of these women had sold themselves to survive.

"I am worried that some of these orphanages may be underfeeding the children, plus abusing them, physically and mentally," said Silvio.

"Silvio, you have rekindled a flame in me which has barely burned for the last ten years. I was an orphan in Poland toward the end of the war. My parents, brother, and sister plus all of my relatives were murdered by the Nazis.

I was taken in and lived with an old Gypsy woman who knew my parents. She was teaching me to read minds and to make potions and medicine from plants in the forest." Bernado poured two more glasses of wine.

"I returned home one night and found her and her dog killed and her lying under the eaves of her burning thatch roof house. I can still see her as it were yesterday, with the thatch from the roof falling on her as it burned. I could not help her. I walked into town and started to live in a tumble-down house. I was thirteen years old." He took a deep swig from the wine glass.

" I was caught trying to steal food, by a well-meaning policeman and taken to a church orphanage. He thought the priests and nuns were very caring and good people."

Bernado stopped talking as the memories were still upsetting.

Silvio looked at his emotion-filled face.

"I have heard some nasty stories about those orphanages in Italy.

Some young boys and girls raped by the priests."

"That happened to me," said Bernado in an emotion-filled low voice. "I would not feed pigs with the food they re-cooked every day. It smelled putrid. One Priest was chasing the little boys. He was extremely cruel with the cane as well."

As the conversation described some hearsay of other orphanages, Bernado had a flash of inspiration. "I would like to start some sort of tribunal which would check the well-being of the young children in the orphanages now. I would pay to have some unbiased inspectors to go to the orphanages in Italy."

He thought for a short while.

"Is there an orphanage in or near Anzio?"

Silvio went quite red.

"Yes, there is one. It is in an old monastery in a small nearby town." "What are the conditions like there?" Silvio spluttered.

"Very poor I think."

"I will start there if you can get me to see this place."

Three days later they met to visit the Orphanage five kilometers from the outskirts of Anzio It adjoined a small very old village. As they drove toward the orphanage they could see it was a rundown looking old building with a church a short distance away. The complex was situated on a large block of land covered in weeds. Only the outer perimeters of the church were mowed back. The church was in far better condition than the orphanage. Silvio had a council health inspector with him, Frank Bruzza.

They walked through the door of the orphanage into the offices. A nun rose from working at a desk and asked if she could help them. "I am Silvio Fiori mayor of Anzio; this is Frank Bruzza our health inspector. The other man Bernado is a benefactor for the poor orphans."

The nun's face lost some color.

"I will go and find father Luigi."

She left the desk and walked out through a door. Two other nuns had heard the conversation. They had worried looks on their faces. They sat and fidgeted at their desks.

The nun returned with a Priest. He was a short squat man. He also had a worried look. Bernado started to feel uncomfortable as the thoughts of the kindly policeman handing him over to the priest in Poland flooded back into his brain.

"To what honor do I owe this visit from the Mayor of Anzio?" Silvio looked at the man and noted his look of discomfort.

"We have started a program of reform in the orphanages in Italy. We are conducting random inspections of the facilities of the premises and conditions such as cleanliness and food of all orphanages. We are doing this to all orphanages, either church or state-run facilities."

"I refuse your request. You cannot come barging in here unannounced" snarled the priest, his face becoming exceedingly red. "I beg to differ with you. I have a permit signed by the government here which gives us the right." Frank Bruzza produced a signed form.

"You are not coming inside this orphanage" The priest stuck his jaw out.

Bernado confronted the nasty priest.

"I was bought up in an orphanage in Poland near the end of the war after my family was murdered by the Nazis. Since that time, I have prospered and am prepared to spend some money to make sure that the children do not suffer like I had to."

“No, you cannot see inside the orphanage it will upset the children.”

Frank Bruzza looked at the priest with contempt.

“If you refuse to admit us, Bernado and the mayor will stay and wait while I go and get the police, and inform the newspapers that we are inspecting your facility. I am sure they would like to send some cameramen and reporters to check.”

The priest had a look of fear; he knew he could not fight the state and news-papers.

As he strode forward to open the door he said with venom.

“The bishop shall hear of this. I pity you when he finds what a devious way you have used to enter a house of God.”

The men followed the angry priest. The first room was the mess hall with the tables and wooden forms. The smell coming from the cooking area bought back bad memories of the Polish orphanage.

The kitchen had a foul smell of rotting food. Pots and pans were not washed properly.

The few children working there were undernourished and dressed in tattered clothes. They had bites from bedbugs and the lice showed in their hair. Their eyes showed no emotion.

Silvio and Frank were horrified. The children in the yard were in the same condition. The sleeping area with the filthy blanket and thin mattresses on the steel-framed rusty beds smelled of urine and fasces.

The priest had an extremely worried look on his face.

"This is all we can afford for the children. The church does not send us enough money."

"I will be checking on that when I go and see the bishop," said Silvio.

The priest sneered.

"What else should we do with these children? Most of them have been born outside the church. They are bastards in the eyes of God. No other person would want them."

The men were horrified at this remark, especially from a man of God.

"We will be back in one week. If this establishment had not been upgraded and cleaned, I think you may be visited by the police. A Priest who has mistreated children would not be very welcome in our jail" said Frank with conviction as he faced the red-faced priest.

As they walked out the door the smell of the orphanage followed them.

"I have been to better smelling pigsties on farms than that place," Said Frank.

"I feel so ashamed that I have not checked on this before," said Silvio with anger in his voice.

"Well, I have checked one before. I was put into an orphanage in Poland when my parents were killed. I think this one is even worse."

When Bernado was dropped off at the house he walked to the rear entrance and climbed the servant's stairs. He visited the laundry and removed all of his clothes except his underwear. He wrapped a towel around his waist then went to his bedroom and had a long shower. Silvio was going to visit the Bishop of Anzio. Bernado was going to accompany him.

Silvio and Bernado walked up the steps of the brownstone building, Basilica di Santa Teresa. When they entered the church, he noticed a body preserved in a glass case at the altar.

Silvio took some holy water on his fingers and crossed himself as he walked into the building, Bernado did not. He almost felt Father Mark from the orphanage watching him.

A Carved figure of Christ stood in a grotto-like canopy held aloft by four columns. The canopy had a circle of blue glass set above a hole in the roof of the canopy. The effect of the blue light shimmering on the statue was quite spectacular.

A young priest noticed the mayor and walked to the men. "Can I help you"? He asked politely

"We need to see the Bishop on an important matter". Silvio said.

"Have you an appointment".

"No, I am sorry we do not. This matter is very important." The men had not phoned for an appointment because they had a feeling that the bishop would fob them off.

"You had better follow me to his office"

They followed the young priest through the Cathedral to the offices at the rear of the building. They stopped at the entrance to his office where two nuns were typing.

One of the nuns looked up. “Can I help you, Mr. Mayor?” Silvio took a deep breath.

“Yes, it is very important that we have a meeting with the bishop.” The nun called on an intercom. The Bishop answered. “I have the mayor and another man to see you.” “I am very busy” tell them to make an appointment,” Silvio called loudly into the intercom.

“I am sorry monsignor; this is very important. If you do not want to see us, we may have to go to the newspapers and police about this problem.”

The Bishop opened the door to his office and stood back. He had a grumpy look on his face, he was not amused at all. The priest from the orphanage had phoned the bishop complaining about the invasion.

“I am not happy about the way you barged into the orphanage and threatened the priest and his staff.” The pompous man said, ‘’ You had better come into my office.” He said curtly.

They walked past him into the large office. He shut the door firmly behind them.

Silvio looked at the Bishop. He was not overawed by the man of God.

“We were very unhappy to see the way the orphanage was being run. The priest remarked that the children were being born outside the church so the conditions in the orphanage did not matter. The priest then said that the church did not give the orphanage enough money to purchase food. Is this so?”

“Of course not, the orphanages have plenty of money to purchase food.”

"Have you visited the orphanage?"

"No not for some time."

"Have you ever visited this orphanage?"

The bishop's face reddened, he was in a very uncomfortable place. He was starting to sweat. He was unaccustomed to being talked to in this manner.

" I have a huge workload and a large area to look after."

Bernado looked at the bishop with contempt

"So, you have not visited the poor waifs in this orphanage? I was placed in an orphanage like this in Poland when I was thirteen years old. My parents had been killed by the Nazis. The policeman who took me to the orphanage genuinely trusted the priests and nuns would look after me and feed me well" He let out a sigh.

"I was raped by a priest in the orphanage on several occasions, as were quite a few of the other boys.

This priest was a sadist. He liked caning young boys for his satisfaction. Some boys complained to the senior priest when they had been raped and were severely caned by him for telling lies. I am no liar." The bishop had a look of horror on his face. Here were some people who had seen the squalor of the orphanage. One had even been living in one and now was evidently in a position of authority in the city.

Bernado looked at the bishop with a steely gaze.

"I would like to see the books and donations given to pay the wages and feed and run this orphanage. I will get my accountant to check the figures to see if the amount is enough to run this facility properly. If it is we will check to see where the rest of the money is going."

The red-faced bishop reluctantly agreed to send a copy of the orphanage accounts.

"I would not like to have to go to the newspapers about this shameful episode. I think you should contact some of your peers and tell them I am conducting an inquisition into this matter. There will be plenty more visits to see if the children are well cared for. These unfortunate children did not ask to be put into care."

The bishop nodded his head, "I agree. "

"There is a large parcel of land around the old monastery. Why aren't the children being taught to grow their own food on this?" "We are fearful that they would run away if they were let outside." "I was of this opinion when I first went to the orphanage, but where would I have gone? People in Poland did not want extra children during the war. I escaped when I was being raped once again by the priest. By this time, I was strong enough to get work."

Bernado continued the conversation. "Build a fence around some of the land adjoining the monastery and then start to teach the children to strive to help themselves."

The bishop agreed to look into the matter.

"I will pay for the fence and purchase tools and seed and some grapevines and fruit trees for the children to start to grow their food. You can send me the bills when this has happened. I am not just targeting the church. State-run facilities are in my sights also."

The meeting ended with a promise that Bernado would have the books for the monastery within the week.

As the men walked to the car Silvio said,

"Shit, my family and I will probably be excommunicated from the church." He had a half-smile on his face as he said this. "I think not. Just think what a story this would make in the newspapers. This would be a worldwide problem. We have been walking among some eggshells and have just trodden on our first rotten egg."

A courier from the Bishop bought the accounts for the orphanage to Bernado's office at the casino. They arrived three days after the meeting.

Bernado took the accounts to his accountant for him to study them.

The accountant walked to Bernado's office with the accounts later that day.

" I have found some very clumsy transfers of money to other persons from these payments. Over half of the money allocated to the orphanage has not been spent on looking after the children. I think we should hand these documents to the police." Bernado pondered on this for a while. "I think I should first visit the bishop again."

Bernado drove to the cathedral. The bishop was more cordial as he greeted Bernado. "I think I should apologize to you, I had no idea that the old monastery orphanage was in such a bad state. I have been given false misleading reports about this facility."

Bernado agreed with the bishop that this would be a worldwide problem.

“I have got the accounts with me; my accountant has identified clumsy transfers of money from the orphanage funds to three different families.”

Bernado laid the papers on a desk and pointed to the monthly transfers.

“Who are these people? “

The bishop was horrified,

“These are the two Priests families. The other is the family name of the Mother superior’s family.”

“My accountant wanted to hand these papers to the police. I asked him to let me show you first. This rot has possibly been happening to other such facilities.”

“I would prefer that you let the church handle this matter. I will discuss this with the Vatican. I will assure you this matter will be checked more widely when handing them money for expenses in the future.”

“Have you thought any more about the garden?”

“Yes, two men are working at the orphanage as we speak. We will purchase the tools some fruit trees and seeds for the garden then send the account to you. I am glad you mentioned this. There is a chance that the left-over fruit and vegetables could be given to some of the aged and poor families to help with their diet as well.”

“I would dearly like for you to request for admission forms to be printed so the employees I am about to hire as inspectors will be able to check on other orphanages also.” The bishop promised he would ask.

As Bernado left for home he had a deep sense of satisfaction that he was now able to be in a position to make a change to a lot of the less fortunate people in the country.

In his mind, Bernado was formulating a trip to visit Poland. For a long time. He had wanted to be able to confront Father Mark. He had a burning desire to find the last resting place of this parents and clan. He was going to place a memorial stone with their names at the place they had been buried.

CHAPTER 15

Bernado visited the local newspaper office and placed an advertisement. This would be running for three weeks in the main Anzio newspaper. Bernado was looking for staff willing to travel to conduct inspections on state and Church-run orphanages.

The Bishop of Anzio pestered the Vatican for the right for Bernado's inspectors to visit and advise church orphanages in Italy. The Vatican had been informed of the terrible conditions to which the children of the old monastery were subjected to. The two priests and Mother Superior were removed from duty.

There had been no publicity of the conditions in the old monastery orphanage.

As much as Bernado would have liked to have the can of worms opened. He did not want to take on the church and embarrass it publicly. There was too much to be done to help others less fortunate.

Fifteen men and one woman visited the casino office for interviews with Bernado and Silvio. One man stood out from the rest. He had been taken to an orphanage just before the war ended. He had been told that his parents had been killed in a bombing raid. This facility was run by a very caring priest and good staff. The priest made a point of checking if there were relatives of the children, who were in a position to take the children into their families.

Pepi Andriani had been told by the priest one day that he had found his family.

They had been captured and taken away and had been looking for Pepi and his sister since hostilities had ended. Pepi and his sister had been reunited with their parents.

Four other men and one woman were hired. They were to work with the government and the church.

In the government, some people should have been doing this job, and were, as in the church situation, people who were lazy and did not care.

Pepi and Bernado would set off for a week to ten days trip, driving through the lower part of Italy checking the orphanages they had pinpointed on a map.

Bernado would show the form with permission to check the orphanages, which had been granted to him from the Vatican. There was sometimes a reticent attitude to allow entry. When Bernado offered to help with gardens and fruit trees, this attitude was usually quelled.

Some of the better orphanages already tilled their food crops and helped the poor of the town with free food.

There were huge variations as to how the poor unfortunate children were cared for.

This was usually evident by the condition of the buildings at the orphanage.

The people who received this food would offer to help with some of the heavier work in the orphanage gardens and grounds. This was a win for both parties.

Some of the children of the orphanages were chosen and adopted out to these families, to be cared for as the people's children.

Two orphanages flatly refused to allow access to their facilities. One was church-run. This was a dreary old building with fretting walls and unpainted doors and window frames.

The building looked the part to be in a horror movie.

The other state-run building was no better. It was situated on the edge of a small town among overgrown trees that hanged over the walls.

The lack of maintenance as in the other building was starkly evident.

Bernado had traveled to the nearest large city which had a bishop in residence. The men visited the Cathedral. After waiting some time, the bishop heard his complaint. He then checked the official inspector's form. The bishop thought for some time. "Would it help if I traveled out to see this orphanage?"

"Yes, it certainly would."

The bishop consulted his secretary and told her to cancel all of the day's business.

During the thirty kilometers trip, the three men spoke of the good and bad orphanages they had inspected.

"I must admit that I have never visited this orphanage before. The local parish priest keeps me informed."

"This is a pity Monsignor. Sometimes the priest's visits are too long a time apart, or the priest himself does not visit and lies about it. We are prepared to wait until you have a quick check of the orphanage accounts."

The bishop called down on an intercom and spoke to one of the nuns. In a short time, a young nun came to his office with the papers.

"I will have a quick check of the papers as we travel to the orphanage."

The grumpy priest running the orphanage reluctantly allowed the three men to enter the facility.

The bishop nearly vomited when the smell of the stale recooked food was discovered in the kitchen. His face went very white. He took a scented handkerchief from his pocket and held it under his nose.

The sleeping and toilet quarters bought a very angry response from the bishop.

The priest looked at Bernado with a foul stare, which could almost kill.

"The church has been withholding money to buy proper food." He spat out to the bishop with venom in his voice.

" I think not. I have looked at our accounts before coming to the orphanage. I want to take your accounts back home with me," this bought a change of attitude from the Priest, he tried to make excuses.

"If your books are in order and it is a genuine shortfall of funds, I will employ some people locally to fence an area next to the orphanage where the children can grow fruit and vegetables. I have done this in many places before." He stared at the priest.

"If your accounts are not in order, you can rot in hell," said Bernado, the bishop reiterated this statement. The priest was visibly agitated.

A short while after the car left the facility; the bishop who had been thinking deeply spoke.

"I feel so guilty for the way those poor children have been miss treated. I should have visited these places and have made things right. I felt as if I have just swept the lives of these poor children under the carpet."

"I assure you Monsignor you are not the only one. We have a state-run facility which has the same problems. We have been denied access. This is a greedy monster problem. I was placed in an orphanage like this when I was thirteen, a priest was raping the little boys. I was one of them. I managed to escape."

The visit to the State-run facility was somewhat more forceful. The town Mayor and the police chief and two of his senior officers attended to obtain entry.

The manager of this facility was restrained by the police. Bernado was given the entry keys by one of the female staff members. The busy looking plump woman accompanied them through the facility.

"I have known that there were some bad problems here. I had suggested that I would not have fed my pigs with the food given to the children. The manager always insisted that this was all he could afford."

"I have heard this story before so many times."

"Yes, this man lives in a large house with servants. His children have good cars and also have nice houses. "The woman said.

As they inspected the facility one of the police officers checked the books.

When they returned to the office the police officer asked the mayor and Bernado to step into the manager's office.

There was an array of papers sorted on the top of a large antique desk.

Red pencil underlined pertinent purchases and grants made by the manager. These expenses had no relation to any dealings made to run the orphanage.

"You are coming back to town with me and the police chief." The man had a look of fear on his face. "I have business at home to take care of," Said the man in a shrill voice.

"If I have my way it will be a long time before you can conduct any business at home."

The Mayor turned to the woman.

"Can you run the orphanage until we fill the position of manager? You could apply if you want to. I will send a van filled with some decent food for the children as soon as I return to town."

The woman assured the mayor and police chief that she could care for the children.

As Bernado and Pepi were driving back to Anzio Bernado reflected on the last few day's work.

"It gives me great pleasure to be able to remove the terrible people who are in reality stealing the food from defenseless children. I would like to take a trip back to Poland when the weather in Poland starts to fine up. I want to find where my parents and relatives were buried after the Nazis murdered them during the war. I want to check on an orphanage there. I am looking for a priest with a scar on his face that I gave him when he was attempting to rape me."

The children were pleased to see him as he entered to door. They came running and fought to sit on his knee.

"We have some very bad news Daddy. Mummy had to have a man come to look at Esmerelda and Punta, they both were sick. Mummy said that the man took them away to go to heaven."

Rina went on to explain how the dogs were ill and could not walk. A veterinarian had checked them and had said they both were in pain.

He had taken them to a small outside room and had euphonized them. There was no cure for their problems Frank and Bobby had then made two coffins. They had dug two holes in the small rose garden near the outhouses and had conducted a funeral with the children and Donna Gabriella present.

Both of the graves had new white crosses at the head with the dog's names carved into the timber

"They have gone to heaven now," she said to the children Bernado was saddened by the news. He had known the two dogs were not very well. He had tried to convince himself they were getting better.

Donna Gabriella hobbled down the stairs.

"How was your trip."

Marta and Rina were with the children. Bernado recounted the stories of being banned from entering the two orphanages. “Some people should be shot for treating small children like that,” said Donna Gabriella with venom in her voice.

“These poor children have enough problems without being beaten and starved. How could people put their greed above the welfare of these children?”

That evening when they all walked to the casino for dinner Bernado noticed that Donna Gabriella had to use the walking stick more.

“Are you ok? Your leg seems to be giving you more problems.” “No, I have not noticed it. There is nothing wrong with my leg!” Insisted Donna Gabriella, as she winced in pain at each step.

The children left to go home early with the women. Bernado wanted to catch up with the staff and find out if all was running ok.

As he sat and drank a glass of wine at the bistro and talked to the men, Bernado noticed the large crowd of people who were tourists.

“Is there something like a sporting event in Anzio at present?” “No there are just more people hiding from the cold in our northern countries.”

“I have not noticed this lately.” “You have not been here very often,” said Luigi with a laugh.

“I feel I am doing some good work with the orphanage inspections. We found two more terrible places where they would not let us inside. We finally gained entry. Some real monsters are stealing the food from these small children.”

This night was Marta's night. The girls, as always amicable, worked this out amongst themselves. This was better than offending one of them.

After the stress of the trip, dealing with the nasty greedy people Bernado was looking forward to the night with Marta. He had been imagining what he could do to make the lovemaking more memorable.

Marta had gained a small amount of weight. Her breasts were fuller, but not excessive. She was still a very beautiful woman. Bernado was in bed when she finally entered the bedroom from her shower. She looked at the bedclothes atop the bed, In the middle of the bed there seemed to be a long tent pole holding the blanket in a tent above Bernado's body. Marta pulled the bedclothes off to show Bernado's long hard Bierwurst sausage.

"He looks as if he is ready for action tonight."

She then giggled. She lay next to Bernado; he carefully rolled over on top of her.

She reached for his hips to pull him inside her. Bernado pulled back, and then just touched the tip of his Bierwurst in the cleavage of her warm home spot. He carefully manipulated it, making sure not to let too much inside.

"Come on don't play, around push it inside me"

"I will later, just enjoy it."

"Hurry up I am losing the urge" She yelled a short time later.

"You are telling little lies; you are moaning and trying to slide upon him," He laughed.

Bernado slid some more inside her then pulled it out.

"Hey leave it inside me you rat."

He slowly pushed his Sausage the full length inside her. It took almost a minute to do this Marta let out a series of loud moans as the Bierwurst Sausage entered her.

"Quiet you will wake the children."

"I do not care; just you get to work lazybones."

Bernado laughed. He carefully rolled Marta on top of him. Marta started working so the sausage was moving deep inside her. She wriggled her hips occasionally, He was getting ready to climax. She pulled back almost letting the sausage out,

"This is my turn now; you slow down until I am ready" after some time Bernado's testicles were beginning to ache. Marta sensed this and started to move more assertively. She was making funny squeaking noises every time she moved, this turned Bernado on. Marta got louder with her moaning and moved more urgently. He kept in time with her. They both climaxed in unison. The climax lasted almost a minute. Bernado could recollect himself adding to the yelling and moaning.

It had been a long time since the sex had been as satisfying as this. He rolled Marta on her back and left his tool inside her. After a very short while the Bierwurst was rock hard once more. This went on for three more sensational climaxes for both of them.

As they lay exhausted on the bed cuddled together

"I have some good news for you. I am pregnant again. So is Rina.

We are about three weeks apart."

This was such a turn-on; that Bernado made love to her again, this time there was less urgency just a lot of gentleness and cuddling.

The following morning at the breakfast table Donna Gabriella gave Bernado a sly wink.

"You must have a bit of Italian in you, Bernado, you are doing a good job of filling the house with laughing children." Bernado laughed. "You do not mind." The old woman smiled.

"As long as you are happy my son. "

Bernado bought up the subject of retracing his past to pay back favors, and to check the orphanage which even now caused him to have the occasional nightmares. Marta and Rina could accompany him. The children would have a tutor and a new maid in the house.

As he walked through the rear of the Casino to check with Luigi and Pierre, he stopped at the marked graves of the two performing dogs which in a way were part of his history.

Their graves in the dirt plot among rose bushes backed by the boundary wall were in a convenient position as Bernado passed this way every morning when he walked to work.

He looked at each grave with the wooden cross with the name of the dog and the date of its passing. A low picket fence had been added to show the boundary of each grave.

Bernado had a lump in his throat as he recounted in his mind the companionship and the acts these two friends performed with him. As he walked past each of the two graves he said the name of the dog and wished them to be in doggie heaven with a big bone. His thoughts went to Shandor and the man he killed. He then went to see the other two dogs and gave them both big cuddles. They hobbled around him wagging their tales.

Bernado was at a meeting with Luigi and Pierre. He poured a measure of Glen Fiddock scotch into three small glasses. He then sat down and passed the two glasses to the other men.

"I am about to go back to Poland to try to find the mass grave where my parents and relatives are buried. I would like to have a grave marker built on the place where they are. I will have a brass plaque cast with all of the people's names on it.

I also have a devil in my mind to bury at the orphanage where I was kept after they were killed."

During the discussion about the everyday business, the casino was going from strength to strength. Tourists were flocking to Italy, especially the warmer climate areas as Anzio.

The car was packed. Bernado and the women took turns to kiss and hug the children. Bernado then started the car and drove off slowly. The children were madly waving; the two children had tears in their eyes, but still waved. Donna Gabriella joined in with enthusiastic waving.

CHAPTER 16

The early June weather was bringing the wild-flowers into bloom along the roadside. Farmers were working in their fields. A small pretty inn in a small town in Austria was the first-night stopover, the town looked like an advertisement for a postcard, all of the buildings were well cared for, and many had window boxes with pretty flowers growing in them. The drive had been quite stressful with the tight corners and steep inclines.

Sleep was all that was on their minds as they unpacked a small case with toiletries and a change of underwear each.

The breakfast was in an old room with heavy adzed beams in the ceiling. The meal was exceptional, with a huge choice of food. Before leaving this town, the car was filled with petrol.

Rybnik, the town in Poland where Bernado had been abused in the orphanage was reached in the late afternoon. Bernado had a feeling of doom about this town as they drove through the streets. Almost all of the bombed-out buildings had been restored. Occasionally one of the building allotments was left as they were with the bricks tossed back off the road into the other parts of the wrecked building. They found a nice hotel and showered to freshen themselves up ready for dinner. The feeling of doom still hung heavy on Bernado's mind. There was the killing of his parents and clan, the nice woman Zelda who had taken him in, and the Orphanage where he was abused. Bernado had a horrible feeling that there may be little resolved by this visit.

As they all lay in the large bed together Bernado explained the feeling of dread.

“I feel as if I am going to meet the ghosts from my past tomorrow. I am worried that they may still be there to haunt me.”

He spoke for some time of the atrocities he had witnessed and had forced to be part of when locked in the orphanage. Both women snuggled up together with him and reassured him that he was doing the right thing to try to put the ghosts of his past to bed and forget about them.

The church still stood proud with its tall steeple and bell tower. Bernado walked through the door of the church, He had an uneasy feeling and flinched as he walked past the small room where he had met father Mark’s persuader for the first time.

A young priest walked out of a door and greeted him.

” May I help you, my son?”

“I am looking for a father Mark who was here some years ago.” “I am sorry but there is no priest with this name at this church.” He thought for a second.

“I will check the church books,”

“Is there still an orphanage in the large building?”

“No that was closed two years after the war. There was some sort of problem there. The church was taken to task about this.”

Another older priest joined them.

“You look worried my son; can I help you.”

"I was placed in this orphanage when I was thirteen years old. The Nazis had murdered my parents and relatives in the woods near a small town near to here." "You had better come to my office." The older priest pointed the way.

"Bad things happened in the orphanage. Were you involved in any way?"

"Yes, I was. I was raped by father Mark almost three times." The older priest's shoulders dropped. He had a look of sadness. "The church finally heard what was going on in the orphanage from an old man who came here one day with the bishop. He had reported that he had been a friend of a lad who had escaped from here. He had been to the bishop and had finally made him believe his story. The lad had stabbed the priest in the eye."

Bernado had a flash in his mind. Stefan the clothes seller had walked all of the long-distance to the church to try to put right the wrong being done here.

"I think I know who had come here. I stabbed the priest with a sharp nail in the face when he was trying to rape me once again."

"Your poor man, this has been on your mind giving you torment for the last few years."

" A thing like this is not easily forgotten."

"If you are looking for some compensation, I will call the bishop and make an appointment for you to see him."

"I am not looking for compensation. I have taken on a task to check both state and church-run orphanages. I have a team of men I have employed with my own money to do this. We have found some bad orphanages where the children are fed with food not fit for pigs. I have permission to do this from the Vatican."

The old priest had a sad look on his face.

"There are many things in the world which need fixing, I am proud to meet you because this problem is high on my idea of a fix list."

"What happened to Father Mark?"

"I was told he went to jail. I have heard he died in there. Father Paul was removed from the church. The orphanage was then closed."

Bernado was almost going to ask to see inside the old building but realized that just walking through the church past the door where father mark would have kept watch had been traumatic enough. As he walked through the passage leading to the main entrance he pushed on the slightly ajar door of where Father Mark would hide. The room was now empty. The table where Father Mark had had his way with him on one occasion was not there. A sorry heavy load was being lifted from his mind.

Bernado left the ghosts of his past remain in the closed doors of the now deserted orphanage.

As he got inside the car, he recounted his meeting with the two priests.

"I was told Father Mark died in jail. I hope someone got to him." He said through gritted teeth.

He drove off through the town looking for where Stefan had lived. He stopped the car momentarily. The houses had all been repaired and painted. He showed the girls where he had lived.

Small children were playing hopscotch on the street outside the house. A young family with children was living in Stephan's old house, as one of the small children ran into this house and returned with her mother. She had fallen and grazed her knee.

They stayed at the hotel again for the night. The sumptuous evening meal and a bottle of nice light wine helped take some more of the worries about his early life in the orphanage away.

The next day they would travel to the town where he had been taken with Stan to sell the pigs many years before.

The short trip bought back memories of being in the Model T Ford with the friendly policeman. They drove around the town, then went to visit the ruined cottage where Zelda and Pepi were meant to be buried. He recognized the ruined house.

The policeman had been right. There were two graves near the ruins of the house. Each had a plaque. One said Zelda the healer. The other just said, Pepi.

Bernado opened the car door and then walked to the two headstones marking the graves; he felt the moist tears run down his cheeks as he remembered Zelda's kindness and Pepe's aloof attitude.

Memories of the proud Shandor came to his mind. As he walked to the car he took his handkerchief and wiped his eyes to clear the tears.

The farmhouse was as he remembered. He drove down the rutted driveway and stopped outside of the house.

Small children were playing with toys outside in the dirt; they ran inside to get their mother as the car stopped.

A handsome blonde woman came to the door; she had food stains stuck to her apron. “Can I help you?” “I am looking for Stan and his wife.”

The woman called back into the house,

” Poppa there is someone to see you.”

Stan walked out of the door. He had shrunk in size; he looked at Bernado with suspicion in his eyes, and then asked,

” What could I do for you?”

“I am the young gypsy boy you helped many years ago.”

Stan looked harder,

“You seem to have grown up.”

Bernado laughed. Stan’s wife came to the door.

Bernado returned to the car and took a large box with sweets and Swiss chocolates from the car.

“These are for you for helping me when I was in trouble many years ago.

Stan’s wife took the large box, then asked Bernado and the women inside the house.

Bernado told Stan of his plan to search the woods to try to find the place where his parents had been murdered.

“My sons all came home after being held by the Nazi’s, thank the lord. He crossed himself reverently. One boy is on the farm, the two others are working in the town. One of them goes fishing in the small river where your parents were killed. He has seen where the burnt-out wagons and horse bones are."

Stan gave Bernado directions on where to find his son in the town. They all were treated to homemade cake and strong coffee before they left.

Bernado drove through the village to find the house. He stopped the car. He went to the door and knocked. A young woman answered the door of the house. She carried a child on her hip; another was in a crib in the kitchen. Bernado told the young woman what Stan had said about the horse bones and burnt-out wagons.

"My husband will be home in about ten minutes if you would like to wait for him."

A young man rode his bicycle to the door of the house. He had a quizzical look on his face when he saw the expensive late-model car parked outside the fence.

Bernado opened the door of the car and got out, then walked up to the young man and introduced himself. He then asked him about the burnt wagons. "I have often wondered where they came from. My father said a Gypsy clan was murdered by the Nazis during the war."

"I was one of the clan; I was off foraging for food and saw the soldiers murdering my parents and relatives. I have come back to try to find where they are, so I can put a marker on their grave."

"If you would like to take me, I will show you where the wagons are. There is a road nearby. I will tell my wife that I am going to show you the wagons."

The young man walked into the house to tell his wife where he was going, He quickly returned.

Rina got out of the front of the car to let the man into the front seat. Bernado asked for directions then drove off.

After driving for some time, the man told Bernado to turn down a narrow track between the trees. The track ended at a small clearing in the forest.

"The wagons and horse bones are only about two hundred meters." They all left the car and started to walk, following the young man. The forest opened up to another clearing. On the ground were the rusted parts of the caravan wheels, axles, and springs. Melted and burned crockery and pots and pans lay amongst the remains of the caravans in the green grass of the glade.

Bernado had a flashback of memories; he imagined he was under the bush watching his parents being murdered. He went to the area where his mother had been killed and dropped to the ground sobbing.

Tears poured from his eyes. The two women came and comforted him. The young man stood at a distance waiting. "This is where my mother was murdered. I can still see the young lads stabbing her."

He gained his composure and stood up. He slowly turned around in a circle looking. He finally worked out where the trucks had headed to. There was an odd-shaped tree he remembered from the fateful day. Bernado headed off. Soon he was in the small clearing in the woods where the trucks and other vehicles had been parked.

He could see the trees and forest in his mind as clearly from the day he watched his clan being tossed into the grave. He turned to the right then walked through the low shrubby bushes and was then in the clear land of the burial place.

The surface of the soil in the glade was slightly irregular; even after all of the years. Bernado crouched and looked at the ground. “This is where they were all tossed in a hole and buried.” He said with extreme emotion in his voice.

He knelt in a half trance, as he recounted the horrible events of many years ago.

Bernado then stood up and turned; he looked back to where the grave was and then walked back to the three others.

On the way, back to the small village, Bernado finally found his voice again.

“I will go to Rybnik and have a monumental mason make a gravestone and inscribe it with all of the names I have written on this piece of paper. I will start the caption with,’ The Rominski Clan’, murdered by the Nazi’s 1943.”

Bernado gave the young man a large denomination banknote. The man was embarrassed and refused to take the large sum of money. “Without your help, I would have been searching for days for my parent’s last resting place. Please take this money and buy something nice for your wife or children.”

The man thanked him very much, he then accepted the money.

That night's dinner at the hotel was a somber event. Bernado was deep in thought recalling in his mind the events which had happened all of the years before. He spoke occasionally about different things he had shared with his parents when he was young.

The monumental mason lived in an old house just outside of Rybnik. His yard had an area with rocks waiting to be cut with his cable saw. A barn-like shed was nearby. The noise of the wire saws cable cutting through stone came from within.

Bernado knocked hard on the door to no avail, the noise in the shed was quite loud. He opened the door and walked toward the man who was pouring some grit into the receptacle supplying the wet grit to the rock cutting wire.

The man turned and noticed Bernado. He had a shock as he had not realized that another person was in his shed. Bernado walked to the man. The man turned off the saw so he could hear. "Can I help you? "Asked the man,

"Yes, I have a large job for you if you are interested."

"Any work is interesting to me. I only get work when someone dies. No one has died in the last three weeks. This is almost a record for this town".

"My parents and relatives were murdered by the Nazis during the war. I have finally found their grave. I would like a large memorial stone made for this grave with all of their names cast into a brass plaque."

Bernado handed the man the list of names he had compiled. The man read the list,

"There are many names on the list. This will be expensive. I do have the material and the facilities to make the brass mold."

"Money is no objection to me. I have returned after fifteen years to try to set things right for them. I was hiding under a shrub when my clan was all killed. I found the man who did this and sent him to the devil."

The man thought for a while.

"I could have this done in three days. Where is the place where you want the gravestone set?"

"It is near a river, some thirty kilometers from here".

The man sat at a bench and then took a piece of crinkled paper. He outlined the stone he would cut. He pointed to some offcut pieces of stone on the end of the bench.

"Pick out what colored stone you would like. There is a nice brown Italian marble there."

Bernado sorted through the stone and chose the brown marble. Next, the man started writing down some times and figures to formulate a quotation.

Bernado studied the quotation.

"I will pay you half as much again if there has been a good job done,"

"I always strive to please my customers."

"My parents and relatives were Gypsies. We were trying to escape from Poland when they were caught."

"This makes no difference to me Jews or Gypsies or any other people they should all have a final marker at the head of their resting place."

"I will pay you extra so you will work quickly. I am now living in Italy and want to return home."

Bernado shook hands with the mason then left.

While waiting for the man to finish the job, Bernado and the ladies drove through Poland to visit some of the larger cities as tourists.

On the morning of the third day, Bernado drove to the mason's home. He walked through the open door of the shed.

"I am just polishing the Plaque before I fix it to the tombstone." said the mason.

Bernado looked at the plaque as the man moved the plaque across the polishing wheel. The man turned the polishing machine off and handed him the finished black plaque with the risen gold colored brass lettering. Bernado read through the names. The list ended with Georgiou the lost gypsy boy.

All people of the clan were accounted for. "You have done a very good job." The man smiled, "Wait until you see the stone I have cut." said the man with pride in his voice.

The large marble stone had been carved so the plaque would fit inside a carved out square. Flowers were carved around the top of the stone.

"I am very impressed."

"We could leave soon. I will get some lunch to take with me." Bernado had thought of this and had a picnic basket packed in the car.

"You can share our lunch I have had extra packed for you."

The man and Bernado loaded the heavy tombstone with the plaque fitted into the rear of a heavy van. This took a considerable effort on Bernado's part. He was getting soft from the good life. The man had a home-made trolley with small rubber-tired car wheels on it to carry the heavy load to the gravesite. This was tied securely in the rear of the van.

After half an hour of driving, they found the narrow track leading off the main road. The small track was driven into. The van followed close behind.

The two vehicles stopped in the clearing. The mason got out of the van.

"Right let's see if I can get any closer with the van."

The men walked off toward the burnt-out caravans. It was possible to drive to the caravans in his high clearance van. Even the rest of the journey was not impossible. They walked back to the vehicles.

They all sat on a rug on the ground and had the picnic lunch, before setting out again.

Bernado spoke to the man of the atrocities he had witnessed years before when his family was killed in this place. The meal was a somber event.

After the lunch Bernado walked ahead of the van, directing the driver past logs and other obstructions in the shrubbery. The two women walked with him. It was a quiet, sad trip.

The van was able to get to the gravesite; there were a few sprigs of shrubbery hooked underneath it, nothing serious.

The rear door of the van was opened and the foundation slab to sit in the ground was gut busted out of the van. This had a keyhole in it to take the tombstone.

The ground was hard to dig to make the rectangular hole for the cast foundation.

Bernado was certainly not as fit as he had used to be. Sweat poured from his brow as he stood in the sunshine helping dig the hole by swinging a pick.

The keyhole stone was levered into the rectangular hole. The tombstone was then laid back onto the trolley and wheeled to the waiting keystone. The mason then went to the van and half-filled a steel bucket with cement and sand mix. He added some water from an old battered oil drum and mixed the cement with a large trowel. The sloppy mix was poured into the slot in the keystone. The tombstone was then fitted into the keyhole and cemented in place. Bernado stood back with the man, Marta, and Rina to inspect the job.

A small lone cloud covered the sun; a strong gust of wind rustled the leaves of the surrounding trees, a flock of pretty light orange birds with grey backs and wings with black faces landed on the ground where the grave was.

Bernado looked up at one of the trees. He was sure he could see a vision of his mother and father showing in the leaves. They were holding hands and looking down at him.

Within two minutes the clouds parted and the sun came flowing down with sunbeams showing through the trees. The small birds took to flight and flew off into the trees

The stonemason was a bit shaken,

"I am sure I felt someone watching us when the cloud came over the glade, even the birds landing was quite spooky."

Bernado asked the girls if they had felt anything unusual. They had both experienced some sort of moving event.

They rode in the rear of the van on the way out of the glade to the car. They sat on some folded sacks. The mason had his tracks to follow.

When they arrived at the car Bernado took his wallet out and paid the man.

"You have made a mistake you have paid me twice as much as I quote you."

"I said I would pay extra for a good job. My people seemed to approve from the signs we had after the tombstone was set in place." "Yes, I have had the feeling they did. On some rare occasions when I have fitted a tombstone I have felt or seen some sign. This one was truly different. Thank you very much for the extra money for the job."

The man opened the door of the van, slid into the seat, and then drove off back to town.

Bernado and the women sat for a while in the car.

"I had a vision of my mother and father standing together framed in the leaves of one of the large trees nearby. I think I have their approval for what I have done."

He started the car.

“I have laid a lot of ghosts from my past to rest because of this visit.”

He thought for a while as they drove along the narrow track to the road.

“I feel as I have had a load of suffering and guilt lifted from me now. I have marked my parent's resting spot, and learned of the fate of the priest in the orphanage.”

CHAPTER 17

They drove through Anzio to their home. The trip had taken ten days.

Bernado felt happy at being able to show some sort of gratitude to his Rominski clan for his existence.

He had played the setting of the gravestone, the eerie events and vision over and over in his mind for the last two days as they were returning from Poland.

When the car stopped in front of the house, the children had spied them from the upstairs window and came running out to meet them. “Father, Nonna has fallen down the stairs and is in hospital,” said Johan with a sense of urgency. The new maid was standing at the doorway. Marta waved then called loudly to the maid. “We will take the children with us to the hospital to see Nonna.” The maid waved then returned inside the house, shutting the door after her.

The children climbed into the car and kissed each person.

Bernado drove off.

Donna Gabriella was propped up in bed with a large pillow behind her back. She had a large black eye and other bruises on her face. She still had a fire in her eyes. She was not defeated by this new problem.

“My stick slipped off the top of one of the stair treads. I should have been more careful.” Bernado then the two women gently hugged her and kissed her. The children also kissed her.

“I think when you come home, we will set your room downstairs for you. I will see Frank about putting a shower and toilet in the room for you if you would like,” said Rina.

“Thank you, my family. I have had some close calls before when I have been coming down the stairs lately.”

Bernado left Marta and Rina with her. He walked to the nurse’s station and asked to see Donna Gabriella’s doctor. The nurse paged the doctor on the intercom. After waiting ten minutes a young tall good-looking doctor asked Bernado who he was. He shook hands

“Hi I am Dr. Martini “

“I am enquiring about my adopted mother Donna Gabriella.”

” What has she told you.”

“Just that she missed the top of the stair tread with her stick and then fell.”

“I am afraid it is worse than this. She has cancer in the bone of her lower leg.”

Bernado was shocked by this revelation,

“How long has she had about this.”

“She has known for a few months. I have suggested that she have it operated on. If we did so she may lose the lower leg. When she heard this, she refused.”

“We have been worried about her lately. I have noticed that her limping has been worse and that she has been in pain when walking. She has just dismissed my concerns.”

The doctor walked back to the room with Bernado.

"I will ask her nicely to explain herself of what I have told you." Bernado agreed with this.

Bernado walked back to the room with the doctor.

"What do you think of my good-looking doctor," said Donna Gabriella. With a smile. "You are very lucky, "said Rina.

The doctor looked at Donna Gabriella sternly. "I think you have something to tell your family" Her demeanor dropped somewhat.

"The doctor has informed me that I have cancer in my leg bone. He said that they may have to take my leg."

The two women had tears in their eyes. This was also their adopted mother. "I was putting off telling you. I did not want you to be worried." "We will pay for the best doctors to look at the problem," Marta said, as she cleared the tears from her eyes.

"We have already done this. We would like to operate to see what we can do. There may be a chance of giving this cancer radiation therapy; we could slow it down from growing." Said the doctor.

Donna Gabriella responded.

"I think I will agree with this. I am enjoying the new family and children too much to want to die. Two new babies are coming soon. I have to see that they get the right names." The doctor agreed for Donna Gabriella to be discharged the next morning to go home. She would need a wheelchair for a short time while her bruised hips healed.

The following morning an ambulance delivered her to the house. Marta and Rina had taken her bed downstairs to a room that had a view of the street. The rest of her belongings were to be taken when she was in the house so she could help rearrange the room.

The orderly from the ambulance wheeled her up the front steps. “I am so pleased to be home in my house. Thank you.” Marta guided the orderly to the new bedroom. He turned and left the house.

Donna Gabriella inspected the room with the bed.

“I think this is a good idea. The children can come and see me without having to climb the stairs.”

She slid onto the bed with help from Marta.

“Could you please bring my clothes and other things from my old room?”

The moving room job took some time and effort. Finally, with the help of Maria the new maid, and Bernado the task of moving the clothes and furniture was finished.

The people Bernado had hired to check on the Orphanages had reported for him from the first fortnight-long trip through Italy. The can of worms that Bernado had opened was wriggling. The reports from the inspectors showed that over half of the orphanages were rorting the system in some major or minor way.

The offers of the garden and fencing had been taken up by all. The inspectors were traveling on a further inspection of the same facilities in three weeks to see if the money was being used for the gardens and fencing.

The Church had reversed its attitude to the forceful inspections and were all now enthusiastically condoning them. Bernado had received many congratulating letters from lowly Priests to some very influential Bishops regarding the inspections.

Both Marta and Rina were now swollen with the unborn children. Bernado was redundant. The Bierwurst had no place in his women's life.

Bernado had taken to staying at the Casino late. He was enjoying the Friday striptease shows. He missed having Donna Gabriella with her witty descriptions of each act being with him during the strip shows.

One evening an exceptionally beautiful woman stepped onto the stage and captivated the audience with her demure teasing routine. She did not do cartwheels and other show-off tricks to show the patrons with what she had had for breakfast that morning. The show was all tease and slight peeps. The crowd erupted in applause when she had finished.

Bernado was captivated by this beautiful tan-skinned woman. Her body was a light coffee color as many of the Italian women were. He met her after the show and asked her to come and sit with him to have a drink. She agreed.

Martina had originated in the north of Italy. She had come from a small mountain village. She could not leave this place quick enough when she was a young girl.

She had found living in the city extremely hard until she had her first break acting in a blue movie. "I had felt much shame for starring in this movie then, but it had placed me in front of people's eyes for other work."

Bernado was feeling a great desire to be with this woman. "Would you care to come upstairs with me, I will show you the view from the landing."

They walked up the twin stairs Bernado from the left Martina from the right. Bernado had walked out of sight from the ground floor. They walked toward the end of the long passage and then up another flight of stairs to where the living rooms they had used before moving in with Donna Gabriella.

Bernado opened the door. They both walked into the room. He carefully closed the door.

Martina came into his arms. Bernado was about to take her to bed.

"Have you got any music here?"

"Just the radio,"

She found the radio and turned the switch on; finally, she found some slow music.

"I will give you a special show for this music."

Bernado was having trouble walking; the Bierwurst stick was rock hard.

Martina looked with surprise at the huge swelling in the front of his trousers; she smiled as she lifted her eyes, but said nothing. She started to dance slowly to the music, removing a piece of her clothes' in time to variants of the music. Bernado was throbbing with desire as he watched.

Finally, Martina had just a pair of sheer panties covering her. Bernado picked her up and carried her to the bed. He laid her on the sheet and then tore his clothes off. Martina removed her knickers, laid back slightly lifting her partly opened legs. She was ready for him.

The striptease show had aroused Bernado. He could not wait to be inside her.

They came together like two wrestlers, each looking for a superior hold.

Martina screamed when Bernado shoved the Bierwurst home in one push. He could not wait for a second longer to have her.

A cat and mouse game ensued with each trying to gain ascension over the other. The lovemaking was extremely noisy.

The coupling lasted for over an hour. Bernado was extremely exhausted.

Martina dressed slowly, after she finished dressing and redid her make- up she kissed him soundly on the lips.

"That was a very memorable ride. One of the best I have ever had. Thank you."

Guilt flooded over Bernado. He showered and checked his clothes for signs of Martina, like lipstick marks, or the smell of her exotic perfume. His legs felt shaky as he walked down the stairs. He avoided the crowd and quickly left the casino.

Rina was checking the children when he arrived home.

"You are late tonight, what happened?"

"I got tangled up with the boys. We had some business to discuss. Then I ran into Three Fingers, Frankie. You know how he can talk!" As he left the guilty feeling came back. He had a feeling Rina did not believe him.

As he woke the next morning the guilty feeling engrossed him, but he could not get the sexy Martina out of his mind. Just the thought of her gave him a huge erection. He resolved not to see Martina again; she had a contract for four more shows at the Casino every Friday night. This would be a problem.

Like a dog smelling a bitch on heat, Bernado could not keep away from the strip show where Martina was performing.

He had not tried to find where she was living.

This was remote from the Casino and constituted a guiltier feeling when he thought of it. He had to have her again.

Martina was the star attraction at the strip show. A few minutes before her show started the crowd in the room swelled considerably.

The room was full. As she came onto the stage, she looked at Bernado and smiled then raised her eyebrows. He was sitting in the second row of chairs.

He felt the Bierwurst acknowledge her presence. He was glad he was not standing in the tightly packed crowd.

The striptease show in the upstairs room was spectacular.

Bernado was extremely aroused.

The sex afterward was magnificent.

Martina had just finished dressing in front of Bernado when the door to the outside opened and Marta and then Rina walked into the room.

Bernado felt an icy hand grip his heart.

Rina stepped back to the doorway and closed the door to stop Martina from leaving the room.

Marta looked at Bernado with a withering look, when she spoke, it was with an icy voice.

"We are not married. I am your business partner and Rina, I, Donna Gabriella, and the children are your family. If this liaison with this porn star and stripper continues, this is all gone." She turned to Martina.

"As of now, your contract is null and void. I and Rina do not want you here anymore. If you cause trouble, we have some friends who will make your life hell. You need to believe me."

Rina opened the door; she then stepped away from the doorway.

Marta continued.

"Go to the cashier downstairs I will phone them and tell them to pay you what we owe you. Martina ran out of the door and ran down the passageway to the stairs.

Bernado did not move, He stood by the bed like a naughty boy who had been caught doing something very obnoxious

Marta picked up the phone and called the cashier. She explained that because of unforeseen circumstances Martina had to leave her employment. She was coming to collect her wages.

Marta turned to Bernado. "Now where does this leave us?" She stopped talking. She glared at him.

"You have options on your plate."

She stopped again to stress her point

"There are two main ones."

She paused to make her point once again.

"You live with us and the children with Donna Gabriella as we have all done so as a family, or you can live here in the Casino and screw every Bimbo when you like."

"There are other options you may think about."

"Which one is it going to be?"

Bernado was in a tight spot. His family came first.

"I do not know where to start to apologize. I have done a stupid thing, which seemed like fun. I did not consider your feelings; I did not know what your feelings would be, considering the fun we all had at the circus years ago. I love my family and adore both of you and the children. I would be pretty stupid to jeopardize this for what was just casual sex."

Rina had her say. "I had a feeling that you were lying to me when you said about the meeting with the boys last Friday. I did some discreet checking and found you had followed a girl upstairs. It does not pay to lie to a woman. We have a sixth sense about those sorts of things."

Bernado tried to keep out of the women's way. This did not work. The household routine and conversations were still the same as before he was caught with Martina. He had a slight feeling in some ways that there was some tension.

Donna Gabriella was admitted to the hospital for a biopsy of her cancer to see if it had progressed. The prognosis of the biopsy was the cancer was a slow-growing one. She opted for radiation therapy on her leg.

As the weeks of radiotherapy passed the treatment was affecting her, but the sense of life and humor still prevailed, even when her hair started to fall out.

She bounced back from the radiation treatment. She took to having long walks with her stick and did not show the problems of the soreness she had before the treatment. Her wispy hair was again covering her scalp. She was the boss of the house once more.

Bernado entered the back gate of the Casino one morning and could hear one of the dogs howling. His morning ritual was to check the two remaining dogs and make a fuss of them before feeding and watering them.

He quickly undid the door to their room. Esmerelda was lying stiff on her dog bed. Carmen was licking her and then howling. Bernado had tears in his eyes when he went into the Casino. He found Frank and asked him to dig a grave for his lost friend. The three women and children attended the doggie funeral as Esmerelda was lowered into the grave in a small coffin. It was a sad event. The children were crying, as they played with the dogs almost every day.

A week after the funeral Bernado had his daily check to see and feed, Carmen. She had also passed away. She had seemed to give up wanting to live when Esmerelda had died.

This was the end of links to Bernado's early life from when he had escaped from the orphanage. Many of the good times of long ago flooded through his head as the last dog was buried amongst the rose bushes.

He thought of Shandor and the heinous Nazi commander he had killed, then Stefano killing him.

How things had changed from that time, the two attractive women and two beautiful children. There was the dynamic thriving business of the casino, and then the privilege of being able to change the lives of many of the poor unfortunate children in orphanages.

His life seemed to be a series of different events that went from better to better. Maybe his parents were watching over him from above.

CHAPTER 18

Three weeks after the last dog had died there was a new life. First, Marta had a daughter. She was named Adrianna; Adrianna had not been home for more than a fortnight when Melinda was born to Rina.

Homelife had resumed to its normal cordial friendly way. Donna Gabriella seemed fitter than she had for a long while. Bernado had some workmen in the house to fit a small lift in a room at the back of the stairs. This could take three people at a time. This gave Donna Gabriella more confidence to go to the babies upstairs.

The two older children nearly wore the buttons off the controls in the first week.

The novelty of the lift finally wore off.

Bernado visited the Bishop of Anzio. The bishop received him cordially. "I would like to expand our network of checking orphanages further Monsignor."

He paused for a while

"The orphanages in Italy are mostly changing their ways for the better."

He paused once more waiting for the bishop to answer.

"I would like the help of the church to expand to other countries in Europe, for checking to see the conditions the children are living in there."

The monsignor thought for a while.

"The publicity which has followed the way some children were kept in some orphanages has traveled by word of mouth throughout Italy. I am sure that this message has traveled further than this into other countries"

The Bishop rose from his chair then turned to look at a large map of Europe on the wall.

"I, myself have heard the priests talking about the changes you have started. I would hope that these changes may be taking place with our neighbors. "

"One would hope so monsignor, but I would not think we can guarantee this."

The Bishop promised he would bring this matter to the Vatican council during his next visit.

"Another waiting game, "thought Bernado as he left the Cathedral.

That evening at the family meal Marta and Rina began discussing the education of both Johan and Gabriella.

Bernado suggested that the children should not be separated to go to an all-girl or all-boy school; He wanted the children to learn to look after each other as they progressed through school. "I am against the church education of segregated children. I will never forget the orphanage where I met up with the church. If this is the way that children are treated by them. I would rather the children have a private tutor."

The women disagreed with this. The children had been segregated long enough from the playground and other children's activities. They had played with the children from Lola's brother's family. They had not attended Kindergarten with other small children.

Donna Gabriella thought for a short while.

“I know of a good school which is non-denominational. The children would have Christian values taught by different faiths. But not have them rammed down their necks to create fear.”

She searched for a table for some magazines. She picked one up and turned the page to an advertisement for this school. She showed them all of the facilities described in the ad.

“I think we should all travel to this school tomorrow with the children.”

The next morning the three women took the children to the school to have an interview with the principal. This school had an extremely good reputation scholastically. It was also very expensive.

The children ran inside the house and came to sit on Bernado’s knee. Johan was the first to talk.

“Daddy we have been to a school today to see the teachers.” Not to be outdone Gabriella added.

“They have some chickens and rabbits at the school”.

“They have a small farm area where the children learn to look after different animals. The children loved the school. The teachers seem very nice. Much nicer than the grumpy old nun’s when I went to school. “Donna Gabriella added.

Bernado was secretly happy. He did not admit it. He wanted to let the women make these decisions. The school was five kilometers from the house. Rina and Marta could take turns to drive the children to school, he thought.

“They have a small bus which picks up the children every day,” said Donna Gabriella.

The whole matter had been settled.

Rina phoned the school and confirmed the booking for the two children. Bernado was pleased. The children were very dear to him. He wanted the best for them.

There were no tears as Johan and Gabriella stood in front of Bernado in their new school uniforms. They were both very proud of their new clothes. They were ready to go to school and meet new friends.

The clock in the hall chimed. It was nearly time for the first day on the school bus Marta and Rina walked outside to meet the bus with them, the children eagerly boarded the school bus. They went to the rear window and waved as the bus started moving.

That afternoon Bernado was working in his office at the casino when Frank Brazzi knocked on the half-opened office door. Bernado stood then went to the door and opened it.

“Come in Frank, good to see you.”

Frank did not smile.

“I have some bad news Bernado. Some do good parole board woman has recommended that the Vince Corrigano shit be released from jail. I have vehemently opposed this.

I did receive confirmation that they are looking into my recommendation.”

This was worrying news.

“Look I just came to let you know in person instead of phoning you. With people like him, one never knows what might happen when he is finally released." Bernado had a worried look,

"I hope sanity prevails with the parole board."

"The dopey woman I have been speaking to said he had been a model criminal and had found religion and had turned to god." Bernado sneered.

" I do not think any god in our world would want him!"

Frank tried to reassure him.

"If I get my way, he will just about be too old and ready to meet God when he finally gets out of jail. I know a lot of things he has done that were only hearsay and not admissible in court when he was committed. I know they are true".

Frank left the office Bernado was extremely worried

Two days after the visit Frank phoned Bernado.

"I have managed to have the parole officer changed for the Corrigano case. The new officer is an ex-cop who knows all about what Vince and his mates got up to." Bernado thanked Frank. "Some other news is that Donna Gabriella's rotten relatives have just been let out of jail. I do not think you would have any more problems with them. They both did not enjoy their stay in jail; I would not think they would be in a hurry to return."

Bernado was at the Casino checking on how the business was running, when he left his office he walked through the gaming area to check the crowd. Three Fingers Frankie and Mildred were playing at one of the tables. When they had finished Bernado walked over to them.

"Could I talk to you privately?"

He asked Frankie. “Sorry, Mildred.” She looked at Bernado.

” Hey, that’s ok I will play some blackjack while you and Frankie fix the world.”

She waddled off to the blackjack table.

“Is something on your mind Bernado?”

“Yes, I have news that Vince Corrigano has turned to god and may get out of jail soon,”

Frankie laughed.

“I don’t think any god in any heaven would need a little shit like him. Just leave it with me.”

Frankie walked off to meet up with Mildred at the blackjack table.

A week later Frank Brazzi phoned.

“There must be a god. He certainly did not want Vince Corrigano. He was working in the laundry at the jail and got caught up in one of the spin-drying machines in a freak accident and had his neck broken.”

Bernado felt a sense of guilt. It did not last too long. He had visions of Vince trying to kill him or one of his family members.

He thanked Frank for the news.

CHAPTER 19

Nearly two years had passed since Vince met the devil. Donna Gabriella was still very fit. The cancer was gone or was in remission.

Bernado had bought the children a small dog. The dog was a small intelligent terrier. The children would play with the dog for hours when they were home from school.

The two younger girls were also enjoying the young dog, even though they had the occasional nip on the fingers when they woke the dog when she was trying to sleep.

When the school bus had dropped the children off in the afternoon Johan and Gabriella would often put Mitzi the dog on her leash and walk over to the casino to see Bernado in his office. The office was situated away from the din of the gambling floor and also accessible from the rear of the casino.

The family had not thought of Donna Gabriella's niece or nephew for a long time. It appeared that they had evaporated into the far distance.

The children were crossing the road one evening after school to walk to the Casino and see Bernado when a small dirty old car had driven slowly along the lane Johan had the leash for Mitzi in his hand. As the car passed the children it had stopped. The children started to walk past the car. The door quickly opened. A man leaped out and grabbed Gabriella and then pushed her through to the rear seat of the small two-door car. He quickly followed her into the front seat, the door slammed, and then the car sped off driving erratically down the road.

Johan at first did not know what to do. He then ran screaming into the casino towing the bewildered Mitzi with him. He ran to Bernado's office.

"A man in a car has just taken Gabriella" he cried. Tears ran down his face.

Bernado felt as if an icicle had pierced his heart.

He picked up the phone and called Frank Brazzi. After a short conversation, He arranged to meet Frank at his house across the road.

He left the Casino carrying the crying Johan and towing the bewildered Mitzi by her leash. He crossed the road then entered the house.

Rina heard Johan crying and came to investigate. Bernado yelled,

"Gabriella had been kidnapped."

Donna Gabriella came into the room, followed by Marta.

Donna Gabriella had turned an ashen color.

Bernado explained what Johan had told him about the car and the man jumping out and grabbing Gabriella.

He noticed that Donna Gabriella was having trouble breathing. Rina also noticed this and ran to the phone for an ambulance. Marta lay Donna Gabriella back on the thick carpet and watched her intently. Rubbing her hands and feeling her brow as she waited.

Frank Brazzi and two policemen walked into the room through the open door.

He spoke to Johan and asked about the car, Johan said it was grey and old.

He sent one of the men to walk up and down the street to see if any neighbors had seen the car.

He then noticed Donna Gabriella lying on the floor. “I think Donna Gabriella needs CPR she has problems breathing”.

He started to administer CPR while they waited for the ambulance.

The ambulance seemed to take forever. In reality, it was eight minutes. A stretcher and Oxygen bottle was bought. Frank stopped the CPR while Donna Gabriella was given medication under her tongue. She was strapped into the stretcher .Rina asked the ambulance officers if she could ride in the ambulance. She wanted to go to the hospital with her. They agreed to take her.

Frank carefully questioned Johan about what the man looked like. “Was he an old man?” Johan thought for a second.

“Not old, but older than daddy.”

“What color was his hair?”

“He had a cap but it was grey around his ears and sort of blond just under the front of the cap he had something over his face so I could not see him properly. The other person had this also.” “What was the color of the seats inside of the car?”

“They were red; the gear lever was on the floor.”

“Very good Johan you are very clever. Did you notice any name on the car?”

“I do not think so. There was a silver thing on the bonnet” Johan thought for a while.

’The car was very small and had funny wheels.”

“Could be a Morris Minor, a Fiat Bambino, or a Baby Renault,” said Frank to the other officer.

“I remember the two people have white gloves on their hands. The one holding the steering wheel and the one who took Gabriella also had gloves.”

Frank picked up his radio and then called the station with a description of the car.

The telephone rang in the house. Bernado picked up the phone tentatively. He was wondering if the kidnapper was on the line. It was Rina phoning from the hospital. Rina answered. She was crying. “Donna Gabriella has just passed away.” She said between sobbing.

“She had a massive heart attack just after she reached the hospital, and could not be revived when she was in the operating theatre.” She started to cry once more.

“The doctors had tried hard to revive her.”

She added after a short while. Bernado relayed the message to all in the room. Marta and Johan burst into tears, Bernado was also shocked with tears running down his face.

Frank offered to send the police car to bring Rina home. He spoke to the officer standing next to him; Bernado told Rina about this. The officer then walked outside to the car. He then drove off in the police car to the hospital.

Rina arrived home with the police officer. Her face was red and her eyes swollen from the crying.

Marta cuddled her to comfort her as she cried as well. Bernado was dazed. He had tears in his eyes and found it hard to concentrate.

Three Police Patrol cars were systematically covering the street area in an ever-increasing circle from the casino area. Frank had his new police handheld radio. It crackled to life A message was relayed that a grey Renault car with red seats had been found in one of the back streets some three kilometers from the casino. The car had been reported stolen from Rome.

Bernado had regained some composure.

"Do you know where Donna Gabriella's niece and nephew are?" Frank thought for a short while.

"I think they are living in a poor area of Rome. I see your reasoning.

They would be blaming you for their bad fortune."

Frank picked up the radio and called the Police Station. He asked the officer to contact Rome and ask for a patrol car to check on them. They would find the address through the parole board.

They were waiting for an hour for confirmation of the officer finding them at their address when the telephone rang.

A muffled voice asked to speak to Bernado. He tentatively took the phone from Rina.

"We have your daughter. If you would want to see her alive again, we would want two million US dollars, in old bills. If the police are to be bought into this, you will never see her again."

Bernado could not recognize the voice as it was muffled by a rag or something else over the telephone receiver.

" How do I know if she is still alive?"

He then heard Gabriella ask to speak to him.

"Daddy I do not like it with these bad people."

"Right is this good enough."

"What do you want me to do. "

"In two days at noon, you are to bring the money in used bills to a red van parked next to the Anzio Plaza Fountain in the town square. You will park your car well away, and walk to the fountain with a soft airline bag with the money inside.

I will have explosives in the van with the little girl. If I see any police, or if the other person tells me on my radio that there are any police coming, I will detonate the explosives and blow myself and the van to atoms. The little girl will be inside. I have nothing to lose, I do not care. Just remember that there will be only you and the bag of money if the money is not in the bag. I will blow up the van and you as well."

Bernado explained the conversation to Frank.

"This sounds a bit dopey. How is he going to get away if you take Gabriella? Even with the explosives if any, we could follow him then nab him when he gets out of the van"

"I will get the money ready. I do not want any stuff-ups."

Frank was thinking.

"I will keep all of my officers informed about the van. We would not like a diligent policeman trying to give him a parking ticket for parking next to the fountain. Tourists will have to be kept away as well, in case there is an explosion."

Frank walked outside with the two officers to his car. Bernado was with them.

"Well Bernado I am sorry to say, this is going to be a stressful waiting game."

The men got into the waiting police car. The Police car drove off toward the station.

The three children were still crying, both the women had red eyes and tears running down their cheeks as well. Bernado tried to comfort them all; he was badly in need of assurances himself.

No meals were served that night. The sobbing children were put to bed, the dog tried to help the children by licking them. She was bewildered by all of the sadness and sorrow.

Both of the women slept with Bernado that night. They finally drifted into a fitful sleep all cuddled together.

The next morning when they woke there was a surreal feeling that this had not happened. The gravity of the double tragedy hit home hard.

Bernado found it hard to think and did not want to move from the house and family. At lunchtime one of the girls from the Casino arrived with some plates filled with sandwiches. They picked at the food as they talked about the double tragedy.

Bernado had phoned the bank about the money; the cash would be ready the next morning.

They all had a fitful night's sleep; the children were restless and would wake to cry once again.

At ten o'clock he went to the car and drove it to the bank. He had trouble concentrating on the surrounding traffic. He felt as if he were in a bad dream. He walked into the bank and felt as if every person was watching him. Bernado asked the teller to take him to the bank manager. He gave a short explanation of Gabriella being kidnapped; the manager was horrified and gave his sympathy for the family.

He handed over the old large battered airline bag. The manager counted out the wads of hundred-dollar bills. Bernado thanked the manager, then took the bag and then picked up the two million dollars in the used US dollars and then carefully stacked them into the bag. He closed the bag and then walked from the bank.

Just before noon he drove to the edge of the square and parked his car. The area around the fountain was deserted except for the red van.

Bernado stopped the car, some distance away from the van. Then got out holding the bag as he shut the car door.

He walked carefully toward the van holding the bag in front of him to show he had bought the money.

The window was down and Gabriella was sitting in the seat. As he arrived at the van he noticed a masked man was partially hidden behind a curtain in the rear of the van, with only his head, arms, and torso showing. His face had a dark-colored stocking pulled over it with eyeholes cut in it. The grey-blue eyes stared out from them.

Bernado looked into the van.

Between the seats were five sticks of Dynamite taped together.

They had insulated wires leading into them.

On the end of the wires was a small black box with a red blinking light with a silver aerial sticking out of it.

"Hand me the money."

The man snarled. Bernado reached past Gabriella and handed the bag of money to the masked man. He ducked back behind the curtain.

Gabriella was tied to the seat. The door was wired shut on the inside.

Carefully Bernado undid the ropes then carefully lifted Gabriella, who was crying out of the window. As he was doing this he could hear the man rustling through the cash in the bag.

He felt like running from the van but slowly walked back to his car carrying Gabriella.

Frank was hiding behind his car. He had a radio with him. When he arrived at his car, he opened the door to let Gabriella get inside. He then walked to the rear of the car where Frank was crouching.

"I saw some dynamite and a black box with an aerial and a red-light blinking."

He thought for a second.

“I would not run in toward the van, He might just want to go out in a fiery explosion.”

Frank was talking to the other police ’There is some sort of bomb in the car. The explosive has a box with a blinking red light. We should wait for a short while then send the bomb squad in to have a look.”

Marta and Rina came to the car and then left with Gabriella to take her back to the house.

Bernado waited with Frank to see what happened.

After nearly an hour the army bomb squad men with their shields and body armor carefully approached the van.

They opened the driver’s side door and then carefully cut the wires leading from the black box. He did not try to look into the rear of the van in case there was an armed man inside. The canvas curtain into the rear was tied together with twine through the eyelets. The Dynamite was removed to be passed to a heavily insulated drum.

As the man did so, some of the wire fell out. There was no detonator on the end of the wire. The dynamite was five candles covered in a heavy brown greased paper, one of the men dismantled the box. One of the men was talking on the radio all of the time, describing the procedure.

“This sender unit is a part of a child’s toy with a blinking light. There is only the battery and light inside. The dynamite is just candles covered in Greaseproof paper”.

The man said.

The bomb had been a hoax.

The bomb squad men stepped away from the vehicle Police offices swarmed to the van. The rear door was locked. It was levered open with a tire lever. The officers had pistols drawn ready. There was no one in the van.

There was just the rear cargo part of the van with a thick carpet on the floor, and the tied together canvas at the other end.

The officers were bewildered. Frank and Bernado walked over to the van.

One of the police pulled the thick carpet out of the van. There was a trapdoor with hinges on the floor of the van.

One of the police lifted the trapdoor to find that the van was parked over a large stormwater grate. The van was entered and then taken out of gear, and pushed forward; the grate was lifted out of the road.

A steel ladder bolted to the wall led down to a large drain.

The kidnapper was long gone.

Gabriella had not seen the faces of the kidnappers as they had stockings over their heads all of the times, she had seen them. Most of the time they had her she was locked into a tiny room with some food and water. They had not spoken to each other in her presence. The red van had also been stolen in Rome.

The kidnappers were not as dopey as they had thought.

The plan was very cunning.

Bernado was not so worried about the money. This could be replaced. The outcome was better than he could have envisaged as most kidnappings ended with a missing or murdered victim.

The Rome police visited Donna Gabriella's niece and nephew. They had a couple staying with them in the small rented flat who verified they were home all of the time during the last four days.

Other people in the adjoining units also verified their alibis. It was noted the nephew had blond hair with some grey around his ears. This was all they had to work on. Nobody in the residential units had seen a red van.

People in other units had been questioned. Nobody knew anything. This lack of cooperation was normal for this type of accommodation in this dismal part of Rome.

The police tried to check the names of the people visiting. They drew a blank. They visited two days later to check on the people again. The flat was empty. All clothes and personal items had been taken.

Once again not one of the neighbors had seen anything happening in or around the flat,

CHAPTER 20

A week later Donna Gabriella's funeral was held. The family was very saddened having to attend this event to say goodbye to their adopted mother and grandmother.

Donna Gabriella's funeral was a huge gathering of people from dignitaries to the lowly street sweeper.

Many people in Anzio had been helped by her or knew her in some way. People were standing in rows with their heads bent low in prayer outside the door of the cathedral. There was no more seating or standing room inside the large building. A loudspeaker had been set up to broadcast the Bishop as he conducted the funeral service.

It was a very long drawn out service in the Basilica Di Santa Teresa, Anzio by the Bishop of Anzio. Bernado, Marta and Rina, and the children went to the front of the cathedral.

Many people talked of Donna Gabriella as their real savior in their times of sorrow or need. Other dignitaries had small speeches they read extolling the good deeds she had done for the people of Anzio.

After the service Donna Gabriella's coffin was carried to a large black hearse by Frank, Tony, Enzo, and Bob, they all had red faces and tears in their eyes. The hearse then drove off slowly, carrying her body to the family crypt in the Anzio cemetery.

A huge following of cars and some busses followed the hearse. There were limousines with the rich and famous right down to little old Fiat Bambinos and motor scooters with the less wealthy. The poorer people rode in the free bus service provided by Bernado.

During the funeral service, Donna Gabriella's body was placed in the family crypt next to her long-dead husband. There were hundreds of people at the cemetery.

The Casino was closed in respect of Donna Gabriella All mourners were invited to the wake to celebrate her life. Many people from the Mayor of Anzio, the Bishop of Anzio, and many others of all walks and trades in the community spoke at the wake. Bernado did not realize how much humanitarian work she had accomplished in the city.

Possibly without the stressful kidnapping, she would not have died when she did.

Bernado was contacted by Donna Gabriella's lawyers a week after the funeral. They were to visit the lawyer's office for the reading of her will in three days.

Donna Gabriella had never discussed her other business assets and transactions with her new family. It had always been thought that her money had been left to her by her husband.

They knew that Nonna Gabriella was one of the two daughters of the casino owner. No questions were ever asked about any other family members.

As they entered the lawyer's office, Lola and her beau were sitting patiently in the waiting room. Bernado and the women joined them. They were called to come inside of the office by the receptionist who had risen from her desk, then approached them. They entered the office then sat at the front of the large ornate desk.

The lawyer cleared his throat. He started to read off a form in front of him. The form had a list of the properties that were currently owned by Donna Gabriella. The property portfolio was huge.

Many of the esplanade properties around the casino were owned by her, plus other hotels and businesses. Her assets were in the billions of liras. She had indeed been a very canny businesswoman. She also had an extensive Blue-Ribbon share portfolio. The cash reserves in the bank were very large.

Bursaries were made for all of the children to be held until they were twenty-one years old and also a provision for any extra children who may be born.

Marta and Rina were included in the will. Both of them received a similar huge inheritance from her cash reserves, including all of the jewelry. Individual expensive items of great value were named for each of the women.

Bernado was named as the inheritor of all of the properties, plus her home and contents.

Smaller amounts were left to individuals like Lola and other people in her life.

The extent of her fortune amazed all who were at the reading of the will.

Bernado thought about the niece and nephew. Their greed had cost them billions of liras. No wonder they were angry. If only they knew what she had accumulated over the years?

Life started to resume its normal course during the following weeks.

Bernado, the girls Marta and Rina, and also the children could feel Donna Gabriella's presence in the house.

Shadows on the wall and movements outside of one's peripheral vision were talked about. This did not bring an uncomfortable feeling at all.

They all knew that Nonna Gabriella was watching over them.

For many weeks after the kidnapping, one of the women drove the children to school each day and then picked them up when lessons had ended.

The feeling of paranoia remained.

Johan and Gabriella did not want to walk Mitzi outside of the yard. Bernado offered to provide a bodyguard, Marta and Rina were uncomfortable with this idea.

The daily normal lifestyle was slowly returning. Six months had passed since the kidnapping.

It was Rina's turn to sleep with Bernado. After they had made love, she cuddled up to him. "I have some news for you. You are going to be a daddy again Marta and I are both pregnant again." she cuddled closer to Bernado as they both went to sleep.

It was not unusual when they were discussing some event or other decision with the children to end the conversation with, "What do you think Nonna?". Her presence was still felt in the house.

Frank Brazzi called at Bernado's office one morning. Bernado asked him to sit down. Bernado liked Frank and was pleased to see him. "I have some news from the USA about Donna Gabriella's niece and nephew. The Las Vegas police were investigating the murder of two Italian nationals. They appear to have been Donna Gabriella's niece and nephew." Bernado cocked his ears up. This was news he wanted to hear.

"The two had the Casino skimming racket working in some of the Las Vegas Casinos. They had skimmed off a lot of money. The Casino owners caught them out. Before the police could be informed, the American mafia had them killed. Both of them had single shot to the back of the head. The mafia way of warning others" Frank paused for a short while.

"Their bodies were found just outside of the city in the desert next to the main road. They were probably left there for a warning to others who would try to take on the might of the American Mafia. We found out when immigration became involved. Interpol had matched their fingerprints." Bernado thought for a short time.

"I have been worried about them since Nonna died. We have kept the children off the streets and even stopped them from traveling to school on the school bus. The children were sad about this as they had many friends on the bus."

The family had always been worried that these crooks may take it upon themselves to try another kidnapping, or some other payback against their family members with some way to get more money, following Donna Gabriella's death.

After hearing this news, the children were now once again allowed to use the school bus to take them to school.

They were very happy, as they had missed being with their many friends on the bus.

Bernado wanted to do a trip through Europe to check on the orphanage program. The first baby was due in six weeks, the second two weeks later.

Bernado called Pepi Andriani and asked him to come to the casino so they could plan the trip through to Romania and then to Bulgaria. This trip would cover some of the other Christian religions other than the Catholic faith. He was interested to see how the Orthodox churched in some of these countries treated their orphans. Bernado and Pepi visited the Bishop to discuss the planning of the trip

"I would like to travel through Austria then Hungary. I would then visit Romania the go to Bulgaria."

The Bishop frowned when Bernado stopped talking

"I would keep my visit to Austria and Hungary if I were you. The two other countries would be too dangerous to visit. Romania has a despot of a dictator and Bulgaria is controlled by Russia. I would not want to visit either of these countries."

As they were walking to the car Bernado bought this subject of not visiting the two other countries to Pepi

"I think I would like to visit these two countries by myself if it were at all possible. They may be where there are large problems with orphans. I will ask when I am in Austria or Hungary."

CHAPTER 21

The trip up through Italy was interesting; The steep climbing roads kept one concentrating as they drove. They stopped at the border to Austria where they had to travel through customs. The main object of this visit was to visit orphanages in Austria, Hungary, and Romania. Bulgaria was too far out of their way.

They booked into a nice inn for the night just over the Austrian Border.

Traveling through Austria to Vienna took most of the following day. They found the St Stephens Cathedral on Stephens Plats at three-thirty pm in the afternoon.

The men parked the car then walked up the steps to then enter the large ornate building. They spied a priest in the distance. They walked to him, Bernado then asked for directions to the Bishop office.

As they followed the priest they marveled at the ornate fittings in this huge building. They finally entered an office. The young nun at the desk asked if she could help.

"I have a letter from the Vatican allowing for me and my workers to check the conditions of orphanages. We have covered a large part of Italy and have found some very well-run orphanages and some very poor examples which have been run by priests and others who have stolen money from the church and the state-run orphanages, which should have been used to purchase food. I wish to have an audience with the bishop about these matters."

The young nun listened attentively. She opened a book which was used for audiences with the Bishop. Would 1.30 tomorrow afternoon be suitable?"

Bernado assured her it would be. He handed over the letter from the Vatican for the nun to read.

"I think the bishop would be happy to talk to you about these problems" She smiled at them as she closed the appointment book. "We will see you after lunch tomorrow then."

As the men drove through the city, they found a good small hotel Das Tyrol. The car was driven to the rear of the hotel by an employee. Their luggage was taken to their rooms for them. Bernado was next door to Pepi. They were going to have a shower and meet to go to a restaurant with a floor show. Bernado had learned some basic German during the years at the Casino, whereas Pepi was quite fluent with the language. Austrian had a few dialect problems he was unsure about.

They wandered along the street and found a large beer-garden restaurant. This venue had a floor show with singer's comedians and dancers. The beer flowed quite freely as they ate their meal and laughed with the crowd. They wandered back to the hotel at 10.30 pm.

The nun smiled as they entered the office. "The Bishop is looking forward to talking with you. He has heard of the good work you have done in Italy."

She rose from her desk.

"Follow me I will take you to his office."

They followed close behind her to a large office. The nun knocked on the door. Then opened it when the Bishop called. “Enter.”

The bishop was a large man of ample girth; His hands were soft when he shook their hands.

“I have been following your travels through Italy with great interest. I must say that you have met some challenges. I have instructed the church in Austria about the vigilance they should have, regarding what you have uncovered in Italy.”

The two men sat down. The nun excused herself then closed the door of the office behind her.

The Bishop put his pudgy arms on the top of the desk, then folded them, showing off the large Bishops ring.

” We have also uncovered some of the problems that you found in your investigations”.

Bernado thought for a short while.

“I am pleased with this. I can speak from experience when I was nine years old. I witnessed my parents being murdered by a sadistic Nazi Commander. I tried to look after myself but failed. I was taken to a church-run facility in Poland. The conditions were very poor. Over the years I have prospered from good luck and had thought I should give something back by trying to make sure children were not subjected to the same treatment I had been”.

The Bishop had a map of Austria with the names and addresses of all of the orphanages in Austria.

“If you would like, I will send one of the young priests with you to inspect some of these facilities. They are both state and church-run facilities. I am not hiding anything. This is a full list of the orphanages in Austria."

"I would like the chance to see what other countries are doing about orphans. I am thinking of trying to visit the church in Romania."

The Bishop frowned then unfolded his arms and leaned back in his large chair.

"You would want to be very careful about this. Romania is a communist country run by a dictator."

He looked at Bernado searchingly,

"How old are you?"

"I am thirty-eight."

The Bishop cleared his throat.

"If I were thirty-eight, I would not take my life and your friends into the dangerous world of the regime of Nicolae Ceausescu. Many people have gone missing in this country." He looked intently into Bernado's eyes.

"This is where orphans are being treated badly. If you were to try to meddle with this problem there you may find yourself locked up in a Romanian jail, or you could be executed by one of his many firing squads. Hitler and Stalin were both gentlemen alongside this monster."

Bernado thought for a while.

"What is happening to the orphans in this country".

"From what we have been told, the unwanted children are being kept locked up like animals in farm pens. They have developed many problems from the lack of food and love." Bernado scratched at the hair behind his ear.

"Is there nothing to be done about these children?"

"I have heard that some people in the US and other countries have adopted some of them. They have had huge problems trying to get these poor children to accept family life. People with a lot of patience have succeeded in bringing some of these children back to a normal life."

"What can be done for them?"

"The Romanians in power are selling these children to try to save money from having to feed them. I would not like to become involved in this can of worms. 'The United Nations' and other agencies like 'Save the Children' are the people who should handle these problems. They are too frightened to come to the country to check the appalling conditions these children are living under."

"What is the church doing in Romania?"

"The church is under extreme duress. Ceausescu does not recognize religion. Christians are in hiding. He has an alliance with the Orthodox Church. They have been beaten into submission and most have joined the Iron Guard. They are very bad people."

As they all arose together Bernado told the Bishop they would like to visit some of the Austrian orphanages. "I am pleased that you have asked. I shall be happy to provide a Priest who has some experience with these facilities."

The bishop reached the desk; he took a small notebook from the desk. He turned the pages of the small book slowly as he read the names.

“Ah Father Damien would be the right person. He helped reform some of our orphanages following the edict we received from the Vatican about the work you were doing”.

The bishop returned to his desk then sat down. He pushed the button on a small intercom.

“Could you please page father Damien and have him come to my office”.

While waiting Bernado and Pepi talked to the Bishop about some of the horrible conditions the orphans had to endure.

There was a soft knock on the door.

“Enter.”

A tall blond, good looking young man entered.

“You wanted to see me, your eminence.”

“These are the people from Italy who started the reform of the Orphanages.”

The young Priest smiled.

“I am so pleased to meet the people who took this job to their heart.

Some of our orphans also were living in very bad situations.”

The Bishop smiled at Pepi and Bernado.

“I would like you to accompany Bernado and Pepi to see the reforms we have conducted at our orphanages”.

“I would be proud to help.”

“You can go with them now if you would like”

“Thank you, your eminence”. The young priest bowed as he left.

As they walked from the cathedral to the car father Damien was full of questions about the orphan situation in Italy and other countries they had visited.

Father Damian was a wealth of knowledge about all of the cities they visited during the next five days. All of the orphanages that were visited had gardens and children dressed in good clothes. The cooking facilities and other rooms of the orphanages were clean. The children attended school and other classes such as cooking, woodwork, dressmaking, and a motor mechanic course. Pepi showed great interest in this conversation.

“We could be doing more of these courses in Italy to give the children a start for a trade to go to when they leave the orphanage” Bernado agreed with Pepi. The education for finding work was not a major part of their reform.

The evenings with father Damien were enjoyable. There was a small problem. Father Damien had an eye for the ladies, and a thirst to taste the local wines. This made the evening meals and conversation with the table filled with guests very interesting.

At the end of the evening's meal, there was no further consorting with the ladies and others by any of the men.

“I have always enjoyed female company. Why would I not enjoy the privilege of talking to them? This is part of my job.”

The fourth day of traveling took them close to the Hungarian border. Bernado drove through the Austrian town and drove to the Austrian-Hungarian border post

There was a line of traffic on the road leading to the crossing.

He pulled into a parking bay near the main Austrian offices.

"I just want to see what is involved in getting a permit to travel into Romania to visit some orphanages." "This would not be a good idea".

Father Damien Said. He had a worried look on his face.

"I hope you do not want to try to drive through Hungary and cross into Romania."

Pepi was not too keen to cross the Romanian border.

"I would like to see what Hungary is doing about the orphans, but I will not be going with you to Romania".

"I have no intention of taking either of you into danger"

Bernado concentrated on driving for a few minutes

"What I will do is to apply for a visa to cross the Hungarian border into Romania and to have a Romanian government guide accompany me to see what the conditions are really like in Romania. They can only say no. I will travel by myself; I have no intention of putting both of you in danger."

Pepi and Father Damien followed Bernado into the offices. Father Damien did a lot of talking to the Austrian officials.

"I do not know what the Romanians will say about this idea. I have my doubts as to whether they will agree. I certainly will not want to go to Romania."

The border guard said.

Bernado thought for a while.

"If the government officials are selling these children to people in other countries, tell them that I would be willing to buy a busload of children to take them off their hands. You could mention that I have come from an orphanage when I was young and I would like to help other orphans".

The man picked up the telephone receiver and dialed a number. He spoke for some time speaking Romanian, finally, he hung the receiver back onto the phone set.

"The official I was speaking to has suggested that you fill out an official form for what you have suggested you would want to do.

Add how much would you be prepared to pay for a busload of orphans to the form?"

The man shuffled through his desk and found a form to obtain the visa. The form took a quarter of an hour before it was all filled out. A price per child was written on the form. There was also a suggestion that the official would be able to act as an interpreter speaking either polish or Italian. The man suggested phoning the border post and asking for Peter in two days. He handed Bernado a card with his name and phone number.

As they drove back to Vienna Father Damien suggested to Bernado that he thought he was doing a stupid thing to put his life at risk in the country which was under the rule of the despot Nicolae Ceausescu. “These regimes usually only last a few years until there is a revolution that tosses these people out of power.” “What happens to the children in the meantime?”

“What happens to other children in the world? Hundreds are being born into poverty every day. I would not cross that border for any reason.”

Pepi was also quite adamant about not crossing the border into Romania. “I have a family back in Italy. I do not want to go missing for a wasted cause”.

Bernado thought for a while as he drove the car. “I will see what the answer is when I phone the guy at the border crossing in two days.

Father Damien was taken to the cathedral He and Pepi stayed outside when Bernado went to see the bishop.

“I am very impressed as to the conditions in your orphanages I visited. The trade courses are a very good innovation for the children to find work when they leave. I will instigate this in Italy when I arrive home.”

The bishop was very pleased to hear the compliments. The children are also helping to pay for the running of the orphanage with the work they are doing while learning” “I will be leaving Pepi in Vienna for three days while I drive through Hungary to find if the reforms have been taken up by their church. I have applied for a visa and a Romanian government official to accompany me into Romania to check on the children in their orphanages.”

The bishop sighed and stood up from his desk. He went to a map of Romania on the wall. He put his finger on an area of the map. "I will sound callous but here in Romania, there is a coal-mining region. I have had reports that children as young as ten years old are working in the mines. Boys and girls are all together in the orphanage. They all have to work. The older miners have free range for sex with the older girls and boys. I have prayed for these children. I would not interfere by sending any of my people into this dangerous country. I would never forgive myself if one was to disappear."

He sat down at the desk once more.

"A Man of your talents would be far better off lobbying the United Nations to save the children. I know from what I have heard, you threw a few cats among the pigeons in our church before you got action.

Look what you have achieved now."

"I was going to see if I could buy some of the orphans and bring them out from Romania."

The bishop leaned back and studied Bernado.

"You are only talking of twenty to thirty children.

If the Romanians think you have that sort of money, they would possibly take your money then kidnap you for a huge ransom. The children would not leave the county at all. You may never leave, even if your ransom is paid".

Bernado was deep in thought after the conversation.

"I think you would be right monsignor. I have not thought of the consequences. If the Dictator is as bad as you say, I think that I may be held for ransom. The lobbying the UN and making a loud noise may be more beneficial than me going missing''.

Bernado and the bishop rose together. They shook hands. “You can find ways of getting things done. This is a rare gift. Do not waste this on a lost cause”.

As he left the office Father Damien walked in to see the bishop. Bernado walked to Pepi

“The Romanian trip is off. The bishop pointed out the fact that I would possibly be held for ransom. We will drive into Hungary tomorrow to see if the reforms have been taking place there.” Pepi smiled. He had looked very worried.

“Thank god for the Bishop. I visualize myself stuck in Vienna wondering if you were still alive.”

Father Damien joined them for dinner that night. He knew many influential people in Austria. When he introduced Pepi and Bernado and said what they were doing with the orphans in Italy, a military-looking man with a tailored mustache sitting at their table offered to pay for the wine and food for the night.

Bernado rose from the table and addressed the people sitting. He told some of the horror stories about the starving children in orphanages they had found.

One man at their table had met Bernado on numerous occasions at the Casino. Bernado could just remember meeting him.

The new people to meet at the casino were vast.

He mentioned in his speech the plight of the children in Romania. All of the people at the table warned him from going there.

When they arrived at the border crossing to Hungary Bernado first parked the walked into the office that they had visited two days before.

He asked at the counter for Peter. The man heard him from his office. He came to the counter.

"I submitted your application to the Romanian officials and got a very quick reply. In effect, it states that they do not want foreign meddlers in their country. They are looking after their orphans without any other countries help".

"Thanks' for the trouble Peter. I was speaking to the bishop in Vienna. He informed me that I may be very lucky to get out of the country. Many people have gone missing there."

"I thought it would have been a very dangerous thing to visit Romania while the political system was ruled by this despot," Peter said.

As he left, he thanked the man again for his trouble

The passports were checked and the visa signed. The gate was opened for them to travel into Hungary.

It was mid-afternoon when they arrived at the cathedral in Budapest. The bishop agreed to see them on short notice. The bishop of Vienna had contacted him about the visit and had explained as to the reason for them coming.

Bernado and Pepi were ushered into his office by a nun. The bishop was a tall thin man with a shock of black hair with a bald patch in the center. His face was brown and weather-beaten and his grip when shaking hands was vicelike. He has a pronounced hooked nose.

He started speaking in Italian.

"I understand that you are the man who took the church to task about the orphan situation" He looked angrily at the two men. Bernado and Pepi looked uncomfortable and were ready for a dressing down by this saturnine looking man. The Bishop smiled broadly.

"I am so pleased to meet a man who by his convictions took the pompous uncaring people to account regarding these children. I have been a man of the land. I would rather be out among the people talking about their problems instead of hiding myself behind this large desk."

Bernado bought up the problems of the orphans in Romania. "I was going to try to get permission to travel to Romania to visit some orphanages. The permission was refused. The bishop of Vienna had changed my mind when he described what was being done to the orphans. He was worried that I may never get home. I would just be another missing person in a foreign land." The bishop stood, turned, and then walked to a large map of Europe on the wall behind where he sat. He pointed to the red dots on the map of Romania.

"Here is where all of the orphanages we know about. The children in some areas are slaves. They start working at about ten years old. They work for twelve hours a day. They are the lucky ones. Many others are housed like animals and never get outside to feel the sun or have any exercise." The Bishop paused.

"I have tried to talk to some of the Orthodox Church people. They are too frightened to talk out. The catholic church is in exile." The bishop turned then returned to his desk. He stood behind the desk looking at Bernado as if he wanted an easy answer. “The bishop of Vienna and I were talking about this also. He suggested that seeing I tossed the cats among the pigeons in the church in Italy and by persisting getting results, I should take on the United Nations about these worldwide problems.” Bernado said.

The bishop turned once more and pointed to another dot on the map.

“The area here is a large coal mining district with hundreds of workers. All of the children past ten years of age work in the mines pushing carts and digging with picks and shovels. Both boys and girls work at this hard work. The older miners have their way with some of the older girls and boys. I still think they are better off than the poor children who are kept like animals in worse conditions than prisoners in goal.”

“Surely there must be some way to have these children helped”. The Bishop nodded his head. He had a sad look on his face. “You would remember World War Two? What about the Jews and Gypsies? Where were all of the helpers then, when all of the people were systematically being slaughtered?”

This observation bought back the memories of Bernado’s past. He had to agree with the Bishop.

“I feel so helpless; I have at least made some small changes to the way the orphans of some countries have been treated. I have heard that after the war the English bundled hundreds of orphans off to Australia on boats. Many of these children were mistreated by the brothers and priests in some monasteries which were meant to care for them. Some years later it was revealed that many of the children had parents back in England. The parents were not told about these children. They thought they had died during the war".

Bernado said with emotion in his voice.

Bernado thanked the Bishop for his help with his reforms to the orphanages. He was ready to return home. He had a fire in his belly about the Romanian orphans.

CHAPTER 22

Bernado and Pepi took turns at driving. Both men discussed the options that were on the table for help to be found for the Romanian orphans. Both men were looking forward to getting home to be with their families. The trip took three long days of driving to finally arrive back in Anzio.

After they had driven through Anzio to Pepe's house. Pepi took his luggage from the car and waved as Bernado left for the Casino. The trip had taken a fortnight. Bernado felt so happy that the Orphanages he and Pepi had visited had progressed so well after they had been visited by the officials of the local government and the church.

As Bernado walked through the door of their house Johan called loudly.

"Daddy's home."

The two women and the children ran to meet him. Two dogs barked a greeting also. There were cuddles kisses and pats for the waiting crowd. Bernado searched in his large loose bag and found gifts for the children. It was like Christmas he was Santa doling out the gifts.

Bernado picked up the new puppy.

"Where did this come from?"

"One of the children's school friends was giving away puppies. Gabriella bought her home one day" Rina said with a smile.

Marta and Rina seemed to have swelled up much more with their pregnancies. She kissed Bernado. He ran his hand over her tummy. “I just felt him kick” Marta smiled “Who said it was going to be a boy.” “I am just working on the law of averages”. “We shall soon find out if you are wrong” She laughed. This will have to be the last one. I think I am getting too old to become a mother again after this one.”

“I think the same applies to me,” said Rina.

Homelife turned to the normal daily routine. Bernado had told his story about the orphan problems in Romania. The women were very shocked at the stories re recounted to them. Johan and Gabriella were very upset about the mistreatment of the orphan children.

“I am going to see the Bishop of Anzio in a few days and ask if he could arrange an interview to be able to talk at the United Nations Building in the USA about the reforms to orphanages and orphans we have implemented in Italy and other European countries. Many Asian and African countries have huge orphan problems since there have been civil wars in their countries.”

The next morning Bernado drove to the Cathedral to inform the bishop of his recent visit to Austria and Hungary.

The bishop was pleased that he had come to tell him of the recent events.

“When I was in Hungary, I tried to cross the border into Romania to see what we could do about the huge orphan problems in that country”.

"I am very pleased that you did not do so. I think you would not be here talking to me now. You have achieved so much in Europe. The regime in Romania would have been your demise. We have had priests with a fire in their belly go to Romania to try to put things right. They have not been heard of since that time."

They had a long discussion about the Hungarian and Austrian method of teaching the children a trade so they could find work when they had left the orphanage.

"I am pleased that you have had this visit to these other countries and have seen the reforms that your campaign has bought about. We should start to have teachers from the local communities visit the orphanages to teach the children trades also. The gardens have been a godsend to both the orphans and the poor of the nearby towns with the fruit and vegetable they have grown." The Bishop said.

"I have been thinking of traveling to the USA to talk at the United Nations if the church can arrange this for me. There are so many orphans in Africa and Asia left from the civil wars which have and still are being fought in these countries. The message could be put to the people who are delegates from these countries."

"I will contact the Vatican and see what they can arrange re you visiting and talking at the United Nations".

The Bishop said.

Bernado had a good feeling of satisfaction as he left the Cathedral. The world needed to be told of the dire situation most of the orphans is living in.

His mind was on this subject as he slowly drove. The car home.

This would be another waiting game for the Vatican to finally make up its mind. The weeks passed by. Bernado spent most of his time in the casino.

He had just returned from the Cathedral visiting the Bishop.

Johan and Gabriella were at the door of the house when the car pulled into the circular driveway. They ran to the car.

"Daddy, come quickly. Mummy is ready to have her baby."

Bernado rushed inside of the house. Rina had Marta's bag packed.

The maid stood nearby.

"I have just started to have contractions. We had better hurry." She waddled down the steps to the car followed by Rina. Rina was carrying the small suitcase. Marta climbed into the front seat next to Bernado. He started the car then sped off toward the hospital. "I did not know if you were coming home. I was going to call an ambulance just as you arrived."

The trip to the hospital only took a short time. Bernado parked the car outside of the emergency department and rang the bell.

A plump nurse came to the doorway.

"My wife is starting to have her baby".

The nurse took a wheelchair from near the doorway, she then helped Marta into the seat. She looked at the heavily pregnant Rina and raised her eyebrows.

Marta was taken in the wheelchair to the maternity department.

Bernado and Rina followed close behind.

Just as Marta stood up from the chair her water broke, making a puddle on the floor. She was whisked into one of the rooms. A young midwife followed them. The door was closed.

Bernado walked to the waiting room. He was talking to Rina about the United Nations, and the possibility that he may have to travel to the USA soon.

Rina had an odd look on her face.

"I think you should call a nurse. I am starting to have contractions." Bernado hurried to the Nurse Station.

"I think my other partner is also starting to have contractions."

He said to the young nurse at the counter.

A wheelchair was found, and then Rina was taken away.

Bernado was sitting in the waiting room. There were five other men and some children waiting in the room as well.

Three of the men had worried looks on their faces as most of the new fathers do.

"Is this your first time?" Asked a young man who was sitting alone. He was biting his fingernails and looked quite stressed.

Bernado smiled at him.

"No, I have four children. It looks as if I am going to have two more today."

The young man looked puzzled.

"So, your wife is having twins?"

"No, I am living with two women. They are both having a baby today. One was not due for more than two weeks, I was told." The young man had a look of amazement on his face.

The other men who were waiting stopped talking to their children and looked intently at Bernado. "How do you keep up to two women?" One of the other men asked skeptically.

"We have a nightly roster."

This stopped the conversation. All of the other men then looked toward the ceiling.

Bernado was flipping through the pages of a magazine. The plump nurse walked into the room.

"Mr. Rominski, your wife has just had a baby boy".

"I wonder which one." One of the other men said quietly to the man sitting next to him.

Bernado smiled to himself. He was about to get up when another young nurse came through the door.

"Mr. Rominski. Your wife has just had a baby girl."

This set the men in the room talking quietly among each other.

They were looking at Bernado.

Bernado coughed to get their attention.

"These two ladies are not married to me. They were best friends when I met them. I could not make my mind up which one I loved the most. We all moved in together years ago."

The men in the room all laughed at the solving of the bigamy problem. Bernado stood up to leave the room. The other men all stood up and came to shake his hand and congratulate him.

He walked to the nurse's station. The nurses must have talked about the two Rominski babies on the same day. One asked if he was the father of the two children. Bernado laughed. He faced all of the nurses in the room.

"These two ladies are not married to me. They were best friends when I met them. I could not make my mind up which one I loved the most. We all moved in together years ago".

He repeated what he had told the men in the waiting room.

"I suppose it is like having twins on the same day."

He laughed once more.

This started most of the younger nurses laughing.

He noticed that three of the older women had a very disapproving look on their faces.

When he went to the viewing window, two nurses were holding the two babies.

Bernado first went to visit Marta.

"I have just had a look at our baby boy. He is a good-looking baby. I have just seen our baby daughter as well"

"What do you mean?"

Mara asked with a confused look on her face

"Rina has just given birth to a baby girl."

"I bet that started a few chins wagging among the nursing staff.

"It also caused some questions among the men in the waiting room. They thought that I was a bigamist with two wives. I said I loved both of you and could not make up my mind which one to be with so we all moved in together." Marta laughed for a while. "You rat! It hurts when I laugh."

She had a broad smile on her face.

Bernado left the room and then walked to see Rina. He opened the door and walked into the room. She had the lovely baby girl lying on her chest.

"Well, my dear this was like killing two birds with one stone." She laughed when Bernado recounted the waiting room and Nurse Station conversations. "They probably thought you were a Muslim Sheik. OOH, it hurts when I laugh."

Bernado left the hospital to drive back home.

The children were worried for their mothers, Bernado promised to take them to see the new babies and mothers after school the next day.

He wondered what they would say to their friends on the bus and at school the next morning.

As per usual the news of being able to talk at the United Nations was not forthcoming from the Vatican.

Bernado had been to see the Bishop on three more occasions, to ask if there was any news. There was silence from the Holy See.

Bernado took to putting more time at the Casino. He had been neglecting his duties. He did have an ulterior motive. The house was filled with baby talk, nappies, and loud crying. The babies were a fine duet. They did not need the large loudspeakers that the bands used for outside venues. Their decibel count was almost similar.

The new conversation with the two women was that they were going to have their tubes tied to stop any more crying baby business in the house.

All of the people living in the house still felt the presence of Donna Gabriella. Even Bernado would ask her opinion about pertinent matters when he was sitting alone for some days.

The casino business was thriving. The tourist industry in this part of Italy was improving every year. Anzio had an advantage over the Mediterranean coast in France and Spain as the warmer weather was more reliable.

One evening after dinner Bernado received a phone call from the Bishop. He invited Bernado to call and visit him the next day. He did divulge that the church has finally contacted the United Nations about his request to be able to talk about the orphanage reforms which had taken place in Italy and adjoining countries in Europe. Bernado was keen to visit the Bishop the next day. He talked to the family about this before they all went off to bed that night.

The bishop rose from his desk as the young nun opened the door.

He came to Bernado with a smile on his face.

"It takes such a long time for the wheels of the Vatican to start to turn. It was many months past that I submitted for you to visit the United States to talk about your Orphanage reform program." He returned to his desk and sat, he motioned to Bernado to also sit opposite from him.

"I have the forms here from both the Vatican and the United Nations regarding your request to visit and talk of your orphan program. "He reached across the desktop with the two sheaves of papers, he laid each sheave out facing Bernado.

"Here is the form from the Vatican. He pushed this closer to Bernado. This is the acceptance for you from the United Nations." He touched the other form.

Bernado took the first form and started reading.

"The Vatican has offered to pay my fares. There is no need for this. I should be able to be reimbursed from the Government by my tax accountant."

He finished reading the form, then replaced it on the desk.

The second form stated the date in one-month time for him to visit the UN building in New York to give his speech.

Bernado rose from his chair then took the forms from the desk. The bishop also rose.

"You can offer the Vatican the fares for my trip back. I will pay for the traveling myself. It will be a new experience. I have never traveled on an airplane before."

He shook hands with the Bishop then left his office.

When Bernado arrived home, he found the two women busy with the two babies. They were changing nappies, a job which did not interest him. The babies gurgled contently and wriggled when the job was being done.

“I have the forms from the Bishop regarding the trip to America to address the United Nations. I am booked in to talk in about a month.”

The women nodded. the need to repack the behinds of the babies was more pressing at the moment in-case there was another accident before another body function sprung a leak.

Rina took one of the forms, Marta took the other one, they both read them.

“I see the church has offered to pay your fares. Rina raised her eyebrows. “I offered to pay my own. I had visions of sitting in steerage with no room to move. If I have to fly for the first time, I will travel first class.”

CHAPTER 23

The four weeks had passed quickly Bernado and his extended family was in the Leonardo Da Vinci Rome Airport.

Jets were taking off and landing. Bernado had not been in an airport terminal before. The rushing people and other staff were bewildering.

He had not taken much interest in airports or planes before the trip to the United States. They were just vapor trails in the sky with a silver plane in front.

He was amazed at the size of the large Boeing 747 on the tarmac taxiing toward the huge terminal building.

After many kisses and hugs, He eventually walked to customs then along with a series of aisles to the boarding platform. He had asked some of the people waiting next to him if he was heading for the right airplane.

He finally boarded the large plane. When inside he was amazed at the rows of seats. Leading off past the business class seating he was ushered to the first-class seating.

"This is my first time flying in a plane''

He told the hostess

She raised her eyebrows in disbelief.

"I will show you what to do". His carry-on bag stowed away, the hostess then explained about using his seatbelt, he buckled himself into the seat.

More people filed onto the plane; the seats quickly filled up. The doors were closed. He had a feeling of being locked in, with no options to change his mind.

The engines roared as the plane sped toward the end of the runway. He had an unusual feeling in his gut when the plane tipped back and took to the sky. After climbing for some time, it leaned to the right, then flattened out as it headed west. The plane buffeted and shuddered in the air. Bernado held the edges of his seat when this happened. The flight time was advertised as taking nine hours.

He introduced himself to the other passenger sitting at the same seat module. This man was an American businessman returning home to the US.

After the first two hours of flying, Bernado began to relax somewhat. He listened to the music on the earphones supplied. A movie played on a screen on the bulkhead of the fuselage in front of him. He drifted off to sleep with the soft music playing in his ears.

He was woken by a cart filled with food and beverages being pushed along the aisle next to his seat. A pretty hostess asked if he were hungry. He selected a meal then also asked for a glass of red wine.

As Bernado started to eat the meal the man adjoining him struck up a conversation. This man was a representative of the Caterpillar Tractor company. He had been visiting agents in Europe about sales of their heavy earthmoving machines.

Bernado told the man of his invitation to talk at the United Nations assembly regarding the world orphan problems. Chuck, was the name of the representative. He was extremely interested in hearing of the problems Bernado had encountered in his Witch hunt in some of the poor orphanages in Italy and other European countries.

"I have heard of similar problems with orphans in the US. The real problems seem to be with the African American children. Our churches and government seem to want to push this problem under the carpet out of sight."

"One problem we have found in Europe is the lack of communication and checking between the priests and city councils with the people doling out the money for food and maintenance of the facilities. The money is skimmed off by corrupt officials and managers."

Chuck thought for a while

"I have heard of the same thing happening in the US. This is done by greedy people who should be sent to jail and kept under similar conditions."

The aircraft was descending rapidly. Bernado did not like this feeling at all. The plane was enveloped in a dense cloud mass. He looked out of the small window. All he could see was the white cotton wool cloud. He gripped the sides of his seat tightly. Chuck glanced at him then smiled.

"You OK buddy."

"This is my first trip on a plane."

"You'll be OK, it's a few weeks since one crashed".

Chuck smiled at him. At this time the plane descended out of the fluffy cloud. It bounced and shook as it did so.

Tops of tall buildings poked from the streets under the plane as it headed for the airport.

The runway was coming toward them at an alarming speed. Bernado shut his eyes and held the armrests tighter waiting for the crash.

The wheels hit the runway with a screech as the tires started to rotate. The plane bounced slightly, then taxied toward the terminal. He opened his eyes. They were on the ground.

"It gets easier with time. I have traveled on them hundreds of times. Never had a problem. Safer than driving a car, with all of the maniacs on the roads today."

Said Chuck with a smile.

When the plane finally pulled into the terminal Bernado asked Chuck to visit the Casino if he were to ever be in Rome or any other city nearby.

Bernado was not used to the ques of people and the zig-zag fences they had to endure leading to customs.

Chuck walked with him to baggage then customs, explaining the procedure as they walked.

When they came out of the customs there were people from various hotels with cards with the patron's names on them. Bernado noticed a large black man in a uniform with the Plaza Hotel embroidered on his cap. He had a board with names on it. Bernado noticed his name among the others on the list. He walked to the man carrying his heavy suitcase. He introduced himself. The man waved to a lad in uniform nearby and had Bernado's luggage taken from him to the Hotel limo. "Where do yo all come from". asked the large man. "Anzio in Italy."

Said Bernado in broken English.

“I was there during the war”. said the man.

The other three people on his list arrived.

He waved the lad over to take their luggage to the limo.

“Follow me. We will go to the car.”

They followed him to the long, stretched Cadillac car.

He opened the door for them to enter.

He then settled in the driver’s seat and sped off into the chaotic traffic. Bernado had never seen so many different cars fighting for space to move. It felt claustrophobic to him. The other three passengers two women and a man took no notice of this. They just stared ahead, not looking, in a trance-like manner.

The limo pulled into the front of the Plaza hotel. The concierge opened the limo door.

“Welcome to the Plaza,” He said.

They all got out and were met by bellhops from the hotel who took their luggage from them. Bernado followed the other people to book in.

When the process was finally ended Bernado took a lift to the floor his room was situated on. After some working out the room numbers, he found the door to his room. As he entered, he noticed his baggage neatly laying in the cradles near the dressing table.

The trip and subsequent initiation to New York had been stressful. He lay on the bed and drifted off to sleep.

He woke suddenly in the late afternoon. He felt somewhat disorientated from the jet lag and change of time. He took the lift to the lobby looking for somewhere to have a meal.

The meeting at the UN was not for two more days. He would try to find some sort of tour he could take to see the city and also be able to check out the UN building before his visit to talk about the plight of the world's orphans.

After lunch, Bernado asked one of the hotel staff on the check-in counter about a conducted tour of the New York City area. He mixed Italian with some words of English. He would like to be able to stop over at the United Nations building the resume the tour with a later bus. The lady on the counter told him where to go to catch the tour bus. She also gave him a phrasebook to convert from Italian to English.

The double-deck bus was filled with tourists from many different countries. This was evident from their dress and language spoken. Bernado sat next to an Italian lady and her daughter. They came from the Florence area of Italy. After two hours of touring the bus pulled into a bus station near the UN buildings. Bernado bid his companions farewell and headed for the UN building main entrance.

Bernado tried to find the relevant department about his speech the next afternoon. After an hour he was finally directed to an area of the building by a woman fluent in Italian. When Bernado approached the office counter he asked for some person who could speak Italian, German or Polish. The woman spoke on the telephone, after a minute an attractive small thin woman came to Bernado and asked what he wanted, speaking in Italian.

“I have been invited to talk at the assembly at 1.30 tomorrow, the talk will be about the plight of the poor orphans in the world and what is being done about this problem.”

“You had better come with me; I will explain the procedure for you to speak tomorrow. You can speak in any language that you feel comfortable with. The people in the assembly have translators who tell them through earphones what you are saying in their language.” She explained where he should go before his speech. Bernado chose Italian as his language.

Bernado spoke of the reforms he had instigated in some of Europe.

The woman was very interested in the subject.

“I have been involved in the refugee and orphan problems in African and Asian countries.

There are huge problems in these countries, Children are being taken as young as ten years old and taught to kill people in some of the African countries. In Asia, young girls and boys of the same age are being taught to be sex workers.”

Melinda introduced herself.

“My parents emigrated from Italy just after the war. Things were very tough where they had come from in Italy. There was very little food. A similar thing with the young girls happened in her area. Girls fourteen and older sold themselves to the American soldiers so they could buy food for their families”.

Bernado was keen to hear more about the Asian and African refugee and orphan situation from a person who was well-schooled on the subject.

"I am here on my own and have a lot to learn about the conditions of orphanages in these countries. What are you doing tonight?" Melinda thought for a short while.

"Where are you staying"

"At the Plaza Hotel"

"I would like to be able to pick your brain about the reforms you have done in Europe. One is always learning in this business". she said

Bernado smiled at her.

"We thought we were doing a good job of planting fruit trees and having gardens for the orphanages, so the children could grow their food. I recently visited Austria and Hungary. They have taken on our reforms. But have added to them with courses such as mechanics, farming, dressmaking and many other subjects for the children. I do not know why we did not think of this."

Melinda agreed to have dinner with him at the Plaza in the evening.

Bernado waited near the entrance of the Plaza. At six-thirty Melinda appeared. She had changed her clothes and looked like an attractive model. Not the coat hanger gaunt type. One who looked like a real woman. She had all of the right pieces in the right places.

Bernado started by telling her some of his story of when he was a child. He then told her of the trauma he had endured in the so-called caring nice orphanage.

"The main problem we are finding worldwide is the lack of funds in war-torn countries to be able to fix these problems. There is a lack of caring to some degree by corrupt officials.

Melinda sipped a few mouthfuls of her soup.

"Another huge problem is the thousands of land mines set to trap the enemies in these Asian countries. They are so sophisticated that they are almost impossible to detect. The people who set these mines are either dead or have no record of where the mines have been laid. These are a terrible curse as they indiscriminately kill or maim defenseless children and women working in the fields". Bernado ordered two glasses of wine to accompany the main course which had just been delivered by a waiter.

"What about the African countries which have had the same problems with rebels? "

"The situation is very similar. Possibly worse because of the children soldiers used by these monsters. These children have no feeling of love or respect for the life of other people. No person would want to take a child who would kill them at the first chance of a problem occurring.

They both started eating their main course. "I am so sorry when I think about all of these children left to fend for themselves in the world. Some individuals from other countries have come and started to take some of these orphans and teach them love again to prepare them for a later normal life. These people help children learn to cook, sew, and tend fields for growing food."

After the meal ended Bernado asked Melinda to accompany him to a lounge area where they could continue their conversation. After an hour talking of the world refugee and orphan problems, Melinda excused herself. She had a big day coming up at the UN.

"Would you like to come to my room to continue our conversation?" Melinda Smiled "Sorry I am not looking for what you may have in mind".

She then rose from her chair.

"I will catch you tomorrow morning before you give your speech. She smiled at him, then turned and left the room.

The cab driver reminded Bernado of a race car driver as he sped off from the hotel toward the UN building. The weaving out and in among the traffic was quite a harrowing experience. In an early brief conversation with the driver, Bernado found he was Polish. Bernado changed to talking Polish with the driver. He did not let on to his Gypsy heritage. The driver smoked a large smelly cigar as he drove.

The smell of the cigar still hung on Bernado's clothes as he walked through the door of the UN building. He could still smell it faintly as he entered the waiting area of Melinda's office. Melinda spied him as he entered. She walked through to the waiting room, then sat near him on a chair.

"I am sorry about last night, but I am in a relationship with a very nice man. I see no point in jeopardizing this for a one-night stand.".

"That's OK, I should not have made the suggestion".

Melinda arose from the chair.

“follow me I would not want you to get lost in this huge building.” Bernado tagged along behind her for some distance, until they came to an office adjoined to the speakers chamber.

Bernado took a folder from his pocket which had the prompts for his speeches. A door opened. A young man called to him.

“Right, Mr. Rominski. Follow me”.

Bernado followed the young man onto a raised stage. A lectern with glass and jug filled with water stood on it.

“Mr. Bernado Rominski will now speak on the plight of orphans in southern and western Europe’”

The young man stepped back, then turned and left the room. Bernado felt quite alone standing in front of the hundreds of delegates sitting in front of him.

“My fellow citizens of the world. I would like to bring news of the plight of the Italian German, Hungarian, Austrian and Polish orphans in orphanages in these countries.

When I was just nine years old I witnessed my parents and relatives being murdered by a German death squad.

I had been away from my parents looking for food. When I finally returned to camp, I heard gunfire and witnessed my parents being killed. Children my age were running with the soldiers and stabbing my friends and relatives. Most were shot with machine gun-fire. I was hiding behind a bush and witnessed my mother have her throat cut some five meters in front of me.

A truck came and ten Polish prisoners tossed my parents and the others on the tray as they would bags of grain. They were then taken and thrown into a deep hole dug by the prisoners. They then had dirt thrown over them.

I left this dismal place of horror and walked for nearly two days before I found a farmhouse. I was taken to a small town the next day by the farmer. I felt so alone. I had nowhere to go.

I was lucky to be found by an old woman who knew my parents and relatives. She took me into her care.

This woman was a healer. She taught me how to treat people with various sicknesses and other ailments."

Bernado stopped and took the glass then filled it with water. He took a large swallow of the water. He thought of Zelda and Pepi before he resumed his speech.

"After nearly a year with this kindly lady. I returned from the forest one day to find her and her large dog shot in front of her now burning house."

He paused and took another sip of water.

I was alone once more. I found a ruined cottage in the town nearby. I was hungry and cold. I was caught by the local Policeman after I had tried to steal a blanket to keep me warm at night.

The kindly policeman took me to the large town nearby to hand me to the local orphanage. The policeman drew a picture in my mind of kindly priests and nuns looking after the poor children who had lost their parents".

He took another sip from the glass'

"I am sorry to say that the orphanage staff was far from being kind to poor children.

No food in the cooking pot was ever thrown out. It was just recooked over again. This food made me very ill for a few days. The sleeping dormitories were filthy. The beds had bugs that bit us all night. One of the priests was a sadistic pedophile, who loved caning the children. I was raped on nearly three occasions by this poor excuse for a human being.

Bernado pause and took another drink. Recalling the orphanage was still upsetting for him.

"I had found a large nail. I sharpened and shaped this on a sandstone block in the wall of the orphanage and kept this hidden in my clothes to protect myself from this sadistic priest.

I had been in the orphanage for nearly three years. During this time many children died during the cold during the winter months. I had been walking past an office one morning when the priest grabbed me and tried to rape me once more. His hand slipped off my shoulder. I bit down very hard on his finger. When he managed to pull his bleeding hand away, I stabbed him in the face, just missing his eye.

I then ran off toward the outer door. By a lucky chance the door opened. I ran at the older priest knocking him down and escaped to the street.

This older priest was well aware of the younger priest and what he was doing to the little boys.

I started to work with a man clearing off bombed building sites.

Over the years by good luck and hard work I prospered. I have two beautiful women I live with and six children

Through a stroke of luck, I was asked to join the Anzio local council. One day the mayor of Anzio and I were talking. The subject of orphans came into our conversation. We started to run some checks on both the church-run and state-run orphanages. We have uncovered some real monsters starving and beating these poor children.

One priest stated that it did not matter what happened to these children as they were bastards born outside of the church. God did not want them".

Bernado looked at the audience. Many of the people had shocked looks on their faces.

"When I was in Austria. I applied for a permit to travel to Romania. I had been told that there were terrible problems with orphans in this country. My application was declined. I asked the border guards if there was any redress to this decision. The man said that some priests were smuggled across the border. They had a fire in their belly as I had. The border guard said he had heard that they had been caught. No one has heard of them since.

The Hungarian church officials told me they knew of these priests in this story.

The Ceausescu regime was very violent toward religion."

Bernado filled his water glass once more and took another sip.

“Through my association with the Bishop of Anzio I have instigated changes in many orphanages and have paid for gardens to be planted for the orphan’s food at the orphanages, also the poorer people of the towns can take the extra food for themselves. Many of the poor people now help maintain orphanages. Some have adopted children as their own. In Austria and Hungary, the church is now running trade classes for the children.”

Just before stepping back slightly, Bernado asked if there were any questions.

For the next fifteen minutes, Bernado answered questions from the floor as best as he could. The crowd rose then clapped their hands loudly as he left the rostrum.

Melinda met him in the room behind the great hall.

“You have had an interesting life Bernado”.

She said as they walked back toward her office.

“Somehow I have a feeling that you will be visited by many of the delegates from some countries to explain some of your ideas and how you have been able to instigate them”.

“I felt as if I should give something back to the community. The mayor of Anzio bought up the subject of orphans one day when we were talking of other matters. I felt as if I had seen a bright light. We went to the local orphanage and were disgusted at the conditions the poor children were living in.”

Bernado shuddered inwardly as he membered the first encounter with the angry priest.

"When we visited the local orphanage. The mayor was extremely upset at the poor conditions the children were living in. The priest said this did not matter as the children were born outside of the church. This man. The other priest and the head nun were taking almost half of the money to purchase food, then giving this to their families. I think he was sent to jail."

Melinda thought for a short while.

"Would you like to have dinner with me and my partner tonight? He is also working for the UN. What you have done would be of great interest to him."

"I would enjoy that. Where would you suggest we go to".

Melinda smiled.

"I know just the place. There is a restaurant where many of the delegates you spoke to today go to catch up after the days sitting". She told him the address, then wrote it onto a piece of paper from her desk. "I will book a table for us. I will be seeing you tonight then?"

"You surely will."

Bernado rose from his seat then left the room. His head was filled with the thought of who he might be able to meet with at dinner.

Bernado was not very impressed with the New York cab drivers. He was more relaxed on the first jet flight. The cab wove through the bumper-to-bumper traffic, steering through almost impossible spaces. Other drivers tooted their horns and some shook their fists out of the side window of their cars.

The maître d ushered Bernado to the table where Melinda and her partner waited. Melinda and her partner rose from their chairs.

"Bernado this is Mark".

Mark was a good looking blond sporty looking man. He reached over the table and vigorously shook Bernado's hand.

"Pleased to meet you," He said in a rounded Southern drawl.

He then said the same sentence in Italian.

Bernado looked around the large room. Many people were dining in this restaurant. He then noticed some were dressed in strange clothes.

They all sat down. A wine waiter joined them at the table.

"What wine would you like, a white or red".

After some discussion, a wine was selected from the list. "I am very interested in the work you have been doing in Europe regarding orphans". Mark said after they had ordered their meal.

"I was one myself for over three years in Poland during the war. The food was not fit for animals. We only had one thin blanket for our bed, even when it was snowing outside. Many children died of the cold. Our beds were full of biting bugs. The priests were sadists and one was a pedophile. Chasing the small boys. I would not recommend the place".

Mark nodded with a solemn look on his face.

“The work you have been doing now must be bringing you a lot of satisfaction”.

“It has. There was a lot of work changing the church’s attitude. We convinced the Bishop of Anzio to accompany an employee and me to the first orphanage, after the mayor of Anzio and I had called to inspect this dismal dirty place. The priest was an extremely grumpy angry man”. Bernado smiled.

The bishop was no better when he was informed of our unannounced intrusion.

He quickly changed his mind when he accompanied us to the second visit. My friend spoke of informing the press about the horrible dirty conditions the poor children barely survived under.” Bernado smiled again at the thought.

“I used the words that I was conducting an inquisition on the church. The poor guy with me thought he would be excommunicated from the church”.

Mark laughed.

“I bet that ruffled some feathers in the church”.

“It certainly did. The pompous Bishops never visited such places as orphanages. They relied on second-hand knowledge from the priests. Some of these so-called inspectors lied about their visits.” Bernado finished his glass of wine and refilled all of the glasses. “I am pleased to say this does not happen now. My trips of discovery have pulled both church and state-run facilities into gear”

When the meal was finished Mark asked Bernado to accompany him and Melinda to the bar area. Some of the people remembered him from the day’s speech at the UN.

Many people spoke about orphan problems worldwide.

One of the American delegates invited Bernado to talk at a Rotary convention that was being held in New York in two days. Bernado declined as his understanding of the English language was not of a high enough standard.

Many people from other countries were booked to attend this convention. It was a good chance to speak lost.

Other people who were at the UN for his speech talked to Bernado about the orphan crisis in their countries.

This time one of the men acted as an interpreter. He was helped by Melinda.

"Would you consider coming to my country to advise our government. I know there is a large problem with orphans because of the recent civil war".

One of the men asked through the interpreter. He had similar requests from other men and women who had listened to him talking at the UN.

Bernado politely declined their offer to assist.

If you can give me your name and address I will formulate a plan of what we have been doing to help the lives of our orphans. I will word this so you can present this to your governments when you arrive home."

Bernado was handed numerous business cards from many people. He carefully slid them into the top pocket of his jacket as he received each one. He reciprocated by giving his card to the donor.

It was late in the evening when he returned to his hotel. He was extremely tired from the long day. The conversations with the people in the restaurant were very interesting. He went to sleep as soon as his head hit the pillow.

Bernado woke late and drifted to a late breakfast. His flight from New York to Rome was scheduled for 10 am the next morning. He felt somewhat seedy from the late night. He went out of the hotel and hailed a cab to take him to the UN building once more. He wanted to have a meeting with people from the UN Save The Children Program.

Another ride with a maniac driver weaving in and out of the other cars deposited him at the entrance of the building. Bernado walked to Melinda's office. She greeted him cordially.

"Did you enjoy the networking night with all of the interesting people last night?"

"Yes, but I felt like I had a hangover this morning. I had very little to drink I think it must have been the conversation and jetlag from traveling. I have a favor to ask you, could you arrange for me to talk to some of the Save the Children people."

Melinda thought for a short while.

"I have a friend who works in the department. Wait while I Phone her."

She dialed the phone then started talking to her friend. After some small talk about the weather and some office problems, she asked if Bernado could visit the office.

She put down the phone back on the cradle then looked up. "you made some lasting impressions yesterday Mary Jo was at your talk. She will get some of the staff together for you to meet." She rose from her chair showing a lot of her leg under her tight skirt. Bernado was not too proud to notice.

"follow me. I will take you to her office."

She started walking briskly. Bernado kept pace with her. "I would not be able to give you directions to Mary Jo. This building is so large you would surely get yourself lost."

By the time they arrived at the office, Bernado was puffing from the fast walk.

When Melinda turned toward him, she noticed this. "I am sorry I should have slowed down.''

. Bernado laughed.

"I should have looked after my fitness a bit more. I think I have been living the good life a bit too much."

His puffing was subsiding.

The two of them entered the office. They both walked to the reception desk. The pretty dark-skinned girl looked up.

"I have a meeting with Mary Jo"

The girl buzzed a buzzer on her intercom.

"There is a man and a lady to see you."

A sexy voice with a Southern accent answered.

"Tell them to come down to my office." "Just walk down along the corridor to office number ten." The girl pointed to the corridor.

As they walked, they passed a large room filled with cubicles in which many young girls were typing.

Melinda tapped on the glass door of the office.

The sexy voice answered as she opened the door for them to enter.

“Welcome to my part of the world.”

Bernado was wondering what to expect. He had been trying to visualize who would be associated with the voice. He was not disappointed. Standing in front of him was a beautiful woman with honey blond hair hanging to her shoulders. She was moderately tall with high heels. She smiled broadly.

“I was listening to your speech yesterday and thought at the time I would like to meet you.” Bernado was slightly puzzled he could not understand all of the conversations. Melinda asked if Mary Jo could speak in Italian.

Mary Jo smiled once more. “Si Si, The language of love”

She smiled at Bernado as she changed her language to Italian.

Bernado smiled back.

“Would you like to come to the boardroom and meet some people I have spoken to since you asked to meet me? We are very interested in what you have been doing in Europe. We have many problems in the US similar to the ones you have combatted in Europe.” Melinda excused herself. She kissed Bernado on the cheek.

“I am sorry but I will have to get back to my office. It was a privilege to meet such a man as you Bernado. I hope you can change more orphans lives in other countries”

She looked at Mary Jo.

"Could you please take Bernado out of the building when you are finished? I would not like to think he was lost down in the dungeons or something." Mary Jo smiled "It would be my privilege to assist a man who has done so much for the orphans"

Melinda turned and left the building.

Bernado followed Mary Jo as she walked to the boardroom. He appreciated the look as she walked in front of him.

She finally opened a heavy varnished door. There were ten people inside the room. As he entered, they all stopped talking, then stood and clapped.

Mary Jo ushered Bernado to the head of the table.

Everyone sat down.

Each person had a business card with their photo and name plus phone number on the card they stood one by one and introduced themselves then passed on their card to him.

When they all were seated Bernado introduced himself

"I am Bernado Rominski. My family was gypsies during the war. My people were trying to flee from Poland to Romania where we were told the Nazis had not invaded.

We had heard of some of our people being killed by a Nazi death squad. We had found a young boy who had witnessed such an atrocity when his clan was murdered. He had been away from the camp and had returned when he heard gunshots. He witnessed the slaying of all of his clan.

Bernado took a long drink of water.

"I witnessed a similar thing some weeks later. I was foraging for food and returned to camp to find the same man and the young Hitler Youth lads he described, killing my parents and relatives. I was helped by a farmer and his wife who took me to a small Polish town. I was taken in by an old Gypsy woman for nearly a year. I returned to her house one day to find her shot laying under the burning eaves of her house. Most of her animals taken for food. Her cats and dogs had also been shot."

He paused to get this breath. "I was just thirteen at this time. I found an old ruined house in town and had been caught stealing by a kindly policeman. He convinced me to go with him to a church-run orphanage This place was run by some caring nuns and priests. He said he had heard from the local priest."

Bernado took another mouthful of water.

"The people who ran this orphanage were far from caring. I was raped by one of the priests nearly three times, he was doing this to other boys also. Some told the older priest who gave each one six cuts with the cane for trying to cause trouble."

He paused once more the memories of the orphanage were still high in his mind.

"The rapist priest was also very keen to use the cane. Most of the nuns knew this but also did nothing. The food was recooked many times. It smelled worse than a pigsty. We had one blanket on our bed.

Many children died in the cold winter. We were infested with lice and bedbugs. As I was being raped the third time I stabbed the priest in the face with a sharpened nail I had found and kept for my protection. I ran from him and managed to get out of the orphanage by pure luck. I was now sixteen years old,"

Bernado looked hard at the audience to see their reaction to his story.

"I found work clearing bombed building sites. This was hard work but it kept me alive.

Since that time, I have been lucky in business and love. I decided that it was time for me to give something back by challenging the church to investigate the plight of the poor orphans. We have found some monsters running some orphanages. They have been stealing the money for food and other comforts like warm clothes and warm bedding."

He paused.

"I am pleased to say the because of my involvement in this I have been able to instigate changes in the way many orphanages have been run. Most orphanages now have gardens for growing food and coursed in dressmaking, cooking, carpentry, and mechanics. Any spare food is given to the poor in the adjoining towns. Many of these poor people have come to help do maintenance on the orphanages.

Many have taken one or two children as their own."

As Bernado gave his speech Mary Jo translated to the people sitting at the table.

After the speech, all eleven of the people stood and clapped their hands.

Bernado felt quite humbled by this response.

Mary Jo translated the many questions coming from the audience. He learned from her that there was a similar situation in the US as he had encountered in Italy, Greedy people running the orphanages and stealing most of the funds.

Bernado urged some of the people present to lobby the churches and other facilities running orphanages to run audits on these facilities and also have certified inspectors to check on the conditions inside of the facilities. The courses initiated in Austria were talked about. As well as the gardens for food. This could be done for very little cost in many overseas countries also. It was far better to have the children working for themselves than being locked up and starving.

After three hours of talking the people went to the large dining area for lunch.

He sat next to Mary Jo.

As they finished eating, he managed to get Mary Jo alone

"I would feel it a privilege if you would have dinner with me tonight so we could continue some of the conversations we have had today." Mary Jo looked at him.

"Would you like for me to book a table at a nightclub"?

“Yes, that would be fantastic.”

“I will make a call from my office before I escort you out of the building.”

They stopped at Mary Jo’s office on the way out of the building. She made a call to a night club not very far from Bernado’s hotel. She would meet him there at six o’clock in the evening. She wrote the name of the club on a piece of paper and gave this to him.

Walking along the corridors out of the building was not the marathon that he had experienced trying to keep up to Melinda. Mary Jo walked slowly and spoke of her home in Georgia. She described her town and people. Bernado talked about finding money and jewelry when he was cleaning up bombed building sites. He told her of the time training stray dogs and joining the circus. He left out the gory bits and the assignations with the ladies, plus the stealing dogs and Shandor.

He described the beautiful building that he and Marta had restored and how Donna Gabriella had taken him and Marta to be her adopted family and partner in the Casino. He could see Mary Jo was impressed by this.

He kissed her cheek as she left him.

“I am looking forward to seeing you tonight, “said Mary Jo. She then turned and returned to the building.

Bernado was looking forward to meeting this attractive woman for dinner. He went to his room and had a shower. After he had dried himself, he laid on his bed and had a nap.

The day had been very interesting. The people he had met had the connections to possibly implement some of the reforms which had happened in Europe over the last three years.

When he woke, he looked at his watch, he had just half an hour to the meeting with Mary jo.

The night club was not very far from his hotel. He walked to the foyer and ordered a cab. He did not want to walk on the streets of New York, he had heard many stories of muggings and other happenings on the streets.

The maître d on the door of the club directed Bernado to the table where Mary Jo was waiting.

"I am sorry. I hope that I am not late"

She rose from her chair. "No, I am early. I did not want you to get lost in New York, So I came early to meet you". She smiled then sat down.

Bernado had a swift glance at Mary Jo. She was attractive in her working clothes, tonight she had excelled herself.

"Would you like me to order for you? Some of our meals have strange names.

She went through the main menu. Bernado chose a porterhouse steak. Mary Jo opted for a seafood combination. "Red or white wine" She smiled.

"What is your preference?" "I will choose the wine. I prefer a red." He selected a bottle from the wine waiter.

The meal lingered on as they talked about life in general and business.

A quartet of musicians started to play.

"Would you like to dance? "Mary Jo asked with a mischievous smile.

Bernado rose stepped around the table and held her chair. “I am not a very good dancer.” She smiled as he said this.

“I don’t think we will be doing the tango.”

Bernado held her arm as they went to the dance floor.

She came into his arms. He could feel all of her body molded into his. They danced to the slow music for quite a while. Bernado was having a problem controlling the Bierwurst stick. It was getting ideas.

“Would you like another drink”?

Mary Jo accepted his offer. They walked to the bar and each sat on a stool. Mary Jo was listening to the slow music. “This is one of my favorite tunes. Let’s dance again.” They drifted back to the dance floor.

The Bierwurst stick was losing control.

Mary Jo had a dreamy look on her face as she rubbed against it gently.

“Would you like to come back to the hotel?”

“I think that would be a lovely idea.”

Bernado paid the bill. They left the night club and caught a cab to the hotel.

As they traveled up the lift they were the only two riding in the car. Bernado and Mary Jo had a passionate embrace and kiss as it took them to the floor.

When they entered Bernado’s room Mary Jo had a request.

“Would you please undress me, I will undress you”

Bernado was almost lost for words. They slowly undressed each other.

Mary Jo would make most centerfold girls in men's magazines look plain. Bernado took her in his arms, gently lifted her, and carried her to the large bed. The Bierwurst was held between her legs. "Would you be careful, please? I do not want you to hurt me." Bernado laid next to her and gently started to slide inside. She lifted her leg across his body. Bernado was on fire inside but felt a gentleness to Mary Jo. He moved slowly Just letting a small amount inside of her. As he pushed, he slowly put more inside her, He was surprised, it did not hit the bottom. Mary Jo rolled over on top of Bernado and moaned then shuddered as she had a small orgasm. She started to ride him with more vigor. She had another small shuddering orgasm.

"Could you get on top of me now, please? I think we are heading for the glory time"

Glory time alright, Bernado almost stopped breathing the orgasm was so magnificent.

"I do not want to leave you Bernado. I want to make love some more times with you before you go."

"I don't want you to leave. I want you here with me all night." Said Bernado softly in her ear.

They both drifted off to sleep. Bernado woke to find Mary Jo straddling him and helping the now growing Bierwurst into the home spot. The sex was not quite as boisterous as the first coupling.

It was a lovely experience

Bernado woke. Mary Jo was cuddled up to him, lightly snoring. He did not have to move very much to re-enter her, she woke, then pulled him to her and kissed him passionately.

Mary Jo woke Bernado at first light. They made love once more.

"I had better get dressed and go home. I have to work today" "I would like to stay for a week and make love to you like this every night. That was the invitation. They made love once more

"I am sorry but I am booked to fly out of here at ten-thirty. I think if I were to keep this up for a week I might have a heart attack and die"

"What a way to go," Said Mary Jo with a smile, as she started dressing

"I feel quite seedy. I think you have worn me out"

"I am feeling quite sore Bernado, I think we may have overdone it a bit.

As they embraced the last time the worn-out Bierwurst made one more effort and stood to attention.

"I wish I could stay Bernado But I have a job to do elsewhere". She kissed him passionately. She then took a business card from her purse.

"If you ever come back to New York phone me".

CHAPTER 24

Bernado finished packing his clothes and sent for the bellhop to take the cases downstairs to the waiting taxi.

As they headed for the JFK Airport. The cabbie started singing an operetta in Italian. When he finished Bernado clapped his hands then spoke to him in Italian. The man had migrated from the Rome area and knew Anzio very well. Bernado told him about restoring the old Casino. The man had also seen this building on many occasions when he had visited relatives.

Bernado gave the man a large tip when he paid him. He took his cases to a trolley, loaded them then walked to the airline booking bay. He was traveling on United Airlines to Rome first class on a Boeing 747.

After filling all of the forms with the relevant questions. He boarded the plane.

He found his cubicle had a pretty brunette woman sitting next to him.

He thought back to the night before with Mary Jo and started to feel regretful about leaving. He thought of the fantastic time they had together during the night making love.

The Bierwurst sprang to attention once more. Bernado had to shift so his coat covered the front of his trousers so the woman sitting next to him could not notice.

After the plane had taken off and leveled out Bernado started to feel more comfortable. He noticed they the woman was reading an Italian magazine. He spoke to her in Italian.

"Good morning." The young lady looked up and smiled. "Are you from Italy?" "Yes, are you".

"Yes, I come from Anzio"

"You are lucky. That is a very beautiful place to live. I live in Rome. I am in the perfume business and have been traveling to source new products for my business".

"I like the smell of the one you are wearing. It has a very subtle aroma. I own the Casino on the foreshore". "I have been there many times with friends"

"I have not noticed you" The young woman laughed.

She returned to her magazine for a short while and finished reading the article.

Bernado dozed off for a short while and entered a sweet dream of being with Mary Jo once again. He could hear her sexy voice talking to him in his dream.

He woke up with the Bierwurst rock hard.

He was embarrassed in case the young lady had noticed it. She was intently studying the large bulge in his trousers. Her face reddened when Bernado opened his eyes. She smiled at him. He smiled back.

The hostesses and flight attendants walked noisily along the aisle with a large trolley with food and wine. Bernado was feeling hungry.

He had a glass of good wine and a small snack.

The young lady woke. She yawned, and then also had a glass of wine.

Bernado once more dozed off. He was woken by yelling coming from the tourist class. Some women were screaming. He turned to look along the aisle. Three men were standing and holding their small carry bags in front of them. They were yelling at the people to sit still and to be quiet.

A hostess came to the people in first class and urged them to sit still and be quiet. Three men were claiming they had bombs in their cases.

Bernado was extremely afraid. The young lady next to him began to sob quietly. He reached and took her hand to comfort her. “I do not want to die”. She said between sobs. “I think it will be all under control soon.” Bernado tried to comfort her.

The hostess returned to the first class.

“Ladies and gentlemen. Please remain in your seats at all times. These men have made a demand to have a large Columbian drug dealer recently caught by police released and provided with a plane and pilot to return him to Columbia. This man is in Mexico in a high-security jail”.

After half an hour the intercom came to life

“This is your captain speaking. Our US government is speaking to the Mexican officials about this situation. I am sure it can soon be resolved. Please stay in your seats”.

A very long stressful hour passed. No more news was relayed to the people.

The captain's voice came over the intercom.

"Our government has been negotiating with the rebels about this situation. We are sure it will soon be resolved"

The rebel started yelling at people once more. Bernado turned to look. The sounds of small gunfire came from the area of the terrorists, two of them fell immediately. The third was wounded but was still standing. He lifted the small bag and managed to pull a short cord that protruded from the top of the bag. flames shot from the bag and filled the plane.

Bernado's ears were ringing from the explosion. The smell of burnt hair and flesh filled the cabin of the plane. The young Italian girl was clasping onto Bernado tightly. Her hair was singed. One hand held onto Bernado's Bierwurst tightly She looked at him then removed her had with an embarrassed look on her face. Bernado smiled at her. " I think we all have been very lucky" he whispered in her ear.

TheEnd

www.ingramcontent.com/pod-product-compliance
Lightning Source LLC
Chambersburg PA
CBHW070641310726
48982CB00001B/364
9780648312192